From the Banks of Little Bear Creek

DUTCH HENRY

DEDICATION

For My Wife and Wonderful Daughter , Son-In-Law
and Grandchildren

NOTE FROM THE AUTHOR

Just as "Tom Named by Horse" is an historical fiction, so is "From the Banks of Little Bear Creek." However this adventure is far more in the fiction realm than factual. The battles and skirmishes mentioned and lived in this story are true. You'll recognize the historical figures interacting with my fictional family. I promise you'll love the adventure.

ACKNOWLEDGMENTS

Often behind the story there are friends who have helped the author bring it all together. My dear friend the late Bob Hollinger helped with much of the research. All my friends who read my manuscript along the way and encouraged me to publish. Bobbie Jo Lieberman, former Editor of trailBLAZER magazine, who worked her magic in editing my story. My wife, Robin, for her encouragement, critiques and putting it all together and adding publishing to her list of things to do.

A special thank you to Bobbie Jo Lieberman and Troy Locker Palmer, PHG Industries for a great cover. Troy can be reached by email at troy@phgindustries.com and visit her website www.phgindustries.com.

Thank you all.

CHAPTER ONE

June 4, 1869

"Won't we be living high this trip, with Soft Cloud along to cook?" Buck flashed Tom a grin and rubbed his stomach.

Tom stood in his stirrups to shout through the dust. "Nothing's too good for the finest horse ranchers in the territory!" He spun his horse, raced along the herd to the chuckwagon and blew a kiss to Soft Cloud.

"I'm along to cook, Buck, but you will carry the water and gather wood!" Soft Cloud returned Tom's air kiss.

"For your biscuits I'll chop down a forest of cottonwoods and carry a lake of water, one bucket at a time!"

This marked the third June in a row Tom and Buck trailed horses to Denver City. The trip, though long and often rugged, proved to be an adventure the two friends had grown to look forward to each spring. Ranchers there paid high prices for Tom's horses, and last year Tom had fallen short of demand.

This year they had convinced Soft Cloud to join them. On the first drive she had been with child. The second year, she'd insisted their son was too young to make the journey. This year, she simply gave in to the endless pestering and pleading from Buck Hawkins, her dear friend, and Tom Named by Horse, her husband. Now she happily drove the mule team and their chuckwagon south across the prairie with their two-year-old son, Hawk, nestled on the seat beside her.

Soft Cloud thought of the first time she'd called her husband Tom Named by Horse—that awful day three years ago when he and

Buck had ridden away to kill her father, Tall Dog. She'd given Tom that name when she had kissed him for the first time, so afraid she would never see him again. She shook away the thought and focused on the happiness of today. All of them together trailing a herd of fine horses. She and Tom held each other's gaze for just a moment.

Tom rode away from the chuckwagon wondering where Buck had disappeared to so fast. Far ahead of the herd already, Tom reasoned, then his mind drifted to the task at hand and the fine men dedicated to him, his ranch and their new life together.

Buck rode point most days on his favorite horse, Diablo, the tall spotted stallion who had the heart of a mountain lion, feared nothing, and to quote Buck, "could run like the devil." Buck preferred to stay out of the dust. He liked to keep his hat, fancy deerskin leggings and vest as neat as possible. How he could grumble if his shoulder-length blonde hair and goatee ever became dust-caked? Buck, a great point rider, always kept the herd moving at a good speed. He always found the safest, easiest routes with the most water, so Tom obliged him in good cheer.

The three hands who hired on at the beginning of the ranch's second year had all fought the Plains Indians Wars on one side or the other, and then as now, they rode herd. The wiriest of the three, Lone Feather, had fought valiantly alongside Red Cloud in the "wagon box fight" that hot August day in 1867. Coop had served under the late Lieutenant Harris and was one of the three survivors of that bloody day on the trail of Tall Dog. Nineteen now, Coop had grown to be a handsome, tall, strong, dark-haired man. Coop was worth his weight in gold when protecting the herd from the many outlaws and cattle thieves who now drifted into the plains looking for easy profits. And of course Cole, who had been with Tom the day they were overrun by the stampeding herd of buffalo. A Private then, Cole, like Tom, had barely survived the day. Cole was the shortest of the group and even though he was tough as nails and an incredible shot, he suffered merciless ribbing from Buck, who forever offered to find him a 14-hand horse. Cole planned to marry when they returned from Denver City. "It just puzzles me something fierce," Buck told Tom this very morning, "what that beautiful Hannah Miller could want with a short legged, square box of a man who has to stand on an anvil just to wrangle himself a kiss."

Lone Feather lived as a quiet man. Though his allegiance to

Buck and Tom stood fierce, he would never stray from his Ogalalla Sioux roots. Choosing his tipi and campfire over the sod bunkhouse, on moonlit nights he could be seen dancing by his campfire, chanting and waving his long lance high. While Tom had been able to convince him to carry one of the new Winchesters, Lone Feather never traveled without his bow and quiver. On journeys such as these, both he and his favorite Sioux pony wore Sioux paint, as Lone Feather declared he never wanted to be mistaken for a farmer. When necessary, Lone Feather could be a tremendous scout.

Before setting out on their three-week journey to Denver City and back, the duties of the ranch had been left in the capable hands of Still Water, Soft Cloud's mother, and her new husband Buffalo Horn. The years of the Plains Indians Wars had been the toughest on Still Water, who'd lost her sons and her husband. But the past few seasons spent with Tom and Soft Cloud on Tom's ranch had helped her to put some of the pain in its own place—in the past. She was delighted now to serve mostly as ranch cook, and everyone's mother.

Buffalo Horn had lost the bottom half of his right leg in the fierce battle on John Bozeman's Road where the Sioux and Cheyenne had successfully forced the Army to abandon Fort Phil Kearny and Fort C. F. Smith. Still able to ride as wonderfully as any Sioux brave, Buffalo Horn was most happy the days that Tom announced they were going out "gatherin,'" for this meant a few carefree days on the prairie chasing wild horses.

Buffalo Horn's most prized possession was the tired old crutch Buck had fashioned for Tom the day after the buffalo stampede. Though the leather padding on top had long ago become frayed and worn, Buffalo Horn fought as fierce as any brave in battle whenever anyone attempted to repair it.

They trailed 65 horses this trip, four of them sired by Thunder, the powerful black stallion Buck had given Tom while he lay in Still Water's tipi recovering from injuries he had suffered in the buffalo stampede. Tom rode Thunder this trip, so buyers could meet the sire of those fine black three-year-old stallions.

Tom galloped to the top of a nearby ridge and watched the herd move over the prairie. Far to his left, well ahead of the herd, he spied Buck and Diablo.

Riding point fit well with Buck's nature. Not quite able yet to let loose of his youth, Buck rode the edge of the knife in anything he did. During the Pony Express days, he'd ridden eleven months for the great Alexander Majors, dodging road agents and hostile Indians. During those rough and rowdy days, he and Bill Cody forged the beginning of their lifelong friendship. Later there came the months he'd spend on the Missouri border spying with Bill Hickok for General Sheridan during the War Between the States and after the war serving as scout for General Sturgis out of Fort Laramie, helping to tame the plains. Those times and adventures had made Buck Hawkins the man he was today. Ranch life fit him well too, and Tom had become the best friend he had ever known, but nothing could set his blood to boiling like being outnumbered and pinned down, fighting for his life and those around him.

There had been times over the past three years when Red Cloud, Roman Nose, and Crazy Horse had provided Buck with all the excitement he needed, pulling him from the ranch and back into service as a scout for the United States Cavalry.

It had never been the same again, though. Not since the loss of his friend Lt. Harris that miserable day in the fall of '66 when Tall Dog butchered the Lieutenant and his men at the Walls of Buffalo Ridge. Was it the loss of Lt. Harris? Or the brutal slaying of Mrs. Harris later that winter on the snow-covered prairie that seemed to have taken a little temper from Buck's steel?

****

As he rode in the warm sun, Buck's thoughts took him to the lieutenant and his lovely, gentle wife.

Mrs. Harris. A finer, more delicate woman had never lived. She'd understood Buck and loved to participate in Buck's relentless teasing of her poor husband. How Buck loved to torment that poor man, and often Mrs. Harris would play along, sometimes driving the two friends to blows. Buck had never been sure if Lt. Harris had truly been jealous or "just funnin'."

For each of the past three years on the anniversary of her death, Buck traveled to the Miller Farm to visit Mrs. Harris' grave. The grave he had dug himself, through four feet of snow, to sit alone on the bench the Millers had surprised him with, and smoke a cigar. Smoke a cigar and remember that morning, just days after her husband's death, on her porch at Fort Laramie. The day she'd invited

Buck to sit quietly with her, and enjoy one of her husband's cigars, as the three of them had so often done. That morning had been the last time Buck would see her alive.

Still Water had tried for Buck's affection, and he had often been warmed by her soft touch and moist kisses. Kisses he had never shared with Mrs. Harris. Was it simply guilt that kept Mrs. Harris alive in his memory, causing him to be unable to allow Still Water into his heart? The burden of that guilt! He should have been with her. He should have traveled with that wagon train the day it left Fort Laramie, the day before the snows came. Why hadn't the General permitted him to go with her? Damn General Sturgis for allowing her to leave the fort in the winter!

Ripped to the present by Diablo's snort and jolting stop, Buck dragged the back of his gloved hand across his weeping eyes. "Son of a bitch!" Less than one hundred yards ahead sat at least 20 mounted renegades. He spun Diablo about, gave him his head with a "Go boy!" Diablo knew what to do and launched his run—a run Buck knew no horse alive could match. They raced to the top of the ridge, circling back to Tom and the herd. He rode the crest so the boys would have good shooting at his pursuers long before they reached the herd.

Diablo's long legs ate up the prairie beneath them, easily gaining distance. Buck snatched his revolver from its holster and, leaning forward on Diablo's neck, emptied it, firing under his arm at the howling and shooting renegades.

Buck hadn't realized how far from the herd he'd gone. When he finally spied Tom and the others, he hoped they understood quickly they had company about to stop in. Buck yanked free his Winchester, levered a shell into the chamber, twisted and fired a shot into the mob galloping behind him. Diablo knew his job and kept up that eye-burning speed along the crest.

Coop and Cole stopped the herd. Lone Feather charged the hill toward the action, and even from this distance Buck read the delight in the Indian's eyes. Tom dropped to the ground and instantly his new 'Big 50' roared. Again and again, the buffalo rifle launched 50-caliber lead slugs into the startled group of charging renegades.

Buck turned Diablo toward the herd and stopped only after he passed Lone Feather. The renegades had begun to turn and flee as Tom continued his rapid fire into the group and Lone Feather charged on, hurling lead and Sioux insults their way.

Refreshed by this surge of adrenaline, Buck trotted the rest of the way to Tom's side, sitting tall and wearing his wonderful smile.

"You gonna call that crazy Indian back?" Buck stepped from Diablo and slid his new Yellow Boy Winchester into its scabbard.

"He'll come back," Tom's attention seemed only partly on Lone Feather and the fleeing renegades.

They watched as Lone Feather continued his charge up the hill, shooting and hooting. Eventually he stopped his war pony and waved his rifle high, shouting Sioux insults and challenges, to be sure the renegades understood they'd been proven cowards this day.

"That was interesting. Guess this trip could be a bit of an adventure," Buck allowed as he stroked his goatee.

"Reckon you'd best not stray so far next time."

"I was thinking."

"Tell Diablo to walk slower next time you go to thinkin'."

Deciding they'd had enough excitement for one day, Tom told Coop and Cole to hold the herd and asked Soft Cloud to start supper. She flipped down the chuckwagon tailgate, propped it up on its two legs, making a tabletop to mix her biscuit dough and prepare beans for the fire. Little Hawk was relegated to a red woolen blanket at her side. Tom settled down on the blanket, scooped up his son and as he watched Soft Cloud, concern flickered on his face. "You'll have to keep the wagon close by the herd. Tomorrow we'll travel slower, so let's keep the herd tighter."

"You expect more trouble?"

"That was too easy. They're not done with us."

"Sure enough, that good-for-nothing bunch had a good look at what we're all about. They'll be back." Buck snatched up Hawk and perched the boy on his shoulders.

CHAPTER TWO

Sun barely kissed the horizon when they moved out the herd. Soft Cloud guided the chuckwagon near the herd's right front. Tom rode at her side, his eyes tirelessly scouring the surrounding country, his Winchester in hand, new Sharps in the scabbard.

They held the horses in a neat, tight bunch, Coop and Cole guided on point. Lone Feather brought up the rear, Buck scouted ahead, selecting only routes that kept them as far from dangerous ridgetops as possible. In this fashion they moved all through the morning and into the early afternoon hours.

The sun hung hot when Buck returned. "We have a stream crossing coming up." Buck wore unease on his face. "Water's not too high and the stream's only a couple of hundred feet wide. Appears to be good footing. Could also be a good place to hit us when we cross."

Tom pulled his black hat, pushed his hand through wet hair and squinted at the sun. Just then he wished Soft Cloud and Hawk were back at the ranch.

"The horses could stand a break and a drink. Open ground? Could we see them coming?"

"Yeah, lays flat. But I don't know about stopping there. I was thinking more like running right on through and getting away from that low land."

"Gotta water the stock, Buck, and the chuckwagon'll slow us down anyway. Take Cole and Coop and scout the other side. If you see anything, get back in a hurry ... we'll make a stand right here. I'm getting a feeling I don't like."

"Yea, that feelin' of yours always wants to get us in trouble."

He signaled Cole and Coop and they set off at an easy lope for the stream.

Tom trotted to the wagon and pulled up by Soft Cloud, "Put Hawk inside."

"Buck see something?" Soft Cloud tried to busy herself with the reins, but her stiffness told of her worry.

"No trouble, yet. But we're coming up on a crossing. If it looks alright, we'll stop for the night and water the stock."

Tom loped to Lone Feather. "Scout that ridge and beyond in a wide sweep, then hustle back. If you see anything, any trouble, get back here, don't try to tackle the whole bunch on your own." Tom held Lone Feather's look, he knew Lone Feather was easily tempted into a party.

With the men gone, Tom rode herd on the left, Soft Cloud drove the wagon on the right. Together they kept the herd moving toward the waiting stream. An hour later Lone Feather rejoined them, riding a very spent horse, and reported all things clear beyond the ridge to their west.

The flat land by the stream stood thick with young prairie grass, offering easy grazing, and the horses settled for the night with full bellies and thirsts quenched. Soft Cloud started her regular evening routine, Hawk on his blanket, biscuits in the Dutch oven, and beans on the fire. Tonight, prairie dogs roasted on spits.

"Mighty fine shooting, Coop!" Buck delivered a man-sized slap to Coop's back.

"Doggone, Buck, them prairie dogs were just jumpin' into my bullets." Coop flashed a grin.

"Reckon that's why we ain't had no more trouble from them renegades," Cole joked.

"Why's that, Cole?" Buck joined in.

"Well I guess they seen Coop's fancy shooting. I mean, five dogs with 20 shots ain't bad!"

Funny though it was, Cole had to rebut, "Five dogs, five shots."

"Puts me in mind of the time Bill Cody and me got stuck in this town with no money." Buck started on a story. "Well, Bill gets this idea that to get a stake for a card game we'd hold a shooting match. Now this wasn't just any ordinary town. No sir. This was one of those camptowns that followed the railroaders along the Union

Pacific. Full of gamblers, killers, tough, hard-working men, with liquor, rowdy women, and no law.

"Bill was there working for the Union Pacific. He was a scout and a hunter and everybody pretty much knew Bill Cody. Nobody knew Buck Hawkins. Bill had gambled away his scrip the night before, and I was powerful low on funds myself. So we just decided we'd start a ruckus, him and me, and I'd challenge him to a shootout.

"Now the plan was pretty simple. We'd keep gettin' louder and louder 'til we drew a crowd, and then I'd challenge him. After we got the crowd all lathered up for a shootout, Bill would chicken out. Course that would just make me all the tougher and bolder, so then I was to suggest some trick shooting, you see, and then Bill could throw it.

"So I got the crowd all goin' and Bill, he played hard to get. He finally gives in and I start taking bets. Taking bets I could outshoot famous Bill Cody. We raised $500. We decided on six shots each. Four still targets and two moving cans some onlooker would pitch onto the street.

"The trick worked just grand. I bested Bill, six to four. We took our money and headed to the nearest saloon. Bill got in a game, and I was throwing back a few shots at the bar. The night appeared to be going along just swell when all of a sudden I heard Bill in a rough argument.

"He'd had been drinkin' pretty heavy, and for a moment, I figure he must have forgotten about our trick shooting scheme because he calls to me by name. Then he declares he's known me for nearly 10 years and I can vouch for what an honest man he is. Not everybody in that tent saloon was as drunk as Bill Cody and some of 'em remembered losing part of that $500.

"Bill sobered up mighty quick, and jumped over the table, scooped up most of the money and high tailed it out that front door. There I stood! With about 20 sets of coal black eyes bearing down on me."

"How'd you get out of that one?" Coop leaned in so close he looked as if he might jump into Buck's lap.

"Well folks, right then and there I knew I was doomed. There I stood, my back to the tent wall, with more than a dozen drunk, cheated railroad workers slowly inching my way, and I mean to tell you, railroad workers got some muscle on 'em. I knew I was done for. Dang that Bill Cody!

"All of a sudden I hear this ripping sound behind me! Doggone! Didn't that crazy Cody come around behind the tent saloon with our horses and cut open that wall. We flew out of town, dodging bullets and the loudest string of cuss words you ever heard in all your life!"

"I knew there was a reason you always insisted on a fast horse." Tom tossed a wink to Coop and Cole. Laughter filled the camp, even Soft Cloud found the story silly and to her liking. "Tom, please remind me not to bet on any of Buck's shooting." Her soft smile tried to convince Tom the silly story had dampened her worry.

"Buck and I'll take first watch. We'll wake you at two, at first light we head out," Tom instructed the men.

.

CHAPTER THREE

Sidewinder boiled in violent rage when he learned through camp natter 20 of his renegades had been bested by a handful of ranchers. The big man stomped through the saloon, kicked spittoons, flipped tables, and tossed chairs, not caring if they held men or not. His big, hair-backed hands flung unwary men over the bar, sending broken bottles and whiskey exploding into the air. His greasy, long black hair sailed airborne as he whirled from side to side. Loud, beastly roars escaped his froth-caked mouth.

Those lucky, and wise enough to stay out of his reach, soon found exits and regrouped in the muddy camp town street started by Hooker five years ago. The men had seen Sidewinder's rage before. In fact, many of them had been there the day he heard Tall Dog had been killed by Tom Named by Horse. Hateful, vicious rage had so consumed him that day he strangled the man who possessed the courage, and stupidity, to tell him—and gunned down four others who had been with Tall Dog the day he died.

That day Sidewinder assumed the roles of Mayor, Sheriff, and god in Hooker's camp town, which had remained safe for the renegades and outlaws all this time, thanks to the bottleneck trail leading to it. Of course the Army being busy with the Indian wars helped. With Tall Dog gone the inhabitants had shifted their focus to a few stagecoach jobs, cattle and horse stealing, prospecting, gambling and the like.

The camp town had grown to a population exceeding 500. Today even a few legitimate businesses gave it a go—stores, eating establishments, a few hotels, livery stables, and a blacksmith. But mostly it was a town populated by ruffians, gamblers, soiled doves—

pretty much the seedier side of humanity. Having to sidestep a dead body in the muddy street was not an uncommon occurrence.

Exhausted, Sidewinder stopped breaking chairs and tables, arms and jaws. He tugged the bottom of his buckskin shirt, straightened himself up, and collapsed at a table. "Somebody clean this place up, and get me whiskey!"

A bent and crooked, timid, dirty little man, with a much crumpled felt hat, patchy beard and very buck teeth, quickly brought a bottle, and settled in next to Sidewinder. "You gonna send somebody after them horses, ain't you?"

Sidewinder snatched the bottle from the eager man's hand, wrestled free the cork with his teeth, and spit it in the man's face.

"You know, I heard that were Buck Hawkins and Tom Named by Horse running the herd. You ain't gonna get an easier chance to kill those sons of bitches," urged the little man, wiping grimy hands on his tattered plaid shirt.

Sidewinder looked up and down the little man's pathetic frame and had to employ restraint to keep from pounding him into the floor like a railroad spike with his huge, hairy fist. "You wanna go?"

"No ... No, not me ... I just serve whiskey."

Hardly a man in the camp town, or woman, for that matter, didn't know about the seething hatred Sidewinder held for those two. They'd killed his friend Tall Dog. Then six months later, they'd helped the Army defeat Red Cloud and his Sioux, along with Roman Nose and his Cheyenne, on that hot, hot August day. The day Sidewinder chose to fight alongside his Indian friends, not against them.

Nine hours, the Sioux and Cheyenne had charged that little fort made of wagon boxes. Over and over again they charged and each time more braves fell. Sidewinder himself had been wounded four times, and took nearly a year to heal. All the Sioux and Cheyenne nations knew army scout Buck Hawkins and Tom Named by Horse had been there that day and had defeated the spirit of the great Chief Red Cloud. And still Red Cloud remained friends with Tom Named by Horse, who had taken Red Cloud's only granddaughter, Soft Cloud, for his wife.

Ever since he healed, Sidewinder yearned to go to Tom's ranch on Little Bear Creek and kill him. Kill him for killing Tall Dog.

And yet Red Cloud had given Tom Named by Horse his word that he and his ranch would be safe on Sioux land forever. But Sidewinder was not Sioux. He was Cheyenne. Buck Hawkins and Tom Named by Horse on the open prairie, burdened with a herd of horses, was more temptation than he could try to control. Plans must be made, and he would make them.

****

Tom rolled over on the blanket, grabbed Hawk and balanced him on his knee`. He found great joy in that little boy's giggles, and Hawk always had a giggle handy. More like Buck than his own father in that way.

Soft Cloud, as usual, had been up for some time already, and a happy breakfast fire crackled and snapped. Biscuits roasted, chunks of antelope simmered, and a gallon of coffee boiled on the coals. They had at last reached a point where they never went without coffee.

Tom sat on the blanket next to the fire holding his son and watched the camp come to life as the early morning sun dried dew from the spring grass.

"Nary a bit of trouble from horse thieves, renegades, or horses. Just a peaceful night, riding herd listening to Cole try to hum a tune," Coop settled in next to Tom and Hawk.

"Cole, singin'? It's a wonder them horses didn't break into stampede!" Buck howled.

"Oh, I don't know," Soft Cloud defended, "I've heard Cole sing, and I am sure that's one of the many things about him Hannah Miller finds desirable."

"Holy Cow! If she can tolerate his singin', that explains how she could fall in love with a tree-stump-shaped fellow." Buck's grin grew wider.

"Buck Hawkins, what a terrible thing to say!" Soft Cloud shook her wooden spoon inches from his nose.

Cole wandered into camp reading faces, chuckles and glances tossed his way. "If I was an antelope and I knew you were going to cook me, I believe I could die satisfied," he told Soft Cloud with a nod.

"Thank you, Cole. You're the only gentleman this morning to

compliment my cooking. The others are too busy inventing insults."

"Finish your groceries, boys, and let's get the herd moving. Let's shed this lowland before we get visitors." Tom meant what he said, but he also thought it was time to interrupt the banter; Coop and Buck could go on all day.

In short order, they had fresh horses saddled, the chuckwagon packed, and began moving across the prairie away from the lowlands of the stream. A cool spring morning and being well fed and rested, the horses showed their extra energy, which required everyone to be top notch in their duties. Tom positioned Soft Cloud and the chuck wagon ahead of the herd to serve as a calming effect, and hopefully keep the horses focused on the wagon and not on their spring fever.

Tom had experienced a lot of life since the day he'd killed the hated buffalo hunter. He now understood how the world worked. At least the world he found himself in. Even before leaving the old hider dead, he'd known it was a brutal world, and killing was sometimes necessary. But now he also knew other things were so much more important. Like friendship. A kind of friendship that develops quickly and deepens over time. The friendship he and Buck shared had become indestructible; the kind of friendship that means you can count on one another, without question, without explanation. A bond of trust, and loyalty.

He had also learned about love. In his early years, those years spent with the old hider, he had never known love, except for the love he'd felt for the old horse, Tom Gray. He understood now love can come in many shapes, sizes, and temperaments. Perhaps friendship does too, but love is something different, and he understood that love is necessary to make a man complete. Not only complete in the way Soft Cloud completed him. But complete also in the manner in which a man believes, lives, fights, and dies. He thought of Tall Dog. His love of his Sioux ways, people and lands had caused him to become an evil, fierce killer. Tom understood that, and respected him for it.

Tom had already learned the importance of protecting what's your own. Again he thought of Tall Dog. Tom knew he would protect his wife and child, his friends and his horses and ranch, just as stubbornly as Tall Dog had ever fought for what he'd believed was his and proper. He had learned the importance of helping others and how by helping others, you helped yourself. He remembered the time, three years ago, when he'd rescued little Sarah Jane Hartman and the other children from the mines in the high country with the help of John Bradley. Tom thought of the orphanage the Bradleys started on their ranch. The orphanage he visits once a year.

Funny, he reflected, how a good woman can change a man. Soft Cloud, his wonderful wife, from the moment they met, he knew they would be forever together.

Tom hurried his horse to the wagon and eased up to Soft Cloud. "You doin' all right up here?"

"Going along as easy as the day, and Hawk is asleep in the wagon."

"I'm heading up to Buck to have a look over things. You'll be fine?"

"Should trouble come calling, I have your Winchester by my side and two fast, strong mules in the harness."

Tom waved and put his horse into a strong run, pulling up alongside Cole. "I'll be riding with Buck. Swing out and stay close to the wagon."

Not waiting for an answer, Tom sped away, holding a run until finally he caught Buck.

"Howdy pard, what calls you to the lead?" Buck looked surprised to see Tom in such a hurry.

"Just have one of my feelings. Seen anything at all?"

"I hate when you get your feelings. No, and I've been lookin' real careful."

"Something's up, Buck. Got a real strong feelin'."

"Like I said—I hate when you get your feelings."

"I'm sending Lone Feather to scout the territory east of us. Hang back a little closer to the herd. I want you within sprinting distance of the wagon when we get the company I feel's coming."

"Only two more days to Denver, Tom." Buck pulled his hat to wipe sweat from his forehead.

Tom glanced at Buck's saddle. "Where's your Sharps?"

"Got my Winchester. My Sharps's back in the wagon. Gets a little clumsy riding with two rifles under your leg."

"Let's get it, and plenty of shells. I got a hunch you'll need it."

Soft Cloud studied them with worried eyes when they pulled up next to her. "What's wrong?"

"Nothing at the moment," Buck answered for Tom. "But he has one of his feelings."

Cole rode close enough to be within earshot. "We don't like it when Tom gets one of his feelings!"

"Cole, hustle back to Lone Feather, have him do a wide circle. You tell him I'm looking for trouble. You tell him I said something's up." Convinced that trouble was imminent, Tom slid his Sharps into its scabbard and rode near the wagon. He had to chuckle watching Lone Feather gallop his painted pony up the ridge, waving his Winchester and howling.

"What will we do if we are attacked? How will we protect ourselves and the horses?" Soft Cloud looked more worried than her voice would tell.

"Guess we'll fight."

CHAPTER FOUR

Sidewinder pushed his men hard until they sat within striking distance of Tom Named by Horse and Buck Hawkins. His scouts told him the herd was only 40 miles to the south. With two hours of daylight remaining, he ordered they ride 20 miles more in the direction the herd. They would strike in the morning and it would be glorious, for he had with him 30 of his most greedy men.

When darkness finally swallowed the land, men and horses, Sidewinder ordered the exhausted army of outlaws to make camp for the night.

"Tomorrow I will kill the man that killed my friend. I don't care who kills Buck Hawkins, but Tom Named by Horse, I kill!" Sidewinder paced filled with anticipation, and hatred, among the camp fires.

 Men reclined on their blankets and saddles, some playing cards, many simply resting by their fire, a few already asleep. It had been a long, hot day of hard riding. Not all the men in camp were totally loyal to Sidewinder. They followed him, enjoyed the amenities his camp town had to offer—lawlessness, whiskey, women, fast living, but remained loyal only to themselves.

Sidewinder disliked most of the men that clung to him like ticks on the belly of his horse. Most were lazy, cowardly, and worthless. But he needed numbers. This bunch that he had hand-picked were 30 of the most godless his camp town had to offer. He knew when the fighting started, most likely half of them would turn and flee, and if he had the chance, he would shoot them down like scared rabbits as they scattered.

Tomorrow, Sidewinder would have a good day. The man he

hated most on this earth waited a few miles away, outnumbered and burdened with a herd of horses. He would have Tom Named by Horse's scalp, and his horses too! Tomorrow would be the day Sidewinder had waited for far too long. Tonight he would drink whiskey and sit by himself and think of tomorrow, and of tomorrow night, when the scalp of his hated enemy would hang on his Winchester.

****

Lone Feather rode a lathered and spent horse into camp long after the fire had died out. Only Coop and Cole remained awake as they rode nightwatch 'round the grazing herd. He found Tom, Soft Cloud and Hawk asleep under the wagon.

"I found our trouble," Lone Feather told Tom.

"Tell me."

"Maybe 30 men camped four hours north."

"You think they mean trouble for us?"

"Sidewinder's in that camp." Lone Feather nodded.

"That's real trouble for us."

Tom rolled from under the wagon, careful not to disturb Soft Cloud or Hawk. He motioned for Lone Feather to follow; they walked quietly to Buck's blanket. Chilly night air hung over them, but stars were bright and the moon nearly full. Even though Tom knew trouble was coming, he couldn't help but enjoy the peaceful surroundings. A glance skyward led him to the North Star.

Buck slept cocooned in blankets. Tom shot a playful glance to Lone Feather. They took a corner of Buck's blanket and yanked it from under him, sending Buck rolling onto the grass. To their shock, Buck landed on his feet, revolver in hand, hammer cocked.

"Hold on there, Buck! It's Tom and Lone Feather!"

"Thought you had me. I heard you wiggle out from under that wagon. I'm just hoping you never need to sneak into a renegade camp to cut me loose again, 'cause I think you've lost your touch." Buck grinned as he holstered his 44.

"Lone Feather found Sidewinder four hours north. With about 30 men."

"Well, that can't be good. But if you take a good look around, we're not in too bad a spot. They'd have to come a half mile over open ground to get to us. Of course, we do have the horses to deal with, and I reckon they'll try to scatter 'em."

Tom paced away, moving toward the grazing herd. He held pride in those 65 horses. He had personally started each one of them. Those four sons of Thunder would probably be the best saddle stock Denver City had ever seen.

"This is a tough one, boys," Tom worried aloud.

"Move the horses back. I will take Coop and run the herd south. That way you can make fight from the wagon. We have seen Sidewinder's cowards. You, Buck, Cole and Soft Cloud can stop them here." Lone Feather suggested, then danced, waving his rifle, and broke into a Sioux war song.

"By gosh, Tom! Lone Feather has a good idea. If he and Coop can get started right away and push those horses ten or 15 miles back, maybe find a deep ravine to hide 'em in, we'll give those renegade sons of bitches something to think about," Buck's smile announced he was itching for action.

Lone Feather nodded in agreement, and pretended to shoot at imaginary charging renegades.

Tom turned to the wagon and rested his hands on Lone Feather's bare shoulders. "You get Coop, and run the horses into the first ravine you find and hightail it back here! We probably have three or four hours before they hit us. Have Cole help you get the horses started, but he stays with us, I want his shooting eye right beside me when this party heats up."

Lone Feather broke off at a run. But Tom stopped him, remembering the livestock caught in the center of the wagon box fight. "Take the mules. We don't need them gettin' shot to hell."

Lone Feather, Cole and Coop saddled fresh horses. Tom and Buck positioned the wagon atop a small knoll, then pull it over on its side, exposing the heavy floor planks toward the expected rifle fire. Satisfied with the wagon's placement, Tom released the mules to Coop. Tom figured if Cole returned before Sidewinder arrived, they would have three men firing buffalo rifles and Soft Cloud loading. This stood a good chance of coming out all right.

"Been in tougher spots, Tom," Buck tried to bolster him.

"Not with my wife and son part of the dance."

"I know, Tom; we'll be alright. Let's wrap that little fellow in blankets before the dance starts, so he can't get into any trouble."

Tom and Buck watched as Lone Feather, Coop and Cole started the horses on their fast journey to the safety of some unknown ravine. Even in the bright moonlight, it took only minutes for the riders and the herd to slip out of sight.

"Sure hope Cole gets back here before the fiddlin' starts," Buck said.

Even though Tom laid heavy with worry over the safety of his wife and child, he had to admit, deep down inside, the promised excitement of the coming battle had him anxious and ready to go. Much care had given to the placement of the fortifications. Sacks of beans, flour kegs and other miscellaneous items they had stacked against the floor of the overturned wagon, and thus made a wall to hide behind more than a foot thick.

Beneath the axle beams they dug a trench and tucked Hawk safely into it. Soft Cloud laid three Winchester and three buffalo rifles behind the overturned wagon and had the ammunition neatly arranged, to facilitate rapid reloading. Canteens of water were hidden behind the small fortress as well.

"I guess all we need now are some dance partners," Buck said, but no one heard him. Soft Cloud sat by Hawk. Tom stood, arms resting on the wagon side while his eyes searched the northern horizon. Just enough sun crept into the sky to allow Tom to see for miles in the direction Sidewinder and his renegades would ride.

"Maybe Lone Feather was mistaken," Soft Cloud offered hopefully.

"They're coming," Tom said. His mind drifted back to the hot August day on the Bozeman Trail in '67, when he and Buck and 30 other men had fought behind wagon boxes much like this one for over eight hours. Red Cloud and Roman Nose had over 500 braves. Many of those braves died that day. Tom fired his Sharps rapidly for so long, the barrel became so hot he was forced to urinate on it to cool it.

The Sioux and Cheyenne braves charged over and over again, each time leaving more dead Sioux and Cheyenne and more dead horses in the field in front of them. There were so many dead braves that charging horses stumbled over the bodies. In nine hours, almost 300 braves lay dead. Inside the wagon box fortress, four soldiers and one civilian were killed, and two civilian wood cutters were wounded. Finally, Red Cloud was forced to retreat.

It has been said that Red Cloud had been surprised at the white man's ability to fire their weapons so rapidly. Red Cloud had no way of knowing that the U.S. Army had just received a shipment of a large supply of rifles known as 'Allin converted Springfield rifles.' Over 5,000 percussion muskets had been altered to breech-loading single-shot 58-caliber rim fires, which a man could reload in less than two seconds. Red Cloud had been used to fighting soldiers that required 30 seconds or more to reload, giving him time to create an effective frontal attack. No such time was afforded him and his braves that day.

Cole thundered up behind the wagon, yanking Tom back to the present. "Coop and Lone Feather are well on their way, moving the herd along good and fast," Cole announced as he yanked his saddle and gave his horse a smart slap on the rump to encourage him to leave. The stubborn animal walked a few steps and stopped to graze. Cole snatched up his reins and charged him, whipping his rump and startling the poor horse into a gallop. "He's a good horse. I'd hate to see anything happen to him today."

"Time to make the biscuits, boys! Here they come!" Buck chuckled, unable to hide his excitement.

About two miles away, just visible in the red horizon, specks of horses and riders raced toward them at a full gallop.

The men snatched their rifles and settled into good positions behind the wagon. Soft Cloud left Hawk and squatted behind the men, ready to reload. All three were armed with Sharps Big Fifty's single shot, 50-caliber center-fire breech loaders and could rapidly reload themselves from the neat stacks of cartridges Soft Cloud had arranged at each position. The Winchesters, however, she would reload with 15 rim-fire 44s, as quickly as the men emptied them.

They watched as Sidewinder and his men bore down on them. The specks grew larger and soon became riders and horses. It was still unclear whether or not they noticed the overturned wagon, for they continued to gallop flat out toward them.

"What do you think, Tom? Should we introduce ourselves?" Buck asked with a grin, eager to get started.

"Aim high, so the lead carries, and let's tell 'em Howdy!" Tom ordered.

The fifties roared into action. By the time the lead reached the attackers, Tom, Buck and Cole had reloaded; with a smile and a wink Buck, initiated another round of fire.

"Poor Devils don't know what hit 'em," Cole said flashing a smile that rivaled Buck's own.

****

Sidewinder and his renegades were stunned. They had not expected to be fired upon. Their plan had been to surprise Tom and his people, and slaughter them with little or no resistance. While the large balls of lead had found no targets, the well-orchestrated defense immediately demoralized the lazy cowards who made up Sidewinder's Army. The group scattered, and some turned to flee.

"Get back here, every one of you!" Sidewinder bellowed at his men.

Two cowboys ignored the order and ran their horses hard to escape both the defense they'd stumbled into and Sidewinder's wrath.

Sidewinder raised his Winchester shot them both from their horses. "No one leaves! We will kill Tom Named by Horse and Buck Hawkins today!"

Sidewinder orchestrated a confused, pathetic rally, and they charged again. This time, a little more timidly.

****

"Hell, they ain't even going to make it sporting!" Buck said, as he got a clear sight on the lead rider and fired. He watched through the high sight as the big round slapped the man from his horse.

The three behind the wagon fired mercilessly into the advancing group of attackers. With military precision, large bore buffalo rifles fired, reloaded and fired again. With each volley, men and horses fell. Not a single round from the outlaw's Winchesters reached the protective wagon; their attack was ended before they were within range of their light rifles.

"They're pulling back already! Doggone, that was a short dance." Buck complained.

"They ain't done yet, they just had the shit scared out of 'em. They'll be back." Tom reached for his canteen.

"What do you think they'll do next?" Soft Cloud bent low to

check on Hawk.

"My guess is they'll try to flank us." Buck suggested.

"They'd better swing a wide arc." Cole said with a grin.

****

Bill Cody, Captain W. Green, and Todd Harvey had started west from Fort McPherson two days earlier, for Denver City. The rode on orders from General Carr to arrest two thieves who had stolen from the Army. They were to capture the men, and return them and the livestock they'd stolen, especially the General's favorite saddle horse. The morning of the third day, they moved across the prairie in a fast lope when Cody jerked his horse to a stop.

"Listen to that rifle fire! Rifles and Fifties! There's a skirmish going on just over that rise," Cody turned his horse to Captain Green.

"Let's go!" Captain Green ordered.

They trotted to the crest. Directly below them, lay the overturned wagon. They could also see the renegades reorganizing for another attack.

"Todd Harvey get down there to that wagon!" Captain Green barked. Todd Harvey's horse kicked up dirt before the words cleared the Captain's mouth.

"On the hill, Captain! The thieves are attempting a flanking maneuver." Cody pointed to a small group breaking away from the main body of renegades, and climbing the ridge in their direction.

"Let's ruin their plans!" Captain Green pulled his rifle.

"Hold on, Captain. Your rifle hasn't got the range. I've got just the ticket," Cody said with a grin, dragging out his brand new fifty caliber Ballard.

Cody dropped, propped that long barreled rifle on his arm, neatly raised the high sight, and fired.

****

Todd Harvey reined his horse to a sliding stop behind the wagon, jumped to the ground, snatched his rifle, and took position next to his old friend, Buck.

"That's Cody's new Ballard!" Todd Harvey hooted, slapping his thigh and waving in the direction of the rifle roar.

"How did you fellas find us?" Tom studied Todd Harvey for

an instant. They'd ridden, and fought together in the past, but how on Earth did they drop in today?

"We're on our way to Denver City to round up a couple of thieves that stole 30 horses from the Army. We heard your little get-together goin' on, and you know Cody. You can't have a soirée without invitin' him." Todd Harvey let a round from his own Ballard fly toward the totally confused outlaws.

"Nice rifle." Buck complimented Todd Harvey as he reached for the rifle and thoroughly examined it. "Never actually held one of these."

"Me 'n Cody each got us one, brand-spanking new out of St. Louis! Some outfit named Brown is makin' them. They figure if Cody'll kill a few buffalo with it, they'll sell a lot more. Straight shootin' sons of guns, they are! You boys oughta look into gettin' yourselves one, if you're goin' ta keep throwin' parties like this 'n." And he gently but firmly retrieved his rifle from Buck's admiring hands.

Roars from Tom's Big Fifty, sending three shots toward Sidewinder's bunch, interrupted their conversation. "Like what I got." Tom patted his new model Sharps.

"Don't you men realize we are in the fight for our lives?" Soft Cloud said, with more than a little angst in her voice.

"Naw, we ain't," Todd Harvey let another round fly over the side of the wagon.

"I kind of like that Ballard." Cole joined in.

"Here. Have a shot." Todd Harvey handed his rifle to Cole.

Cole eagerly accepted the Ballard, sighted over the side of the wagon, and dropped a renegade with a single thundering shot.

"Look at that! They're going home already! My barrel ain't even warm," Buck complained.

"Well, I thank the Great Spirit, and hope it is over for good." Soft Cloud quickly moved to retrieve her son and pull the heavy blankets from him.

"It's not over. They'll be back, and a little tougher to fool next time," Tom said.

"Yeah, but they're gone now. So which one of us wants to break the news to Lone Feather and Coop?" Buck said, nearly laughing as he pointed to two riders galloping in from the south.

At the same time, Cody and Captain Green stormed down

the ridge toward the small group behind the overturned wagon.

CHAPTER FIVE

Captain Green, Bill Cody, Lone Feather and Coop gathered on south side of the wagon. For a brief moment, they looked at each other with a look that betrayed their inner thoughts. And then finally Cody spoke, "Damn short dance, wasn't it fellas?"

"Dance?" Soft Cloud screamed, "Dance! My child's life was in danger! How can you make a joke at a time like this, when we could've been overrun and all of us killed and my two-year-old son left dead?"

"Naw, couldn't have happened." Todd Harvey spit into the dust, dragged his gloved hand across his moth. "Not today."

Tom showed a sheepish grin to his friends, and gave Soft Cloud a reassuring hug. Reassurance came cheap, though. They still had two days of prairie travel after rounding up the horses, and the danger of another attack from Sidewinder and his bunch remained very real.

Tom held his hand out to Captain Green. "Howdy, I'm Tom Named by Horse. This is my wife Soft Cloud, and my son, Hawk. This here's Coop, and that savage over there is Lone Feather. The short fellow is Cole. Mighty glad you three happened along."

"Glad to be of service," Captain Green returned.

"Doggone Buck Hawkins, glad to be able to return the favor. Remember that day along the Union Pacific with Tall Dog and that survey crew?" Bill Cody gave Buck a man's handshake and an even a harder slap on his back.

Buck flashed his tremendous smile, memories of that day only served to widen it. "What a day that was, but I would have held up better if we'd killed Tall Dog that day. He got to work me over pretty good after that, and Tom here had to save my bacon."

A brief moment of uncommon silence fell over the gathering of friends as they each, in their own way, remembered the events that befell Buck and Tom that summer.

"So you're on your way to Denver City. How about we all travel together? I have a feeling Soft Cloud would like that, and maybe when we get done with our business in town, if you haven't caught the fellows you're after, we can give you a hand," Tom suggested to Bill Cody.

"You folks are going to Denver City? What business is it you're going to do?" Captain Green inquired.

"Takin' 65 fine horses to the auction there!" Buck boasted.

"Be all right with you, Captain?" Cody asked.

"Fine by me, give me a chance to get to know this Buck Hawkins I've heard so much about." Captain Green studied Buck in mock scrutiny.

"I am afraid a two-day journey driving horses is hardly enough time to get to know Buck," Soft Cloud said, noticeably comforted to know they would have added protection.

"Coop, you and Todd Harvey mount up and start out in the direction Sidewinder and his outfit headed. Try to get a handle on how bad we spooked 'em." Tom gave Todd Harvey quick glance.

"We'll do 'er, Tom!" Todd Harvey assured.

"Let's set this wagon right and get to the horses," Tom said. "Take Lone Feather with you. Maybe with him along, you'll be able to find us by the time Soft Cloud has dinner cooked."

"We'll take Lone Feather, but I'll bet we can follow the smell of Soft Cloud's biscuits directly to camp!" Coop swung up on his horse.

Tom and Cole fastened ropes to the high side of the wagon, Captain Green and Bill Cody pulled the wagon upright. In a few moments the supplies were reloaded, and the chuckwagon sat ready to roll.

"We got no mules!" Buck announced and burst into laughter. "We got harnesses, we got Cole's horse, and we got Cody's horse ..."

"If you don't mind, gentlemen, I'll ride my horse." Captain Green interrupted.

With a little effort, and more than a little jocularity, they altered harnesses to fit Cole's and Cody's horses. Soon one Captain riding his horse, and one very heavily laden chuckwagon started across the prairie.

Darkness had just begun to hint it might be time for camp when they drove up to the herd, still in the ravine and grazing contently. Soft Cloud went right to work, and set up her kitchen on the rear of the chuck wagon. Tom started a cook fire, Cole rode out to count the horses.

"Looks like a good herd from here, boys." Captain Green surveyed the milling horses.

"I can ride the hell out of 'em, Captain. But Tom here breeds 'em and schools 'em." Buck said with a wink and a nod of satisfaction tossed Tom's way.

"The Captain's right. You ought to do right well at the auction." Cody agreed.

The men spread blankets near Soft Cloud's fire and began to make themselves at home. Tom, as usual, held Hawk. He relaxed, content to just listen to Buck and Cody spin yarns. Captain Green chose to listen as well. Everybody there knew the business with Sidewinder was not complete, but they also knew little could be done by talking about it while sitting on wool blankets next to a fire.

"Too bad Mr. Majors doesn't have the Pony Express anymore. You boys could get a good price for some of that stock." Bill Cody said.

"You two rode Pony Express together, isn't that correct?" Captain Green asked.

"Sure did. We didn't see much of each other then, but we'd hear high tales and try to best each other." Cody gave a sly chuckle.

"Yeah, I heard tell Cody here got his start as a messenger boy." Buck teased.

"As a matter of fact, I did. I was 13 and weighed 'bout maybe 85 pounds. My mother actually introduced me to Mr. Majors, and every chance I got I was sure to show off my equestrian skills. Soon I became his messenger boy, and I'd carry dispatches between his wagon trains on their trips across the plains. Eventually, I got to ride the Pony Express for Mr. Majors. A finer, more honest man never lived."

"Amen to that." Buck agreed, shaking his head.

"Mostly I rode between Red Buttes and Three Crossings, about 120 miles. A long and lonely trail that required crossing the

North Platte River. More than a half-mile wide, and sometimes more than 12 feet deep. My longest ride, though, happened when I got to Three Crossings one day and found my replacement rider had been killed the night before! So I had to run that extra 76 miles. But by golly, I got to Rocky Ridge on time. Three hundred and eighty-four miles, round trip, stopping only twice to eat and three times to change horses." Bill Cody boasted, deservedly proud of himself.

"Yeah, but you didn't have Indian trouble." Buck said, not to be outdone by Bill Cody. "I came galloping into Reid's Station on Carson River and found no one there, and no change of horses. I did find feed for the horse I rode in on, so I gave him a 20-minute break then started for the next station, 15 miles farther down the river. I figured I was done, having already done 75 miles, but the next rider wouldn't mount up! The superintendent was at the station, and even he couldn't get the next rider to go. So he offers me 50 dollars to make the ride. Now this next leg was known to be dangerous, and there were reports of hostiles about, which is why I reckon the poor fellow wouldn't go.

"A few minutes later, I started out. It was 35 miles through dangerous territory, without a change of horses. I got there on time. Changed horses and headed out for another 30 to the next station, switched horses again and pushed on. When I pulled into Smith's Creek, I'd traveled 185 miles.

"But this tale ain't over yet, boys. They gave me 10 hours rest, then sent me back with the return express. Sure enough, when I got into Cold Springs, I found that the station had been attacked. The keeper was dead and all the horses were gone! I had no choice. I watered my horse, which I had just pushed for 30 miles, and we started for the next station, about 40 miles away. It was getting dark by then, and that part of the road went through sagebrush, high enough in some places to hide a horse. For that whole 40 miles my eyes were glued to my poor, tired horse's ears, watching for any signal of danger. But I made it safely and reported what I had found. I took off for the next leg, and when I arrived at Adobe station, it was under attack! This station was so big that the station man, his two helpers, myself, and 10 horses hid inside. Well, I rested there for an hour, and after dark started out on my own route. Total trip: 380 miles, including crossing the Sierra Nevada!"

"We always agreed that was the toughest trip ever made by

any Express rider!" Cody saluted Buck with his tin coffee cup held high.

Fine stories of days gone by were interrupted when Coop dropped his saddle beside the fire and announced, "All the horses are here! We didn't lose a single one!"

CHAPTER SIX

Three mornings after the incident with Sidewinder, Tom, Buck, Coop, Cole, and Lone Feather drove their horses down Denver City's Main Street. Soft Cloud guided the chuckwagon, flanked by Cody, Todd Harvey. Captain Green followed the herd as it slowly made its way toward the stockyards at the end of town, where the auction would be held in two days.

"I'll need to check with the sheriff on the two we were sent to roundup." Captain Green said. "Cody, Harvey. You're free to stay with Buck and Tom. I'll look you up at the stockyards when I'm done my business."

Tom, Buck and the boys drove the horses along the dusty street to the stockyards and corralled them in the first four pens. Cole, Coop, and Buck set out in search of a saloon.

"Lone Feather, you'd better stay here with the horses. They don't serve savages in any of the saloons here in this 'civilized' town." Tom teased.

"I will stay here and watch your horses. But you bring me a steak dinner."

"Done," He took Soft Cloud's hand and began to turn away.

"Tom Named by Horse! Good to see you again!" Boomed a voice above the noise of the stockyards. Tom recognized Chester Donovan without turning. For the last two years he bought every horse Tom brought to the auction. "I'll not have you folks stay at the hotel this year. You're coming to the ranch with me and the missus," Donovan insisted.

Tom shook hands with Donovan, a big man with a big ranch. Always well-dressed, Donovan sported a white felt hat, a white shirt and fancy vest. His carriage, pulled by a matched pair of white horses, boasted red leather seats.

"I promised Lone Feather a steak dinner, but if you can give me a minute to round one up, Soft Cloud, Hawk and I would be honored to spend the night at your ranch."

Tom left Soft Cloud and little Hawk in the carriage with Donovan and hustled to the Bulls Head Saloon.

He spied his men at a large round table in the center of the saloon. Cody deep in the telling about the time he rescued Todd Harvey from an angry Paiute woman. "Soft Cloud and I will be spending the night at the Donovan ranch. Keep an eye on things here for us, Buck, and take a steak dinner to Lone Feather at the pens." Tom told Buck.

Shots in the street sent Tom, along with everybody at the table, running to the street, weapons drawn. Donovan slumped over in his carriage seat.

Tom and Buck outpaced the others, pushing their way through the gathering crowd. Donovan had been shot but was still alive. "They took Soft Cloud and your boy, Tom. Ten of 'em, maybe more. They surrounded us before I could react. A big hairy bastard told me to tell you he was going to do your wife good before he killed her, and he would feed your boy to the wolves. I didn't even see who shot me ... I'm sorry, Tom."

"Cole, Coop take care of the stock, and get Donovan to a doctor. Buck, Lone Feather come on!" Tom shouted.

"I'm ridin' with ya!" Todd Harvey shouted.

"I'm in too, Tom." Bill Cody said.

Tom saddled Thunder, Buck readied Diablo, Lone Feather took a fresh mustang and, at Tom's suggestion, Cody and Todd Harvey each took a son of Thunder. In moments, they galloped into the prairie outside Denver City.

No words were needed. Keen eyes, followed the trail picked up just outside the stockyards. All five men, experienced trackers and crack-shots with their Winchesters, revolvers and buffalo rifles rode silent, grim painted their faces and posture. There was little doubt they could overpower Sidewinder and however many men he had with him. If they could just catch them before Soft Cloud or Hawk came to any harm.

They followed the trail across the prairie toward low foothills the day long, and into the evening. As the sun slipped low and shadows stretched, Tom allowed Buck and Cody to take lead position, knowing they were the better trackers.

"We have to go on foot now, fellas," Cody dismounted.

Lone Feather glanced at Tom, then left the group to scout on his own.

Cody leading the way, they walked on through the night, into foothills, across streams, and through brush. Cody never lost the trail or needed to backtrack. Tom felt fortunate to have Cody with them that day.

"They split up here." Cody rested on one knee to examine trail sign.

****

Soft Cloud fought with all the toughness of any Sioux brave, but there were just too many. They came from nowhere and shot Chester Donovan, punched her face, knocking her to the carriage floor while someone snatched Hawk from her arms. She wheeled about, jumped from the carriage to the nearest man's horse, wrestled his gun from his hand and pointed it at his head before he could take his next breath. But when the man she came to know as Sidewinder called out for her attention, and she saw the knife already breaking the skin of little Hawk's neck, she relented.

They had been riding in the direction of the foothills for hours now and her arms, tightly bound behind her, had been numb for some time. She hadn't seen Hawk since they'd left town. A rage burned in her chest that she had never felt before. She promised herself that should any harm come to her son, every horrible technique of slow death mastered by the Sioux would be put to use on those cowards who hurt her child.

Where was Tom? Certainly he had heard the gunshots, and surely he would be tracking them. But why had he not found her yet? Was he dead? No, if he were dead, she would feel it. He was coming and he would save her and Hawk.

"Stop here to rest the horses." Sidewinder walked to the edge of the ridge they had just ascended, and surveyed land below. "We wait here until we are certain he follows." Then, with hate-filled eyes, he glared at Soft Cloud. "I will cut the eyes from the face of Tom

Named by Horse."

Soft Cloud returned the hateful defiant stare, and was pleased to realize Sidewinder was unable to keep his eyes locked on hers. This man, she would put to a slow death.

"You are mine." His big hairy hands squeezed her face, she heard her ears pop. Then he smashed her to the ground and crawled onto her. He tried to kiss her, she bit him in the cheek, tearing flesh, and spit it in his eyes. He punched her face, and the world went black.

CHAPTER SEVEN

"Looks like they split up." Buck studied the tracks. "Some continued straight on for those hills out yonder and others headed back to town."

"That's how I see it." Cody agreed. "It don't figure they would take Soft Cloud and the boy back to town. They're headed to the hills."

"Sidewinder wants me, for killing Tall Dog," Tom said. "That's what this is all about."

"You got it." Buck said almost to himself.

Tom walked with Thunder a short distance along the trail headed to the hills. The trail might be difficult in the dark, but he'd already identified their destination, about 20 miles ahead a sharp ridge erupted from lower hills surrounding it. That's where Sidewinder would be. Why would he send half his men back to town? Just as a decoy? But if he wanted Tom to follow him, he was damn sure going to get what he wanted.

"Gotta be waitin' for us on that ridge, Tom." Buck said.

"That's how I got it figured." Tom swung up on Thunder. "I ain't walking anymore. I aim to save my wife and son."

"We're with you. Let's get there before sunup." Buck mounted too.

Tom took the lead and set a fast pace. He struggled to fight visions of what Sidewinder and his kind could do to a woman. By God, if anyone hurt her or Hawk they would have one hell of a price to pay.

"You've got 'er pegged, Tom." Cody pointed to a faint spark of light on the high ridge that could only mean campfires.

Tom had already seen the tiny flicker given off by several small campfires that hung high like so many stars. He knew that could only mean one thing: "Here I am, come and get me, if you're man enough!" Well, I'm coming, you overgrown bastard.

They pushed on at a flat-out run, asking for everything the horses had. At this rate, they would cover the distance that separated them from the ridge in no more than an hour.

All of a sudden, like a streaking meteor, Lone Feather bolted beside them on his sturdy mustang. "They're behind me!" He shouted. "Get ready they're coming hard!"

That's why the two groups! Tom understood immediately. Sidewinder sat on the ridge. He knew Tom would be here by now. He wanted to watch from above as Tom and Buck got cut down.

"Everybody stop!" Tom swept into motion, leaped from Thunder, snatched his big fifty, and landed on his feet. In a second, all five men dismounted. "Lone Feather! Gather these horses and run ahead! Don't lose these horses, whatever you do! On the ground, everybody! Fire at the dust!" Tom barked orders as concisely and calmly as any seasoned cavalry officer.

Each man got away two rounds and then a third, before the dust dissipated. "I guess that changed their plans." Cody chuckled.

"Anybody see anything to shoot at?" Buck asked.

"Not a damned thing." Todd Harvey complained.

Tom focused on what might be a target. Just for a second he thought he saw a sliver of light. Then he realized what it was: conchos, silver conchos. Those stupid renegades put conchos in their hair, on their saddles, sometimes on their hats. "We have targets, boys," he told them. "Look close, you can see the moonlight on their conchos."

"Holy cow, Tom's right. I can see 'em!" Buck fired.

"Let's turn their lights out, boys." Bill Cody let go a shot.

The four big rifles roared time and time again. To Buck, it sounded like a symphony. To Bill Cody, like a dance. To old Todd Harvey, it sounded too familiar ... to Tom Named by Horse, it sounded like not enough.

They shot until nothing was left to fire at. Not a single shot had been returned.

****

36

Even in the darkness, from his vantage point, Sidewinder was able to watch the four men approach his camp. Much called his attention in the camp, but now he wanted to watch his men kill the four below. When he saw them stop and fire at his men, his rage boiled over. "Build those fires higher! I want plenty of light. I want to be sure Tom Named by Horse comes to find me and his wife and breed kid."

How could this be? How could he lose sight of the riders below? The moon hung brighter now than it had been. Sidewinder strained over the edge into darkness below. And he saw nothing. Not even the mostly white, paint horse Buck Hawkins rode. It didn't matter anyway; he had the woman and the kid. "They will come. They will come and we will be ready and I will wear Tom Named by Horse's scalp on my belt!"

****

"Lone Feather, sneak to their camp and stay close. When they see us, every man in that camp will run to the edge of the plateau. I'm counting on you to get in and save Soft Cloud and Hawk when the shooting starts." Tom motioned for Lone Feather to be on his way. As quiet as an owl, and just as deadly, the wily Sioux brave faded into darkness.

"Give me a minute, Tom. I gotta make Diablo as invisible as that Sioux." Buck emptied his canteen into the dirt, creating a puddle from which he grabbed handfuls of mud and turned Diablo from black-and-white, to black.

For nearly an hour they pushed for as much speed as they could manage while staying concealed in the foothills' thick brush. All the while Sidewinder's fires illuminated the ridge to the point that Tom could almost get a count of the men up there. The large fires also made it impossible for Sidewinder and his men to look down into the darkness and see their approaching demise.

When they neared the ridge as close they dare, Tom stopped and studied the fires some 300 feet above them. "We're not going to be able to do much from here."

"Looks like it could be five miles out and around. We got no choice. We must go around and come down at them from the back." Cody reasoned.

"Looks that way." Buck agreed.

Slowly they led their horses along the rocky shelf border of the high ridge, a very tedious process. The footing unsafe, the horses anxious, a slip and fall would prove deadly. The slow pace of their progress tore at Tom's gut. The thought of Soft Cloud and Hawk up there, and yet they could not hurry.

On and on he led his friends, carefully selecting each footstep. Twice, horses stumbled, the unstable earth beneath their feet giving way; only the alertness of the men and the surefootedness of the horses prevented disaster.

Worry overtook Tom. At most, they had an hour of darkness. They needed to attack the camp while still dark, while the fools' fires could prevent Sidewinder and his men to see into the darkness to return fire. Unconsciously, Tom picked up the pace, making things worse, for the higher their ascent, the looser the footing.

When he heard the frightened horse struggle, Tom spun about. The last horse in line, Todd Harvey's horse, had slipped over the edge, clinging to the trail with his front feet and kicking frantically with his hinds. They watched helplessly as Todd Harvey pulled hard on the reins trying to assist the panicked horse.

Tom jammed his fingers in his mouth and released such a loud whistle every man and horse jumped. Todd Harvey's horse, responding to Tom's call, somehow found the footing necessary and leaped onto the trail, nearly on top of Todd Harvey. Tom felt his legs go weak, dropped to his knees. Too much, he thought. Too much depended on him now. He could make no more mistakes.

"Take it easy, Tom." Buck said in the kindest voice Tom had ever heard him use. "We'll get her. We'll get 'em both."

"We're all right back here." Todd Harvey whispered. "Let's move on."

Buck grabbed Tom by the back of his vest, jerked him to his feet. "Come on, son. Pick up your feet and get going." Tom could not help feeling shaky. His legs felt as if they were not his own. Slowly, ever so carefully, he resumed the task of picking trail along the narrow ledge. Higher, ever higher, closer to Soft Cloud and closer to Hawk.

They traveled on, one careful step after another. Sometimes the ledge so narrow the men had to walk sideways. How the horses kept from falling over the side, none of the men could figure. Finally, they were above the ridge overlooking Sidewinder's camp. Tom stole a glance over his left shoulder. They were about 100 feet above the camp and 1,000 yards to the north of it, and just ahead Tom saw thicker brush.

Once in the dense brush, they tied the horses behind. Tom and Buck stood shoulder to shoulder and easily counted their adversary's numbers gathered round the large campfires.

"I make out 14." Buck said.

"Yeah, that's what I get. Can you see Soft Cloud or Hawk?" Tom asked.

"Fourteen to four, that's regular odds for us, Cody." Todd Harvey said.

"Fourteen to five; we got us an Indian out there somewhere." Cody corrected.

"Well hell, Cody, then I can sit this one out." Todd Harvey said.

"How much closer do you figure we can get?" Tom asked anyone who might answer.

"We have good cover for another hundred feet or so, beyond that we'd be in plain sight. I pretty much like it right where we're at." Cody volunteered.

"We're just so far away. I make it a 1,000 yards or more to the camp." Tom protested.

"Tom, I know you're worried about Soft Cloud and Hawk. For Christ's sake we all are, or we wouldn't be here with you. If we try to move in any closer someone's likely to see us, and they'll kill 'em for sure." Buck reasoned.

"Look here, why don't we move down to the end of the brush? We would have clear shootin', there's nothin' between that brush line and their camp, 'cept that downhill slope." Todd Harvey argued for Tom.

It was agreed and they snuck through the brush and stopped just inside the thicket line. They enjoyed a remarkable field of vision, and recognized that most of the men in the camp were either drunk or asleep. Still, Tom could not see Soft Cloud or Hawk. He would feel better if he could at least see Lone Feather. Nothing left to do, but to get at it.

"Ready, Buck?" Tom loaded his Sharps.

"Yep." Buck raised his and checked Cody.

"Ready here." Cody affirmed.

"Me too." Todd Harvey said.

"Everybody picks a standing target; second round the blankets, then fire at whatever is still moving." Tom directed.

The four big rifles filled the night air with a thunderous, collective roar and powder smoke. Before the first rounds slammed their targets, the second volley exploded, and the third just as quickly.

****

"What the hell's going on?" Sidewinder bellowed as the man's chest standing beside him exploded. He grabbed the falling man and tossed him aside. "They got behind us and above us! Shoot back, you cowards!"

The fifty caliber balls of lead rained into the camp at such a rapid pace that half of Sidewinder's men were dead before he gave that order. The other half were just simply stunned as they snatched their rifles and dove for cover.

****

Lone Feather dashed into the camp at the first volley, and with a mighty swing of his war club, smashed flat the man's skull who guarded Soft Cloud. He meant to grab her arm and yank her to safety, but the weight of the dead man, and her arms still tied behind her back made him fail.

Lone Feather dropped, pushed the dead renegade from Soft Cloud, and with the quickness of a skilled Sioux warrior, slashed the leather bindings that held her arms. Soft Cloud could not stand so Lone Feather squatted by her side. They huddled deep inside the renegades' camp, but Sidewinder's men had their attention focused on the hell coming their way from Tom and the others above them.

Lone Feather saw Sidewinder charge him and fired his Winchester. At that instant Soft Cloud recognized Lone Feather, and all that she had suffered that day came rushing to the surface. Unable to control herself she grabbed, and smothered her close friend and wept. It was just enough to knock Lone Feather's aim high and wide; his bullet missed Sidewinder, as the big renegade threw his knife. The blade found its mark in Lone Feather's chest, and Sidewinder grabbed Hawk and a horse and galloped over the ridge, into the black prairie below.

His remaining men fought on, giving Sidewinder time to escape. But between the buffalo rifles raining fire down on them from above and Lone Feather's Winchester biting at them from the rear, they could only give him a very few minutes.

****

Tom ran down the hill amid the waning gunfire and fell beside his beloved wife in seconds. He brushed hair from her eyes and examined her beaten and swollen face, and held her.

They sat together, slowly rocking. They wept desperately, neither aware of their surroundings.

Lone Feather struggled to his feet and limped to Buck, Sidewinder's knife still in his chest. "Can you pull this out without killing me?"

"Let me ponder this a second." Buck led him near a fire.

"Hell, that ain't more than a flesh wound." Todd Harvey said. "Why I remember one time with Cody when this fellow run up behind me…. "

"This is not the time." Cody cautioned with a subtle movement of his hand.

"He's right though, Lone Feather, I don't think it's too bad." Buck said.

"Dammit Buck, pull it out then." Lone Feather urged.

In a fast jerk, without warning, Buck yanked the short bladed skinning knife from Lone Feather's chest before his complaint faded. "Todd, gimme some rags over here so I can tie this thing up."

"Use this knife to scalp him." Lone Feather ordered.

"Happy to." Buck said.

Todd Harvey searched through the camp and found half a dozen canteens still full of water. He brought them to Tom. "Go ahead and help her clean up a bit Tom."

The others busied themselves, checking the horses tied on the picket line just outside the camp. "Twelve horses. I counted 14 men. Sidewinder took one horse. Who took the other?" Buck asked Cody.

"Could've wandered away when Sidewinder cut the picket

line, or maybe they never had 14 horses." Cody suggested.

"Yeah, maybe," Buck said. "But I got a bad feeling about that missing horse."

Buck and Cody stood a moment and watched Tom, as he cradled Soft Cloud, well aware of the fact that he needed to know about his son. They walked together across the campsite.

Tom wrapped a blanket around Soft Cloud and sat facing a fire with her on his lap. Soft Cloud continued to sob. Her dainty body trembled as she struggled to catch breath. Tom held her tight, his head buried in her neck.

"Hate to have to tell you, Tom, but Lone Feather saw Sidewinder get away with Hawk." Buck said.

He looked up at Buck, dust and grit on his face smudged and streaked by tears.

Buck sat on the blanket and laid his strong arm on Tom's shoulder. "We got 'em, Tom. They're all dead." Even as he said the words, Buck realized it was no comfort to his tormented friend and less to Soft Cloud.

CHAPTER EIGHT

As soon as they had light enough to track by, Tom and Buck started on Sidewinder's trail down the slope and out to the prairie. A whole lot of talking had been necessary to convince Cody and Todd Harvey to escort Soft Cloud and Lone Feather back to Denver City.

"Find out if Chester Donovan survived, and take them to his ranch. They'll be safe there. We'll meet back at Donovan's outfit when we've finished this. If you and Todd Harvey need to move on before we return, thank you for this." Buck had told Cody, as they parted company. Tom remained unable to speak, and were it not for his son, he would gladly let Sidewinder's debt ride a little while longer so he could nurse his wife back to full health. But that could never be. Not while his son was in danger.

The sun danced high and burned hot as the two friends traced Sidewinder's tracks. Tom's mind shifted from his tortured wife to his helpless son, out in this heat with that fat son of a bitch. He knew Hawk would be suffering in the hot sun with no water, rest, or shade, as long as Sidewinder had him.

Thunder was as good a tracker as any man or dog. Tom let the reins lay loose; the black horse kept his nose low and followed the trail and scent of Sidewinder's horse. All through the day the two traveled in this fashion, making slow but steady progress, Thunder's nose and Buck's keen eye never lost the trail.

They continuously moved northeast. Buck figured Sidewinder was headed for the camp town in the high country north of Fort Laramie. If that were true, they would have plenty of time and opportunity to overtake him and save little Hawk. Several times throughout the day, Buck tried for conversation. But Tom never responded. He simply sat Thunder looking ahead, scanning the prairie. His rifle loaded and ready lying across his thighs, not in the scabbard.

As shadows appeared on the prairie floor and twilight approached, Buck tried again. "Think we ought to rest the horses? Maybe figure on makin' camp for the night?"

As before, Buck received no answer, so on they rode, into the darkening flatlands. Buck knew Sidewinder had not been able to rest his horse, either. He also knew Sidewinder was a very big man and, even though Hawk was a mere child, his horse carried far more weight than either of their two. Buck reasoned Sidewinder would stop for the night; and if Thunder could keep them on the trail, this could be over soon enough.

They passed through a patch of tall sage when Tom jerked Thunder to a halt. In the same instant Tom pulled the rifle to his shoulder. Both horses stood still and quiet.

"What have you?" Buck whispered.

"Something's just ahead. See in that low spot?"

Buck did see something, perhaps a mule deer or an antelope. But he didn't think it was Sidewinder. They stepped down, dropped their reins to the ground, and crept ahead.

Buck relaxed first, spying a very sweaty, tired horse. "Here's that missing horse, Tom. That fat old bastard knew damn well you'd be chasing him. He left that camp with two horses and your son."

"He's not got a big lead on us. Look here, the sweat on this horse is still dripping off her. Too dark now to be sure of the trail. Either we stop, or trust Thunder's nose," Tom kicked the dirt.

"Not sure what to say, Tom. Either way we lose. Stay here till sun up, and the bastard picks up six hours on us. Continue on, and if Thunder strays from the trail, we could lose it for good. Your call, Tom."

Tom said nothing. Instead, he walked to Thunder and stepped into the saddle and walked on. Buck decided to stay on foot. Every now and then he could still make out clear sign of trail.

Tom sensed that Thunder still ran true on trail. Buck walked alongside, his eyes always on the ground just ahead of Thunder's nose. They walked on through a very long, quiet night. As the sun began to show itself, soft footing proved indeed Thunder had never strayed.

"I'll be damned, there's blood here." Buck jumped in front of Thunder and studied the dirt. "I believe that fat old bastard is nicked. Maybe Lone Feather didn't miss after all!"

Tom leapt down and knelt beside Buck to examine the blood. With the sun's rays just skimming the grass tops, it became possible to see the occasional drop of blood.

"Holy Cow! I wonder if ol' Thunder has been trailin' that son of a bitch's blood all along," Buck hooted. "Sidewinder's bound to tire now."

"He can get as tired as he wants, just so he doesn't die." Tom gave Buck those horribly inhuman eyes he could sometimes manifest. So brutal and cold were Tom's eyes when hatred and rage overtook him, they chilled Buck to his very core. Without a word, Tom remounted and pushed Thunder on, quicker now.

"Tom, we ought to give these horses a break. There's no water for miles in this direction and we haven't rested or watered them since we started."

"They can rest in a little while. It won't be much longer now." Tom's answer shocked Buck.

Buck knew sometimes Tom had an extra sense and he had learned to believe in it. So he pulled his big fifty and slipped in a shell. They rode on again in silence as the sun climbed ever higher. Hotter and hotter the day became, so hot that the rifle barrel lying on Buck's thigh became hot enough to make him reposition it regularly. He turned to glance at Tom, and what he saw worried him. His friend appeared not human, just six feet of muscle and hate. Their horses were exhausted, but neither would quit. On and on Thunder and Diablo marched across a burning prairie. Buck squinted at the sun. It had already passed its zenith and was just beginning its slip from the sky.

All at once, Tom jumped down and took the magnificent stance he used when he was about to fire his buffalo rifle. Before Buck could look across the prairie to see what his target, Tom fired. Buck tried to follow the shot, but Tom's second shot caused him to flinch. But at Tom's third shot he saw a horse and rider fall—perhaps a half mile away! Tom remounted and galloped toward the fallen horse before the smoke cleared the end of his rifle. Buck could do little except to dig heels into Diablo and race along.

"I'll take my son, you bastard." Tom hollered after he stopped Thunder less than 200 feet from the fallen horse.

The fat coward lay hidden behind his horse, and he had Hawk, naked as the day he was born, positioned on the horse's carcass to prevent Tom from firing again.

"I guess you'll give me a horse and let me ride out of here, or I'll cut your little bastard's head off." Sidewinder yelled back. "He's burning up in the sun. Little fella lost all his clothes. He's as red as a sunset, and hot as a branding iron."

"Naw, I don't think you'll hurt 'im. In fact I'll make a bet with you, that you'll cover my boy up right now."

"The hell I will. This little half-breed is bound to die!"

Before the last word cleared Sidewinder's lips, Tom let fly another fifty-caliber shell. The ball of lead found its mark less than three inches to the left of his son, in the carcass of the horse, spewing blood, hide, and hair in Sidewinder's face.

Sidewinder returned fire: three quick shots from his Winchester. One struck Tom in the thigh, knocking him backward. He jumped to his feet and with no hesitation fired back. This round found Sidewinder's exposed shoulder, tearing his arm from the socket. Almost as fast as the shell itself, Tom sprinted to his son. Buck followed without delay, bringing the horses.

Tom sat on the horse and grabbed Hawk. No place on him was free of burned skin.

Sidewinder lay on the ground moaning. "You shot my goddamn arm off! I'm going to bleed to death." He spat at Tom.

"Not right away. But you are going to die." Tom said, as politely as if he were at a dinner table. Then carefully he covered his son with his own shirt and passed him to Buck. "Take him for a walk and make that shirt wet with your canteen. Maybe you can water our horses. I'm going to be busy for awhile."

Buck handed Tom Sidewinder's skinning knife he had pulled from Lone Feather's chest. "Lone Feather asked that you cut this bastard with this knife."

"Glad to oblige." Tom yanked his saddlebags from Thunder. "There's a few things in here I'll need."

"You half-breed son of a bitch, you ain't cuttin' nobody." Sidewinder shouted and began to rise.

With horribly icy eyes, Tom glared at Sidewinder and said

simply. "Lie down. And I don't think I am a half breed! I'm one hundred percent mean." The big man did as he was told.

The puddle of blood in the prairie dust next to Sidewinder's shoulder grew in size too rapidly to suit Tom. From the saddlebag he grabbed a long strip of leather. He put his foot in the middle of Sidewinder's chest, wrapped the leather around the shoulder stump, and with a strong tug, fashioned a tourniquet of sorts to slow the bleeding. "Can't have you dying too soon." Tom said with a grin and his iced eyes burned into Sidewinder's own. From the saddlebag Tom retrieved four short stakes. "I guess I only need three, seems you're short a wing."

With incredible peace and patience, Tom drove a stake by each ankle. He tied Sidewinder's legs to the stakes. Then he did the same with the groaning man's remaining arm.

Sidewinder knew resistance was futile, so he didn't struggle. All he could do was to hope the end would be quick.

But Tom had other plans. With the short skinning knife he cut every stitch of clothing from the big man's body, then sat calmly to watch Sidewinder bake. He was still sitting and watching when Buck and Hawk returned. As if at a family picnic, Tom stood, took little Hawk, and gave him a tender hug and kiss. "You go back now with Uncle Buck. I'll be along tomorrow. Mother is waiting for you." He handed him back to Buck. Surprise showed on Buck's face, but he needed no more instruction. He and Hawk mounted Diablo and turned for Denver City.

As ruthless a man as Sidewinder had been, the terror he felt at the hands of Tom Named by Horse danced on his face.

Tom waited until Diablo was gone from sight. Sidewinder struggled against his bindings just often enough to suit Tom. He sat and watched as the white skin cooked red.

"I have heard many stories of how you burned people alive. I have heard other stories about how you enjoyed raping other men's wives and daughters. I hope you understand, this time, you picked the wrong woman." Tom straddled Sidewinder as he spoke. He leaned forward and stuck just the tip of the skinning knife into Sidewinder's skin, just below the rib cage. "Do you know what I'm going to do?"

CHAPTER NINE

In the darkest hours just before daybreak two days later, Tom rode Thunder to the Donovan's sprawling house. Exhausted, he simply unbridled and uncinched the big horse, let his saddle fall to the ground and gave Thunder a smack on the rump. Then he stumbled up the wooden steps, crossed the wide porch and knocked on the door.

After several moments the Donovans' house servant flung open the door. "Yes sir, how can I help you?"

"I'm Tom. I believe my wife Soft Cloud and my son Hawk are here."

"Yes sir! Yes sir. They are here. I'll tell them you have arrived."

"Are they sleeping?"

"Why yes sir, I do believe they are. I will only be a moment."

"Please, man. Let them sleep. Could you find me a place in the house to rest?"

"Yes sir. Follow me, please. The Donovans keep a spare room right back this way."

Tom followed to the rear of the house. Off the kitchen laid a small room fitted with what looked to be a comfortable bed, dresser, and dry sink. "This'll do fine. Oh, and could I have the pitcher filled with water? One more thing. I have a black horse wandering the front yard. Could you have someone take care of him?"

"Of course sir. I'll be right back with your water."

Tom sat on the bed, pulled off his moccasin boots, deerskin leggings, vest, and hat, and fell asleep before the water made its appearance.

It seemed to Tom he had just closed his eyes when the clatter and hustle of early morning activities of a ranch house kitchen roused him. He propped himself on his elbow, looked through the opened door to the bustling kitchen. He spied the man who had greeted him the night before hurriedly shifting between stove and big wooden table. "Hey fella, do you know where my clothes are?"

"Yes sir, I'm sorry to say, but they were so filthy they stunk my kitchen. I cleaned them and hung them out in the fresh air. I have hot water on the stove and can fill the tub for you."

Well how about that, Tom thought, my clothes made his kitchen stink and I need a bath. "Soft Cloud and Hawk?"

"They have not come down yet, it is only 5:30, but Master Donovan likes his hot breakfast by six. Why don't I fill your tub?"

"Donovan's okay then?"

"Master Donovan was shot in the stomach the day they took your wife and son, but he will be all right in another month or two. If I get your water now, you and he and everyone else can have breakfast together at six."

Tom watched from the safety of his large bed as the Donovans' house servant poured steaming water into the wooden tub at the foot of his bed. "What's your name?"

"My name is Newly, sir."

"Well Newly, if I crawl in that tub, do you think you can dig a bullet out of my thigh?"

"No sir! Not me, sir! I only carve on dead meat. But I can get Mrs. Donovan, she's an old hand at carving out bullets."

"Give me a chance to get in the water and a towel over my lap before you fetch her."

Newly helped Tom into the tub, carefully placed a pillow on the hard wooden edge to cushion Tom's wounded leg, handed Tom a bar of lye soap, a brush and rag, and strategically placed a towel over his midsection. Then he turned and darted from the room.

Tom noticed there was no door on his bedroom! There he sat, naked, in a tub of water next to the big open kitchen, the table stocked for breakfast. In clear view of everybody sitting down to eat!

Mrs. Donovan rounded the corner, never a glance at the table. "Let's have a look at your leg. Soft Cloud will be down in a minute, just as soon as she has Hawk dressed for the day. His sunburn is coming around nicely. Oh my, this looks infected already

... I think Soft Cloud will need some time. Perhaps you could stay a few days. Yes, I think you should stay here a few days ... Oh my, this leg will take some work. Now you stay right there. I'll hurry back with the things I need."

"I'll wait right here, unless my water gets cold."

Tom would recognize those footsteps any day, anywhere, anytime.

Soft Cloud walked softly into the room, face swollen, eyes puffed, arms bruised. Gently she sat Hawk on the bed, dropped to her knees and hugged Tom. Tears began flowing again for both of them.

Mrs. Donovan paused at the doorway. "All right now, Tom, I think we can get this done quickly. Soft Cloud, would you mind going to the other side of the tub and holding his hand? Okay now, Tom, here I go."

She dug her instrument deep into his thigh, he felt it bump the bullet lodged in muscle. With amazing deftness, she tugged out the bullet.

"Holy cow! Holy cow! That hurt worse than when it went in!" Tom howled.

"Let me scrub this good with the lye soap. It's going to burn." Mrs. Donovan warned.

Tom's face showed such fear and anxiety that Soft Cloud was forced to laugh. She began with a muffled giggle, and when Tom looked at her in disbelief, she burst into hysterical, outrageous laughter.

"This is not funny." Mrs. Donovan's words and face displayed her seriousness and concern. "His leg is infected, and I need to clean it very thoroughly."

At that Tom erupted in wholehearted laughter. He struggled to keep his leg still while Mrs. Donovan scrubbed his wound with a brush much too stiff, but his laughter could not be reined in.

"I sure am glad to find everyone in such great spirits this morning." Chester Donovan leaned heavy on his cane, his eyes bounced first from Mrs. Donovan, to Soft Cloud and then Tom, while a broad smile crossed his own face.

Still laughing, Tom looked up, greeted his friend with a mock salute, and then noticed behind him stood Buck, Cody, Todd Harvey, Captain Green, Newly and two of the hands.

"Well, maybe I should have sold tickets. I could make more money taking a bath than selling horses."

"Tom, stand up and dry, off so I can wrap this leg properly." Mrs. Donovan suggested, paying no attention to either ticket sales or the gathering crowd.

Tom and Soft Cloud looked at each other with tear-filled eyes, tears of laughter, confusion, relief and love. Tom shrugged his shoulders and with a childish smirk jumped right up.

"Oh my goodness! Oh my goodness! Tom, sit right back down. Sit down this instant!" Mrs. Donovan sputtered while the men in the doorway howled with delight. It was no secret how much fun could be had teasing Mrs. Donovan. She sprang up and whirled around. "You men sit down at this table and start breakfast. I was under the impression there was so much to be discussed today. We will join you in a very few moments." It was also no secret how firm Mrs. Donovan could be.

"Soft Cloud, perhaps you could help Tom dry while I go upstairs and gather some fresh clothes from Mr. Donovan's dresser." She turned to leave and then hesitated. "I believe his things will be large around your waist, but we'll make do as best we can."

Tom stepped from the tub, and soapy and wet, he hugged his wife, reached down with one hand, and scooped up his little boy. They stood in silence, embraced each other, the incident behind them now, but the memories of horror would need time to fade. But fade they would for certain under love's shinning light.

Most conversation at the breakfast table had to do with normal ranch business. Donovan was sending his two top hands back to Denver City to try to hire a dozen or so extra hands for spring roundup, which was already a month late.

"Donovan didn't get all your horses this year, Tom," Buck said. "He was outbid on all four sons of Thunder."

"I was sure hoping you'd buy them," Tom said. "Do we know who got them?"

"Sure do," Bill Cody grinned and stroked his mustache, "I got 'em!"

"Don't think I ever rode a better horse, Tom," Todd Harvey grinned.

"Glad to hear that! Thunder passes on good blood. And I believe he's the fastest horse on four hooves." Tom saluted Buck with his coffee cup, honoring the gift from a true friend.

"Except for Diablo," Buck came back.

"A challenge?" Tom sipped his coffee.

"Ya know, I reckon it is." Buck said with a chuckle.

Tom leaned on his right elbow, so he could read Soft Cloud's eyes. He flashed her broad grin. "I'll take that bet, you're gonna regret."

"Done," Buck raised, reached across the table, and shook hands with his partner.

"I'd sure like to see how this turns out, but I need to get to the fort with our prisoners." Captain Green said.

"Sure am sorry for all that happened. But I'm damned glad we were here to help." Cody shook hands all around.

"Same here, fellas. Soft Cloud, you take right good care of that little guy there," Todd Harvey said, "And you and Tom try to keep this worn-out Army scout alive till we meet again!"

Bill Cody, Todd Harvey, and Captain Green thanked the Donovans for their hospitality. Todd Harvey made a show of stuffing biscuits in his vest pockets before joining the others heading out. Buck followed them through the front door and down to the barn. Tom caught the glint in his eyes; maybe it was just a little hard for him to let the excitement they represented disappear.

Tom, Soft Cloud and Hawk spent the morning relaxing on the big front porch. Tom even wrangled a fine cigar from Donovan. Tom had developed a habit of cigar smoking that first winter Buck spent with them in their sod cabin. He had even perfected the talent of propping his feet up on the porch rail and rocking his chair back on its hind legs, just like Buck.

CHAPTER TEN

"So Cole promised to wait until we all get back to marry Hanna Miller? I just hope she doesn't change her mind." Tom bounced Hawk on his good knee while Soft Cloud attended to dressing the wound in his other leg.

"Hold still for me to get this wrap tight." Soft Cloud tried to steady Tom's leg and wind cloth at the same time. "Cole, Lone Feather, and Coop set out this morning. How does your leg feel? When do you think you can travel?"

"How about leaving tomorrow morning, if I can talk Donovan into the use of one of his wagons."

"I'll not lend you a wagon, but I'll make a gift of my two-seater carriage team of white mares in exchange for a foal by Thunder from each mare." Donovan offered.

Tom rubbed the wound on his leg for a few seconds. "I accept that generous offer!" He stood, careful to bear most the weight on his good leg, took Hawk's hand, put his arm around Soft Cloud's waist. "Let's take a short walk and check on our new mares."

"Can you walk that far?" Soft Cloud worried.

At a pace Tom could manage without too much discomfort, they walked across the dusty front yard to the large corral behind the barn. Tom rested his arms over the top rail taking in the beauty of the two white mares. After a moment, he turned, leaned his back against the fence and looked toward the Donovan house. A fine, two-story board house painted white, with a grand full length front porch. The entire yard sat behind a sturdy rail fence.

"The money from selling our horses will be enough to build a house like that." Tom pointed to the Donovan house.

"Sometimes it is hard to believe.... "

She need say no more, Tom understood. He always understood Soft Cloud as she always understood him. He knew she would be tormented by memories of that horrible day in the hands of Sidewinder, but he also knew his wife to be strong. Strong enough to get beyond those memories. Things that should never happen to any woman. At that moment Tom wished he could kill Sidewinder a hundred times more. Would that be enough?

"Hey Tom, I just heard Donovan sold you his matched pair." Buck started down the steps from the house.

"And the carriage too." Tom said.

"I guess ol' Thunder will have an easy walk home." Buck joked.

"It's a two-seater, Buck, you can give Diablo a break too."

"Might just take you up on that. Right now we're supposed to come for dinner."

After dinner, Donovan, Tom and Buck settled on the porch to enjoy the night air, and cigars and coffee. Mrs. Donovan and Soft Cloud busied themselves with conversation about the new house, while they helped Newly in the kitchen. It pleased Tom to hear the excitement in Soft Cloud's voice. He found it difficult to control his thoughts right now, and her laughter was like sweet music, and medicine to him.

They had barely lit their cigars when a Donovan hand galloped into the yard.

"They killed Buster! They just shot 'im right off his horse! Would have shot me too, but I got the hell out of there! Was maybe 20 of 'em! Buster never had a chance." He never bothered to get off his horse. He just announced the news from the saddle, then pulled his hat, pushed his hair back, and wiped his sweaty forehead on his shirt sleeve.

Buck jumped up and turned to Donovan. "Who's Buster?"

"He's my top ranch hand! Where did this happen, Poke?" Donovan shouted.

"We were riding out to check on the boys at the line shack, the other side of Spider Creek." Poke struggled to catch his breath.

The front door swung open with a bang and Mrs. Donovan and Soft Cloud ran out. Mrs. Donovan looked at her husband and Soft Cloud at hers. They both knew what must happen next.

"Did you recognize any of them?" Donovan asked.

"Never a chance, boss. I still can't believe I got away. It's like, seems like they wanted to kill Buster and didn't care much about me."

"You folks been having trouble here with cattle thieves or renegades or such?" Buck turned to Donovan.

"Didn't feel much like bothering you folks with my troubles … not with all you've been through the last few days, but yeah, and we're not the only ones. Every rancher in the valley's been losing stock for the last four or five months."

Soft Cloud pushed her way by Donovan to sit with Tom. Hawk bounded through the door, completely unaware of either the situation or his father's wounded leg, and jumped into Tom's lap.

"Go tend your horse and hitch a team to the wagon. We'll be goin' for Buster's body right away," Donovan said.

"Chester! You're in no shape to drive a team across the prairie! I think the world of Buster too, but I simply won't allow it."

Mr. Donavan slumped in his chair, a lost, desperate color washed over his face.

"We'll go with you, Poke," Buck nodded to Tom.

Soft Cloud jumped up. "What about your leg? … What about me?"

"My wound's not that bad, and I can't let Buck go alone. You'll be all right here with Mrs. Donovan. We'll be back in a few hours."

Poke pulled up to the big house with mules and wagon. Tom leaned to kiss Soft Cloud, but she pulled away. He could not comprehend the shock he felt. Tom saw in her eyes a distance he had not seen before, not even on that terrible day in Still Water's teepee when she'd admitted that Tall Dog was her father.

"Buck, you and Poke will have to go it alone." Tom sat down, gently took Soft Cloud's hand. Tom sat with Soft Cloud long after the Donovans took Hawk inside.

CHAPTER ELEVEN

Twilight carried with it enough chilly air for Mrs. Donovan to ask Newly to start a fire in the living room fireplace. With considerable effort, Tom convinced Soft Cloud to go inside by the fire and rock Hawk to sleep. Even though the room was bright and made cozy and comfortable by the fire, Tom felt a chill from Soft Cloud.

What should he do? He pondered. Although nothing had been said, he knew Donovan hoped he and Buck would at least look into the matter of Buster's death. If Tom insisted on taking Soft Cloud and Hawk back to the ranch, would Buck stay behind and go it alone? He needed more information. "What do you know about the cattle stealing that's been going on?"

Donovan wrung his hands. "It seems to be a well-organized operation. I know we've lost, by our last count, over 300 head in the past two months. All told in the valley, five ranchers have lost somewhere near a 1,000 head. It's big country out there with plenty of places to hide. Hell, there's room to hide a 1,000 head in any number of canyons within a day's ride of here."

"I'm not clear with the workings of a cattle ranch, but what would they do with a 1,000 head of cattle after they had them?"

"Tom, that's part of the puzzle. Ever since we knew we had a problem, someone from the Stock Grower's Association has been watching the corrals and stockyards in Denver City. The new line of Denver Railroad will be operational in a few months. Then we'll be able to ship east, right out of Denver City. For a year now, we've gathered our stock in pens the Association built at the railroad terminus in town and trail them to Kit Carson to load on rail cars.

And it's a sure thing none of our stolen cattle are showing up there.

"Twenty-one ranchers in the territory belong to the Stock Grower's Association. We all take turns sending our top hands on a rotating basis to watch the stockyards and make sure any beef that goes through there was sent by the rancher who owns the brand. Any cattle wearing wrong brands are sorted out and returned to the proper ranch. It's common, Tom, for cattle to get mixed together on the open ranges we have here in the territory. So we just sort them out at the pens, and send them back. But like I say, something's going on. We're all coming up short on our counts."

"They have to be going somewhere. Doesn't make much sense, does it?" Tom said as he gave Soft Cloud a perplexed look.

"That's just it. Even if the outlaws planned on drivin' the cattle out of the valley, someone would see a herd that size or pick up trail or something. But to just disappear like something dropped down out of the sky and snatched them up, why it just plain doesn't figure. That's why I sent the boys to town, to see if we could wrangle up with a few more hands to help with spring gathering, and have some extra eyes out with the cattle."

"It's late now. Let's sort this thing out in the morning." Tom escorted Soft Cloud and Hawk to the room off the kitchen and in minutes all three climbed in the big bed, Hawk sound asleep between them.

"I give you my word, Soft Cloud, I will not leave your side for any reason until you are done with this."

Soft Cloud climbed over Hawk onto Tom, wrapped her arms so tightly around his neck he thought he would suffocate, and broke into tears. For a long time she stayed that way, crying until she fell asleep.

CHAPTER TWELVE

Newly roused everyone in the morning as he hustled to prepare breakfast. Good food was his priority, not quiet. Tom woke to find himself alone. Hawk in the front room wrestled with Buck, he figured that out by the giggles and laughs. Soft Cloud he could see in the kitchen with Newly. Tom limped to the table and started on his first cup.

Soon Donovan joined them, then Buck. A little later, Poke came in through the rear door, grabbed a plate, and stacked eggs, steak and potatoes on it. Soft Cloud served Tom a plate heaped so high, it looked like three meals. A tense air swaddled them all.

"I want to bury Buster today. I want him to lie at rest on the ranch he helped me build." Donovan low voice cracked.

"Want me to gather the men?" Poke stabbed his eggs, never looked up.

"Take three men ... dig his grave in the family cemetery. We'll bury him at noon."

Poke finished in a hurry, retreating by the same rear door he had entered.

Donovan turned to Buck. "I never did see why Buster thought so highly of him. When this is over, I'm going to send him packing. Just something about him."

Soft Cloud took the seat vacated by Poke, put her hand on Tom's thigh and picked gingerly at her food.

"He sure had a lot to say last night on our trip out to fetch Buster and back. He's got all sorts of plans about starting his own ranch one day," Buck said.

"Most hands do. I don't believe Poke'll make it, though. He

always seems to look at things the wrong way, and he never quite gets things done." Donovan wore a look that told Tom he had more to say. He looked over his coffee cup to Buck ... something was on his old friend's mind. Buck's posture told Tom Buck had discovered something troubling the night before.

"Are we ready to head back today?" Tom tossed out, more as a test than a genuine question. Soft Cloud's hand tightened on his thigh, but she said nothing.

"Not sure," Buck started, "If you two aren't in a big hurry, I think we owe Donovan just a little bit, and I have a mighty big curiosity that wants to be satisfied about this cattle stealing business. Poke told me you folks lost about 300 head, and so far, in the valley here, there is something like a 1,000 missing?"

"That's a little what I mean about Poke. Sure, every hand likes to talk about the cattle thievin', but I didn't know that any of the hands knew how many had been stolen. I guess they all talk though." Donovan excused himself, saying he had paperwork at his desk that needed his attention.

"Tom, I'd sure like to take you out to where Buster got it, and look over the site in the daylight," Buck said.

"Think we can get back by noon?" Tom felt Soft Cloud's hand gripping his thigh ever tighter.

"Sure."

"How about we take that fancy rig and matched team out for a run!" Tom threw a wink Buck's way.

Fifteen minutes later, the handsome two-seater pulled by the magnificent matched pair of white horses, started away from the Donovan house. True to Tom's promise, Soft Cloud sat by his side. They traveled the road for about 20 minutes, then Buck steered the horses into tall grass, and followed the trail left by Buck and Poke the night before.

Buck stopped the mares in a low area between two trails, hopped from the carriage, and walked about, suspiciously examining tracks left in the trampled grass.

"I had the stinking feeling Poke wasn't quite square, and I just needed to look into this a little," Buck said.

Tom and Soft Cloud got down and studied the ground. "Tom, there doesn't appear to have been more than two horses here," Soft Cloud offered.

"That's pretty much how I felt, even in the dark last night, just not enough trampled grass to suit me. Look around here. No tracks anywhere except right here. And then they turn around." Buck pulled his hat, scratched his hair, and surveyed the tall grass in each direction.

"You think Poke killed Buster?" Tom hated the thought.

"The man's slippery. I figured him out last night. I'll tell you something else. When he wasn't looking, after we got back to the ranch, I took a good look at Buster. He was shot right in the face. His face is full of powder burns. He was shot close-up, Tom." Buck set his hat on his head, and climbed back in the rig.

****

Tom stood quiet, holding Soft Cloud and Hawk by the hand while they watched the men lower Buster's body into the ground. They shoveled dirt into the grave then paused while Donovan spoke.

"Ten years ago, Buster Kelly and I chose this place to build a cattle ranch. Buster was a great man, always willing to help, never asked for anything. Not even a share of the ranch. He stood as my best man when I married. He helped us fight Indians, blizzards, droughts and outlaws. He never shirked his duties. Hell, he never complained. May God welcome you, Buster Kelly ... I know I'm sure gonna miss you."

Mr. and Mrs. Donovan crawled into the two-seater and rode a quiet ride back to the ranch house with Tom, Buck, Soft Cloud and Hawk.

Back at the house, Newly had set a table, covered with food in the front yard, and he busied himself feeding the hands as they straggled back from the cemetery.

"What do you think, Tom? You want to stay on and help the Donovans catch this cattle-stealing ring?" Buck looked square at his friend.

"I sure do want to get home. We should be gathering horses to replace the ones we've just sold," Tom fiddled with his food. "And I want Soft Cloud to rest and be with her mother."

"Well then, that says it. We'll tell Donovan we're sorry, but we'll be leaving in the morning."

"I am okay, Tom, Buck. If you two feel you should help your

friends, as I do, then you must." Soft Cloud gripped Tom's hand as fierce as a momma bear.

"Are you sure?" Tom studied her, searching for the truth of it. "I mean, I don't know what to think about all that happened to you. Wouldn't you rather go home and be with Still Water?"

"Yes I would. But your friend needs your help ... I'll be fine here with Mrs. Donovan. I'm not at all sure what difference going home would make."

Tom looked deeply into her brown eyes, and standing, holding her hands, he made her promise. "Anytime you feel the need to go home you let me know."

"I will."

When all but the Donovans had gone, Tom approached Chester Donovan. "Buck and I have a plan we'd like to tell you about."

Buck grabbed a chair, spun it backwards and straddled it. Tom sat on the edge of the picnic table.

"You need to hire a new top hand, and it should be me," Buck announced with an air of determination that gave the big man pause.

"Go on," Donovan said, intrigued.

"I figure I need to get into Denver City and work the men at the stockyards and corrals, but I can't push for answers if I'm not your top hand. Call Poke in, tell him you made me ranch foreman and give him the rest of the day off. My guess is he'll hightail it straight to town to complain about the Donovan spread bringing someone new in to be top hand."

Donovan leaned back in his chair, looked out across the grasslands. Tom watched Buck and Donovan, and his mind drifted back to Soft Cloud. How would she feel if he went to town with Buck and left her behind?

Just as Buck had predicted, in less than a half hour after Donovan gave Poke the news, Poke was saddled and riding out the ranch road. Buck and Tom watched from the porch. They looked at each other as if to say "Now, we got it going." Just before Poke rode out of sight, the two men realized he was not headed to town.

"He's not going to town," Buck jumped from his chair, "He's headed too far west!"

"I'll follow him. You get to town tomorrow, and work the

men at the stockyards." Tom raced to the house to Soft Cloud. He grabbed her shoulders and pulled her close, then pushed her away. "If you meant what you said, I've got to go. I've got to go right now and follow Poke. You say the word. If you don't want me to, tell me. Otherwise, I've got to go."

"Go. I'll be safe here. After this is done, we can go home. We will go home ... and build our new house

CHAPTER THIRTEEN

Tom followed Poke's trail for hours by the time the sun began to set, coloring the sea of grass slightly orange. In the distance stood rocky canyon walls where Poke was surely headed. An uneasy feeling tugged at his gut. Could it be this easy? Would Poke lead him to the stolen cattle so easily, recklessly? There had to be more.

Walking might be better, Tom reasoned, concerned he might be getting too close to Poke and might be found out. Even though he hadn't yet caught a glimpse of the man, Tom knew Thunder covered ground faster than any other horse and felt it unwise to press too fast. "You earned a break, Thunder." And after another half hour of walking, Tom felt certain Poke's destination was indeed the hill country just ahead.

******

Buck rode to Denver City in the morning. He stopped Diablo on the south side of the stockyards, sat a moment taking it all in. The Denver stockyards were less than two years old, but were already the busiest in the Midwest. Hundreds of cattle were trailed from here daily. The stockyards and the grasslands outside the city held several thousand head. It took Buck only a few moments to get a handle on how things worked here.

"You the man in charge?" Buck questioned a tall gentleman scribbling numbers on a tablet as he walked a plank, top-rail high along the outside of the sorting corral.

After giving Buck a look that said, "Who the hell are you?" the man put his pencil and tablet in his left hand, removed his hat and dragged his dusty shirt sleeve across his face and over the top of his bald head. "I ain't in charge, but maybe I can help you."

Buck scrambled onto the plank and held out his hand to shake. His hand remained empty. "My name is Buck Hawkins, just wanted to say howdy. I'm the new ranch foreman for the Donovans." Buck watched closely for any reaction this fellow might give up. He was disappointed in the stone face of the tablet man.

"Donovans huh?" He pushed his way past Buck and resumed his counting.

"Yeah, that's what I said. You familiar with the Donovan spread?"

"Reckon I am. Big fancy spread, lots of cattle. You say you're their new foreman? I never thought I'd live to see the day Donovan got rid of Buster Kelly. But with all that's been goin' on, I guess he had it comin'."

"Donovan didn't get rid of Buster. Somebody shot him dead."

The man with the tablet jerked erect, and showed a bit more interest in Buck. "Somebody killed Buster Kelly?"

"Sure did. What did you mean about things goin' on?"

"Nothing much," He pretended to be counting cattle again.

But Buck knew this fella had information. "What's your name, fella?"

"Call me Smokey. I work for the Circle Y. These here are their cattle I'm trying to count. We're shippin' 800 head today. Somebody killed Buster Kelly! Somebody done killed Buster Kelly! Got any ideas who it was?"

"I might. Don't matter though. Donovan wants me to oversee the goin's-on here at the stockyards. He wants to ship a 1,000 head next week."

"You're dressed mighty fancy to work in cattle pens. You'll get them fancy leggings an' vest awful dirty," Smokey taunted.

"Been dirty before. Who do you think killed Buster?"

"What makes you think I would have any idea?"

"You knew 'im real well, didn't you?"

Smokey dropped his tablet, let his arms fall to his side, and took a step toward Buck. They stood so close, their noses nearly touched, "I got cattle to sort, Buck. I'm done visitin'."

Buck figured he'd let that go for now and jumped from the

plank, confident he'd stirred things up in Smokey's mind, and he might just keep an eye on him.

For the next half an hour, Buck rode Diablo around the outside of all the stockyard corrals. By his guess, in the ten large corrals there were seven or eight hundred head, and at least thirty cowboys. A little farther outside of town a herd grazed, waiting their turn in the pens. He put his heels to Diablo and loped out to the chuck wagon. "Good morning there, I'm Buck Hawkins, the new ranch foreman for the Donovan spread."

"Donovan spread? What happened to Buster Kelly?" The cook looked up from his duties of making fresh coffee and biscuits for the half dozen or so hands scattered around the herd.

"Buster was shot dead two days ago," Buck answered, stepping down from Diablo.

The cook staggered back, grabbed his tattered apron and wiped his greasy hands clean. "Buster Kelly, dead? Things are happening too fast around here to suit me." He handed Buck a steaming cup of coffee.

"Thanks. Donovan asked me to poke around, see if I can find any idea who's stealing cattle. Mind telling me what outfit all this belongs to?"

"This chuck wagon, my services, those boys out there riding herd, and that herd all belong to the Bar 7. And we ain't lost a single head to no cow thieves! 'Course I don't get around much to find anything out. Ya know, I ain't moved this chuckwagon off this spot for almost a month. I don't even know who the hell runs the Bar 7."

"You don't say. The way I heard it, every ranch within a 100 miles of Denver City lost cattle."

"It's a little bit like this, Sonny. They that run the Bar 7, whoever they is, aim on keeping what's theirs. Maybe, Donovan could put on a few gun hands, too."

Buck took in the old cook's frame and noticed the bulge under the greasy apron, made by the old man's side arm. He handed the cook his empty coffee cup and settled back into the saddle. "Thanks for the coffee, and the advice. Reckon I'll be seeing you around." Buck started away, then turned Diablo to face the cook. "Where would I find the Bar 7 spread?"

"Twenty miles east. They say you can't miss the main road that leads to the ranch house." The cook pointed east with the coffee pot. "Never been there, myself. Don't never intend to go neither!"

Two hours later Buck and Diablo loped across a small, wooden bridge that straddled the stream on the dusty road leading to the Bar 7 ranch house. From the moment Buck spied the dwelling, he was unimpressed. Even from a distance, he could see the buildings sat in disrepair, and the fences he rode past could all use work. He rode into the yard and stopped at a tiny, ram shackled sod house.

Two men with Winchesters stepped out on the porch.

Buck nudged Diablo a few yards back from the house.

"Need to know who you are, Mister." The tallest man demanded.

Before answering, Buck studied the weather-beaten house. Smashed windows and bits of glass on the porch told him they had been smashed from the inside out.

"Name's Buck, boys. Just looking for a job. Word in town is you'll take on a man good with a gun."

"You dress kind of fancy. Either you're gunman or gambler. Which is it?" The same tall man waved his Winchester toward Buck.

Buck dove from Diablo, snatched his Navy from its holster, and fired two rounds into the plank floor of the porch, inches from the tall man's feet. As he sprang to his feet, Buck fired one round between the feet of the shorter man. Both men fell over backwards in their retreat. "I can deal from the bottom of the deck too, boys." He introduced them to his famous flashing smile as he neatly spun his 44 on his finger and let it drop into its holster.

"Damn! Remind me not to piss him off!" The shorter man said with a grin, and held out his right hand. "Howdy. I'm Farley, and that tall fella, we call Shorty. We run the Bar 7. Come on in for a whiskey, Buck."

Buck tied Diablo to the porch rail, stepped out of the sun, and followed the men through the front door. As his eyes adjusted to darkness, he took a quick inventory. One table, and a few chairs. The cook stove sat piled high with whiskey bottles, ammunition boxes, and other junk. Not much cooking going on here. He noticed two cots pushed against the wall, and not much else. He wasn't sure what he had found, but this was not a working ranch.

Buck waited until Shorty and Farley sat at the table. Then he joined them, choosing the better of the remaining two chairs.

"A hundred a month, keep your mouth shut and do as you're

told. I don't care how fancy you are with a gun, one of us will cut you down if you so much as think about crossing us."

These fellas get right down to business, Buck thought. I guess I walked into the rattlesnake den. Might as well make the most of it. "So, you boys been doing all the outlawin' that's been going on in these parts?"

Shorty levered a shell into the chamber of his Winchester and jabbed it so close to Buck's face it moved the whiskers on his goatee. "What if we are?"

With his finger Buck pushed the Winchester aside. With his grand smile he suggested, "I heard you offer me a hundred a month. I'll take that, and twenty percent."

Shorty jumped straight into the air. "I ought to part your eyes right here. But before I do … what makes you worth twenty percent?"

"I replaced Buster Kelly at the Donovan spread."

The outlaws looked at each other, Shorty sat down and laid his rifle across his lap. "Now that has my attention. Chester Donovan would never replace Buster Kelly. And that man was a real pain in our ass."

There you had it. They might not have killed Buster, but they sure wanted him dead. "It's always been my experience, a dead man ain't much of a bother," Buck said, showing his big smile.

"So you killed Buster Kelly, and you figure to take advantage of the situation you created," Farley surmised.

Farley's reasoning sucked the air right out of Buck's lungs, but he decided to let it ride and see where it took him.

"Don't know about the twenty percent, Buck, but maybe we can work out something. We got close to a thousand head grazing outside Denver, ready to ship to Kansas City. We plan on trailin' to Kit Carson in two days," Shorty said.

Buck sat quiet and listened as Farley spoke. "We always had a problem with that damned Buster Kelly. If he found any brands that didn't match up, he'd pull those cattle and drive'em back to the ranch they belonged to. We always made sure to ship our cattle on a day our boys watched the stockyards. But that goddamned Buster would show up anytime he wanted. The son of a bitch cost us 500 head already. I'm damn glad he's dead. Now, maybe we can run this outfit."

"One thing's sure. Buster ain't gonna show up and reduce your herd size any," Buck walked toward the door to leave. "You boys think it over. I'll be in town day after tomorrow."

On the ride back to the Donovan ranch, Buck pondered over the information he had gathered thus far. Seemed as though Buster Kelly had been killed for interfering with the outlaws' shipments, but they hadn't known he was dead. For just a little while, Buck had been beginning to believe Buster Kelly had been dirty. But now he had to question that fact. If it was a fact. And then, he still had the one thing that was a fact ... There had been only one other horse with Buster Kelly the night he'd been shot dead, and that other horse had been ridden by Poke. Must be that Buster had gotten into Poke's way.

CHAPTER FOURTEEN

Thunder pawed the ground and paced in circles between the house and barn. Sweat dripped like rain from his matted black hair. His saddle hung twisted to the side.

Soft Cloud flew first from the house. She reached Thunder before the screen door banged shut. Unconsciously she righted the saddle and looked down at the dust turning to mud from Thunder's raining sweat. She spun and ran into the barn. "Tom! Tom, where are you Tom?" She knew he was not in the barn but called out more in an attempt to feel useful than to expect to find him.

She ran back to Thunder and grabbed the sweaty horse by the mane. "Where did you leave Tom?" she screamed. Unable to bear the burden, she collapsed in the sweaty mud by the horse.

Donovan hobbled at his best speed with his cane to Soft Cloud. Blood on the saddle and Thunder's condition told Donovan as much as he needed to know. He took Soft Cloud's arm and pulled her to her feet. "Come now, let's go back to the house. I'll get someone to see to Thunder, and we'll send some boys out to look for Tom."

****

Buck rode a tired Diablo into the Donovan yard, still deep in thought about his first meeting with the Bar 7 boys. Seeing a hand walking Thunder to cool him, he was glad to know Tom was back. "Yo, Tom, where are you hiding?"

Soft Cloud crashed out the door. "Buck! Thunder came home without Tom!" She ran into Buck, nearly knocked him from his feet.

She buried her face in his chest, broke into sobs. "We should've gone home, Buck! We should've gone home." She let her legs go limp.

Buck looked down at Soft Cloud, then at Thunder, then to the porch and Donovan, leaning on his cane, and Mrs. Donovan holding Hawk by the hand.

"Get me two of your fastest horses!" He lifted Soft Cloud. "I'll bring him back." With the gentleness of a newlywed, he led Soft Cloud to the porch. "You all take care of her now. Thunder's tracks will be easy to follow. Few horses have feet the size of his." He turned and gave Soft Cloud a brotherly hug and a kiss on the cheek.

He bounded the steps, stopped by Diablo and yanked the saddle. "You tend to this horse as if he were God's own!" He ordered the man who walked Thunder. In minutes he had his gear on the horse who appeared the stronger of the two and galloped out the lane, his eyes glued to Thunder's tracks.

Not a mile from the ranch house, Buck found where Thunder had turned onto the road from the grassy plain. Thunder's trail was clear. The big horse had cut a path of smashed grass and deep divots. Looking ahead, Buck felt certain of the destination: the far-off hills where the big canyons started. He pushed his horses in a low-bellied, ground-covering flat-out gallop, for he had no trouble staying on the trail that stretched out clearly before him.

Evening shadows washed over the plains by the time he reached a stream at the base of the hills. And the horse Buck had pushed hard was spent. "Guess you're done, aren't you, fella?" Buck unsaddled the exhausted horse.

Both horses drank heavily while Buck lay on his belly and splashed water in his face and long blond hair. Thunder had crossed the stream in a single bound and left deep holes where he'd landed. The marks Thunder had made as he scrambled and slid down the hillside ahead gave Buck more clear trail.

He saddled the other horse and, rifle in hand, he walked the hill following Thunder's trail. He made steady progress until darkness overtook them. Squatting on his haunches he turned to the horse. "I reckon this is as far as we get tonight."

At the earliest inkling of sunrise, Buck set out. For several hours their progress was slow but progressively upward, then the terrain leveled. High above the plains, they stood on the edge of a flat grassland plateau, which seemed to go on for miles. In the distance

Buck saw cattle.

"Things might get a bit interesting now." He told his horse and mounted, took off at a lope, careful to keep to the edge of the open grassland. Trees and brush provided ample cover so Buck was able to sneak to within a quarter-mile of what appeared to be a base camp.

Before him a herd spread over a mile wide on the hidden grassy flat high above the surrounding world. Buck studied the lay of the outfit. Some 20 men on horseback rode herd. Trees to the rear suggested the plateau dropped away. A row of military-style tents, neatly aligned, told of a well-organized operation. Three covered wagons waited at the end of the row of tents, a small fire burned by the first wagon. Then Buck saw him! Tom was stretched, beaten and naked, over the wagon wheel of the first wagon! Buck could see the bloody welts on his back from lashings he must have suffered. He could also see four men sitting around the fire near Tom. Those four were Cheyenne!

Buck slipped deeper into the brushy cover, led his horses down over the edge, into the thick brush where he tied them to low branches. He grabbed the saddlebags, heavy with ammunition, slung the Winchester over his shoulder, and snatched his Big 50 from its scabbard. Then he made his way closer to the camp, one silent, careful step after another.

When he had crept to as near as he dare, he lay on his belly and simply watched the camp. It seemed for now, at least, Tom was no longer the focus of their attention.

In darkness the yellow glow of the small fire by Tom and four Cheyenne provided the only light on the plateau.

Buck needed a plan. How many men were in the tents? Twenty or so men rode herd, but how many more made the camp? How could he get the Cheyenne away from Tom without rousting those in the tents? Buck crawled closer to the campfire and stopped a stone's throw outside of camp. Disappointment crept in when he saw the Cheyenne were not drinking whiskey. He had hoped for a little help from a cheap bottle.

The backup plan would take a little longer. Moving slower than a stalking cat, he crawled under the most distant wagon. Without a sound, he shifted one limb at a time and slid forward under each wagon, until he lay behind Tom. "Don't move—it's

Buck." He whispered in Tom's ear. "I'll cut you lose, but don't move until you get my signal. My rifle is right here in behind this wheel. There are four Cheyenne around the fire behind you. When you hear me start the party, dive under the wagon and just start shooting. Kill them all." Buck crawled on his belly away from the camp until a safe distance then jogged with stealth through the brush toward the herd and men there.

By the light of stars alone, he scouted the plateau for exactly the position he needed. Finally satisfied with the high ground he selected, very near the herd, he stretched flat, the Big 50 sighted on the man nearest him, five more shells laid neatly on the ground by his left hand. All he needed now was for several of the men to gather close enough together to afford him five or six fast shots.

Minutes seemed like hours. He knew Tom was hurting, but he needed just the right opportunity, or things would get worse for them both. The men riding herd knew their business and stuck to it. Buck worried the break he needed might not come. Then three riders gathered at the herd's near end. As Buck sighted his rifle, he realized they were going to start a fire. He waited fretfully and watched through rifle sights as the campfire grew from a single spark to dancing flames. Soon a bright campfire illuminated five men who seemed about to brew coffee and take a break.

Buck sighted on the biggest man, and squeezed the trigger. Before the bullet reached its target, he flipped open the breech, ejecting the spent shell, rammed a new one home and fired again. He spent no time enjoying the chaos he created below, but fired four more times. By the light of the fire he knew all five men lay dead or dying. Shouts of the other men as they tried to organize a defense rang loud, but chaos ruled the moment.

Soon shots volleyed in his direction but he knew he was safely out of their range, so he reloaded again and began to fire into the herd. As he had hoped, he started a stampede. He shot into the herd until every sleepy cow was on its feet, bawling and running away. For just half a minute he watched the confusion below. Then, satisfied no one from the herd would interfere with his rescue, he jumped up and raced back toward the camp and Tom.

****

After Buck's first shot and before the second, Tom dropped to his knees, snatched the Winchester, whirled around and killed the four Cheyenne. Men poured from the army tents; he methodically cut them down one by one. Six in all.

Buck burst from the darkness into the campfire light. "Able to travel?"

"Not a one of these lazy no-accounts can swing a lash like the old hider! They hardly tickled me."

"I have a horse in the brush. You grab one from the picket line, cut the others loose and let's get."

Tom snatched the lance that lay by a dead Cheyenne. "For Hawk."

Instead of cutting the 12 picketed horses free, Tom tied them in line and swung onto the first one. "For me."

Buck gave a wave of acknowledgment and jogged into darkness to retrieve his horse as Tom rode away, string of horses in tow, in the direction of the Donovan ranch.

CHAPTER FIFTEEN

Soft Cloud heard them approach the big house and flew down the steps into early morning light. As she stopped sharply in her tracks, relief, joy and surprise flooded over her. There sat Tom holding the lead on a string of horses. Buck, one leg crossed over his saddle, sat grinning.

"Found these out there. Thought we could take them back to our ranch, unless Donovan wants to buy 'em again." Tom spoke to Soft Cloud in a voice loud enough to be heard by Mr. and Mrs. Donovan, who stood smiling on the porch.

Donovan hands wandered into the yard from the bunkhouse to see about the noise and began to examine the horses in Tom's string.

The world around Tom and Soft Cloud faded away. Her soft hands quivered as they traced the bloody wounds on his back. "Tom, they beat you!"

"Things got a little rough there for a while, but they hardly raised a welt." Tom lost himself in her embrace, held tight and smothered her in kisses.

The gathered hands broke out in raucous applause and cheers, those with hats tossed them up. "That's how you kiss a woman, boys!" one hand shouted. There was a time when Tom would not have understood or surely would have been embarrassed, but not today. Encouraged by the cheers, Tom scooped Soft Cloud in his arms, bounded up the steps two at a time, and into the ranch house, nearly knocking the Donovans from their feet as he thundered by. Another round of cheers, hoots, and yee haws rattled the porch frame.

"What did Tom mean when he said unless I wanted to buy them again?" Donovan asked Buck.

"Just that. On our trip back we recognized half the horses as mustangs you'd bought from us last year at Denver City's auction. Got any ideas how they might have ended up in the thieves' camp?"

Donovan limped slowly down steps, leaning heavy on his cane, and pushed his way through the men who examined the horses.

The sun had begun to heat up the morning, and the tired and thirsty horses pawed the dust. The boys from the bunkhouse began to drift away. Buck waited while Donovan ran his free hand over the backs of all the horses tied in the string, and he watched as Donovan's face morphed from the always pleasant, pudgy-cheeked man to a stiff, tightlipped, narrow-eyed angry spirit.

"What the hell's going on here, Buck?" Donovan's dark eyes sliced the air between he and Buck.

"Don't you know?"

"What's that supposed to mean?"

"Seen Poke around this morning?"

"No, I haven't seen Poke! What are you drivin' at, Buck?"

"Want to know where we found these horses?"

"Of course, I do!" Chester Donovan's face tightened, quivered. "Quit playing games, Buck, spit out what's on your mind!"

In a very deliberate manner, Buck laid his hands atop his horse, looked at the string of horses he and Tom ponied in. "Those horses come from your ranch. They were tied on the cattle thieves' picket in a well-organized camp on one of your high ranges, that was running about five to eight hundred head of cattle."

"What are you saying, Buck? You think I'm dirty?"

Buck ran his hands down the front leg of his horse and picked it up. After examining the foot he let the leg drop to the ground.

"I'm gonna take these horses to the corral yonder where they can get water. Then I'll join you for breakfast. If you'll still have me."

Donovan stood like a snubbing post, forced Buck to maneuver around him to take the horses to the big corral. He watched Buck lift the saddle from the weary horse and toss it on the top rail of the of the corral fence. All the horses needed water, and sparred at the long trough with teeth flashing, squeals, and pinned ears. Finally Donovan turned, and with his cane, worked his way up the steps into the house.

Buck finished his duties with the horses, checked his Navy Colt to be sure each chamber held a shell, and it slipped easily in and out his low slung holster. He went to the smaller corral and checked on Diablo and Thunder. Satisfied, he straightened his clothes and hat, scooped water from the trough, splashed his face, and feathered out his goatee. Then with long determined strides, he marched into the house.

As he climbed the wide plank steps, Buck had a feeling in the back of his neck so familiar each time before trouble came to call. He let the door close quietly behind him, stopped a few seconds to adjust from outside brightness, and to take another breath. In three strides he crossed the front room and leaned against the doorjamb to the kitchen. Conversation around the table ceased. He nodded to Tom, tossed a wink and a smile to Soft Cloud and Hawk. Then straightened. He noted the vacant chair and empty plates on the table in front of it, directly across from Tom. Newly darted in and out between chairs shoveling eggs, potatoes and steak onto plates. Mr. and Mrs. Donovan, seated at the end of the table, wore anticipation on their faces and postures.

Poke was absent. Two hands Buck did not recognize flanked the Donovans. Careful to be sure all could see, Buck slipped his finger under the handle of his Colt, raised it an inch out of its holster, and let it drop back. Then he sat.

"Have some eggs and steak, Mr. Buck?" Newly invited.

"Coffee and biscuits too, Newly, thank you." Buck hoisted his plate high.

"Tom will tell me nothing." Soft Cloud complained to Buck. "You tell us, *now*, what happened, and who beat Tom!"

"I reckon that's what I aim to do," Buck started, "soon as I fill my gizzard and swallow a cup of coffee."

Tom looked across the table at his partner. He wondered himself what information Buck had uncovered. On the ride in from the outlaw camp, all Tom got for his questions was a consistent brush-off.

"Fellas," Buck addressed the hands seated by Donovan, "gonna need to ask you to finish your breakfast outside. What I have to say is best said to as few ears as possible."

Buck watched confusion wash over Donovan's face, and he

recorded how Mrs. Donovan placed her hand on his arm. He finished his breakfast, one-well chewed bite at a time, and thoroughly enjoyed not one, but two cups of coffee. He enjoyed the building tension, too.

"Dammit, Buck!" Donovan finally blurted. "What kind of game are you playing?"

"How many hands does the Donovan ranch keep on payroll?" Buck took a sip of coffee as if to let on he had an idea how many.

"Most of the time, 50 to 60. We run 5,000 head, Buck. On one hundred and fifty thousand acres."

"Must be some of your own men are in on the cattle stealing. How else would your horses get up there? And how can you explain the main camp sittin' only half a day's hard ride from your ranch house on some of your best high summer pasture?"

"Does that mean you no longer think I'm dirty?" Donovan sent the closest thing to a glare he could build.

"Never did. Just disappointed."

"Disappointed that I'd be stupid enough to hire a man like Poke?"

"This is a big operation and I don't think I can trust any of your men to help Tom and me sort this out. Hell, I wouldn't be surprised to find the sheriff in Denver City part of it." Buck aimed the tip of his steak knife at Tom. "And somebody at the rail yards knows plenty."

As Tom listened, he knew Buck was tiptoeing around some mighty important fact. Soft Cloud rested her elbows on the table, her face cupped in her hands and Hawk asleep on her lap. Newly kept coffee cups full of steaming brew. Mrs. Donovan now had both arms around her husband's arm. And he was plainly annoyed at Buck's chosen method of parceling out information.

"You know any of the folks from the Bar 7 east of town?" Buck held his voice level.

"That's a big spread. Couple of hombres from down Texas way showed up about 18 months ago and took it over. They're a rough bunch. Never met any of them. They don't really belong to the Stock Grower's Association. I've suspected them all along. You know something?"

"All this started about a year ago?"

"Yep, that's why they're my prime suspects. I was just about to start taking matters into my own hands when I got shot and Buster was killed."

"How many drifters do you have on the payroll?"

"Too many." Donovan answered with a sigh.

"I had the pleasure of meeting Shorty and Farley the other day. They run the Bar 7. They were expecting to meet me in town yesterday, to put me on their payroll."

Surprise lit Donovan's face. Intrigue danced on Tom's.

CHAPTER SIXTEEN

Tom and Buck leaned against the bar rail in the Laramie saloon for nearly two hours when, finally a dusty cowboy ambled up to Buck.

"Buck Hawkins?" The cowboy wanted to know.

Buck turned to survey him. A quick glance revealed an average sized but thin man in well-worn and dusty clothes, boots that appeared too large, a felt hat that in its younger life must've been good looking, and a gun belt supporting a left and right revolver.

"Yeah, that's me, who's askin'?"

"Don't matter who I am. What matters is you're a day late. Shorty and Farley don't like them that's late." The dusty cowboy displayed an air of unauthorized authority.

Tom rested his hand on the butt of his Colt, his fingers danced about the trigger guard. In the corner of his eye, he noticed, two cowboys who had been sitting at a table behind them slowly rise to their feet. He gave them cold eyes and simply shook his finger. They sat back down.

"It couldn't be helped. You here to take me to the ranch?" Buck offered a smile.

"That's right, let's ride."

Buck and Tom turned from the bar.

"Hold on there, Buck." The dusty cowboy protested. "Farley didn't say nothin' about anybody but you."

Buck and Tom looked at each other, then at the dusty cowboy, and together they said, "We're a team."

"Well, you can explain it when we get to the ranch."

The two cowboys from the table followed them through bat wing doors, and two more waited on their horses.

They rode from Denver City at a fast gallop.

After they settled in to an easier speed, Buck decided to make use of the time they all had together. "Hey fella," he asked the cowboy on his right, "you know someone named Poke?"

"Naw."

"Did you know Buster Kelly?"

"Nope."

"How long you been with this outfit?"

"'Bout a day."

"I see. What about these other fellas?"

"We all signed on together, 'bout a day ago."

Tom chuckled inside at Buck's inability to gain information from the talkative cowboy. They rode on in silence, the afternoon sun taking its toll on the horses.

"I need to rest my horse," Tom said, "we had a 20-mile ride into town."

"Farley ain't gonna like us being late," the dusty cowboy protested.

"I'll explain it to him," Tom slowed his horse to a walk, and thought he'd take a chance. "Anybody in your outfit Cheyenne?"

"Indian? Hell no!" The cowboy scoffed.

That gave Tom two possibilities. Either these boys were just too new to know, or what Tom thought was true. He'd carried a feeling in his gut ever since getting shot off Thunder two nights back.

"You two shut up and ride. You can do all your talkin' at the ranch with Farley and Shorty," the cowboy ordered.

It took an hour for the tired old ranch house to come into view, and they plodded across the little wooden bridge. Farley and Shorty sat on the porch, rifles across their laps.

"Good to see ya, Buck. Who's your friend?" Farley waved his rifle toward Tom.

"My friend," Buck said.

Shorty jumped up, levered a shell into his rifle chamber. "Don't get smart with me fancy pants."

"He works for me on the Donovan spread, doesn't talk much, good with a gun, and he does what he's told," Buck stared Shorty down.

"Junior, tend them horses." Farley barked, and the skinny, dusty cowboy began to gather reins.

"Come inside out of this heat and wash down a little of that dust," Farley offered.

Everyone but Junior crowded into the small ranch house. It was cooler inside, and Buck sure liked their whiskey. Tom chose water. The others took a bottle and retreated to the cots in the rear of the cabin while Farley, Shorty, Buck, and Tom gathered at a table.

"Sorry I'm a day late, couldn't be helped. I have to watch when I slip away." Buck explained.

"We shipped 350 head yesterday with no trouble from Buster Kelly, thanks to your good shooting!" Farley slapped Buck's back, hoisted his shot glass into the air, and clinked it against Buck's.

Buck shot Tom an informative glance, and Tom noticed Shorty caught it as well.

"We got 400 more head, and some of the boys think they can have another 100 in a week. Think you can give us a hand and move some of Donovan's stock out to the hill country where my boys can drive 'em to our range?" Farley asked.

"How many do you want and when do you want them?" Buck seemed pleasant enough.

"The Donovan spread runs 5,000 head. I'll take 200 next week."

The cowboys in the rear gave a hoot and raised their glasses, obviously glad to hear business would be good.

"I can handle that. What about the eyes at the rail yard? You know they're watching for fresh brands."

"Got that covered," Farley bragged.

"You paid off the sheriff?" Buck grinned.

"Better. I got the rail yard manager's wife right back here in a dugout behind this cabin. He don't give me no trouble. We're gonna slit her throat when we're done with her," Farley took a sip and flashed a proud squint-eyed look.

Tom snapped inside, sprang to his feet and shot Farley and Shorty dead-on in the face. Buck took his cue, dove to the floor, and shot dead the cowboys on the cots in the rear of the cabin.

"Holy cow! Tom, you could give a guy a warning!"

"It ain't over." Tom pointed out the window at the crowd of outlaws running toward the cabin.

"Looks like this cabin's seen this sort of action before. At least we have their Winchesters. And look at the pile of ammo on the stove." Buck checked the Winchesters, found them fully loaded, tossed one to Tom. "Good thick walls. We can hold out until water and whiskey's gone." Buck found himself unable to hide the excitement he felt at times like this. He loved a hot party.

Tom took position next to the window nearest the front door. "Bar that backdoor."

"What the hell's going on in there?" A cowboy hollered from the yard. Tom peeked out the window. "I count 13, Buck."

"This'll hardly be sporting."

"We just had a difference of opinion with Shorty and Farley," Tom's voice rang sinister.

"What's all this shooting about?" The cowboy yelled back.

"Had to get 'em to see things our way," Buck told them, his smile broadening.

Tom and Buck watched as the men outside, obviously confused, huddled together and then drew their revolvers. "We're comin' in." The cowboy who seemed in charge announced.

"Not armed, you're not," Buck warned.

The men outside stopped for an instant, then dove for cover. Two never made it. Tom and Buck had fired first and often.

Bullets slammed into the front of the sturdy cabin. Tom and Buck slid to the floor and reloaded. The men outside retreated to the safety of the barn and stream bank.

"Sure wish I had my Sharps," Tom said.

"Be handy, wouldn't it? Some of those boys out there can shoot."

"Maybe they'll lose interest."

A fresh volley poured into the cabin walls.

"Maybe, but not yet," Buck shrugged his shoulders.

"Let's talk to 'em." Smiling a smile that rivaled Buck's, Tom dropped to his knees, slipped his rifle barrel out the corner of the window and fired in the direction of the stream bank. As he reloaded, Buck did the same.

They maintained alternate rifle fire at the men huddled in the stream bank until Tom noticed two men sneaking from the barn toward the corner of the house. He yanked open the front door, fell to his belly on the porch planks, and shot them down. Under Buck's cover fire he rolled into the cabin and pushed the door shut.

"That was fancy," Buck's grin punctuated his compliment.

"They were trespassing."

"Could get rough, if this dance ain't over by dark."

"If they stay in that creek bed, they might be able to wait us out."

For a little while gunfire ceased. They watched from the cabin as the sun fell and shadows in the yard stretched. At least they had the sun to their backs. Darkness was their biggest threat. Indians rarely attacked under the cover of darkness, but the men huddled in the stream bank were not Indians.

"We have to get out of here before dark. They could surround this cabin, and we'd never know it. Sounds like they're on dinner break, anyway," Buck said.

"We're not going anywhere without the woman they have in the dugout," Tom's icy eyes told Buck not to bother arguing.

"Got a plan?"

"I'm gonna go get her and we'll take her along."

Tom stood, stuffed two boxes of shells in his pockets, and paused at the back door. "Give 'em something to think about, Buck".

Buck tore the lid from a box of shells and sat it by his knee. "Hurry back." He fired well-spaced, well-aimed rounds at the men crouching in the stream bed as Tom slipped out the back door.

The cowboys in the creek bed concentrated their fire on the cabin, and Buck was all too eager and willing to hold their attention.

Tom found the dugout a few feet behind the cabin safe from gunfire and sprinted to the sunken door. He pounded the door and got no response. "Hey lady, I'm here to save you. Move to the back if you can. I need to shoot this lock." He waited a few seconds to give the prisoner inside time to move, then he aimed his Winchester at the lock on the chain and fired one shot. The bullet slammed into the lock and the chain jumped free. He grabbed the chain and yanked it through the door latch and pushed in the door.

She lay huddled in the damp cold, filthy and not moving. He dropped down in the cold mud and cradled her. "Wake up now. I'll take you home."

She never moved. He carried her to the door, where the setting sun sent a few meager rays of light to the dugout floor. Tom's eyes flooded and he spun about. There in the corner he found a broken jar. The desperate woman had taken a broken jar and cut open her throat.

Those dirty rotten bastards. Why the hell were there so many rotten bastards in the world?

He carried her out and laid her gently on the ground, smoothed her ruffled dress, took his bandana and tied it around the dead woman's neck to cover the jagged, gaping wound. Bending down on one knee, he placed her hands neatly on her lap, kissed her cold cheek.

He stood, checked his rifle was fully loaded, checked his Colt, then bolted at a flat-out-run toward the creek bed. Winchester under his armpit, hand on the lever, he charged the creek screaming louder than a Sioux warrior. When he passed the cabin he opened fire. Propelled by rage, he ran screaming and shooting, directly toward the surprised and confused cowboys in the ditch.

Buck, taken totally by surprise, jumped up, kicked the door open and charged the ditch, firing and hollering.

Some cowboys so unnerved by this frontal assault scrambled up the bank on the other side and tried to run away. None got very far, and those that stayed in the ditch, died in the ditch.

Tom collapsed. "She's dead, Buck."

Buck squatted by his friend. "We'll take her to town and find her husband."

In the barn they found a wagon of sorts. Buck spent a little time testing the wheels and swinging the tongue. "I believe this'll get us to town."

There wasn't much in the way of harnesses in the barn. But with what they found, combined with some rope and some leather straps, they fashioned a usable harness and breast collar for the horse Tom had ridden, which seemed to be the most gentle.

After they rigged the horse, they gathered more ammunition and blankets. Together they wrapped the woman in blankets, carried her to the wagon. Both men were reminded of that day, more than three years ago, on the prairie south of Fort Laramie. The day they'd met during a skirmish with Tall Dog and Black Feather. The day their friendship started with the burial of another dead woman they had carefully wrapped in blankets, and placed on a wagon.

Tom opened the corral gates to allow the horses an escape. Then, for a second, he stood and looked at the sad little ranch house.

"Come on, Tom, let's get the hell out of here."

It was dark and late by the time they drove the broken wagon into town. Light spilled to the street from saloon doors and windows. So did laughter and piano music. They stopped at the brick building with a sign "SHERIFF—DENVER CITY".

"I'll bang the door." Buck jumped down, ran to the door, and started banging.

CHAPTER SEVENTEEN

"Hello in there!" Buck shouted as he pounded the door. No light showed in the barred window to the right of the door. "Anybody home?"

Tom tried to get Buck's attention to warn him the sheriff was coming, but not to the door.

"Turn around, son," the sheriff ordered Buck. "Hands in the air!" The sheriff stood just outside the light coming from a saloon door across the street. Near as Tom could tell in the darkness he was a tall man with wide shoulders and a double barreled shotgun lying across his left forearm.

"Sheriff, there you are," Buck acknowledged, with a slight chuckle and feeble smile.

"Yep, here I am. What's so almighty important to be banging on my door at three in the mornin'? And who are you?"

"Sheriff, my name's Buck Hawkins. The fellow on the wagon there is Tom Named by Horse and we got some mighty important stuff to discuss, if you'll kindly point that scatter gun toward the ground."

The sheriff took steps toward Buck keeping the shotgun aimed as it was. Tom felt his eyes sizing him up as he walked, one careful step after another. Tom sat still on the wagon seat, the horse pawed the dusty street, and Buck stood with arms in the air. Tom held his .44 part way out of its holster, his finger on the trigger guard.

"Okay, Tom Named by Horse, you can get down and join your friend over here by the door. We'll go inside and sort this out."

"Alright for me to let my arms down?" Buck asked with a

shrug and a crooked smile.

"Yeah, go-ahead. Move aside. Let me get to the door."

The sheriff rested the shotgun on his forearm while he used a big black skeleton key to unlock the heavy plank door. He swung the door in. Once inside he lit the lantern on his desk, and two that hung on the side walls.

The sheriff was indeed a tall man with broad shoulders and long gray hair that curled back up on itself at the top of his shoulders and had a neatly waxed mustache and no other facial hair. He wore a flat-brimmed black hat with a snakeskin hatband and long-sleeved white shirt under a black leather vest with a gold-chained watch fob in the right pocket. No spurs on his boots, but his gun belt had two pearl-handled Navy Colt 44's.

The sturdy jail looked like it could withstand just about any kind of assault. Triple thick brick walls, barred windows, and a double-thick plank door. The front room was good-sized, big enough for a pot bellied stove, the sheriff's huge desk and a smaller desk off to the corner. Four chairs sat around a small wooden table in the room's center. On the wall behind the sheriff's desk hung a gun rack on which six Winchesters and two shotguns sat chained.

The back wall was a double-thick plank with a door in the center that led to the five jail cells behind. The door stood open and one customer occupied the first cell.

"Hey, Sheriff, you know I never got my supper!"

"Yeah well, neither did the fellow you killed," The sheriff said.

"I want my supper you, no 'count bought-off tin badge!"

"If you're lucky, you'll get breakfast! That is, if I don't hear one damned word out of you all night." The sheriff slammed the door that separated the two rooms.

Tom and Buck sat at the table and watched as the sheriff started a fire in the stove. "A little coffee can't hurt our discussion, I reckon."

"I think that'll do just fine," Buck said.

When the fire caught, the sheriff strutted across the room, heels clacking on the brick floor, laid the shotgun down on his desk and settled into the big wooden chair. For a few seconds longer he sat behind his desk, reared back in his chair his feet up on the desktop and studied Tom and Buck. Finally he spoke. "My name is

Sheriff Bo Zeller, and the good citizens of Denver City hired me to help domesticate this town. There are a lot of good people in Denver City. We got a railroad now, stockyards, four hotels, eleven saloons, three churches, three General Mercantile stores, and over fourteen hundred permanent residents. We have a Stock Grower's Association, two-stage lines, and our own brewery.

"I tell you that just so you know I like this town. I've been sheriff here for three months, before that I was sheriff in Abilene, before that Dodge City and I'm not dead yet. I just thought you should know. I work at stayin' alive."

"Sheriff, we've been coming to Denver City for three years to sell our horses," Buck propped his feet on the desk and rocked back on his chair. Not to be outdone by the big feeling Sheriff, "We hail from 40 miles southwest of Fort Laramie."

"A little far from home, aren't you?" Sherriff Zeller sent an annoyed scowl at Buck's moccasin boots atop his desk.

"Seem to get a real good price for our stock at your horse sales."

"What would selling horses at our stockyards have to do with banging on my door in the middle of the night?"

"Long story, Sheriff. Figure that coffee's about ready?" Buck glanced at the stove.

The Sheriff clasped his hands behind his head. "Not quite ready to boil yet, start talking."

Buck turned to Tom who signaled for Buck to go ahead.

"Hard to know just where to start." Buck put his feet on the floor and leaned forward, pulled off his hat, ran his hands around the brim, laid it flat on the table top, and pushed his long blonde hair back with both hands. "Tom and I are friends of the Donovans."

"How is Donovan?"

"His belly's healin' all right, but his cattle are disappearing. What's your take on this cattle thievery that's been going on?"

"Tell me yours," the Sheriff said without a twitch.

Tom and Buck exchanged glances again. "Tom and I know a couple boys who won't be stealing cattle anymore. Ever hear of the Bar 7?"

"Sure have, new outfit 'bout 20 miles outside of town. Tough bunch, I've had two deputies watchin' their outfit. What've you got?"

"Well for one thing, on the back of that wagon out yonder we have the dead wife of your stockyard manager. Bar 7 was holding her hostage so they could ship their stolen stock and not worry about brands. I think they said they sent three or four hundred head a few days back," Buck watched to notice if the big flinched.

Sheriff Zeller stroked his mustache. "Who killed her?"

Tom was trying real hard to read this fella. Cold-blooded son of a bitch he was. Who does he think killed her? If he was sheriff and liked town like he said he did, he had to know the stockyard manager and his wife, yet there was no emotion. Unless you count a little twist on the end of a mustache. Tom jumped up and was instantly staring down both barrels of the sheriff's shotgun. "Who killed her? ... Who killed her? ... She killed herself, you bastard, with a broken bottle! Those bastards at the Bar 7 killed her!"

Buck grabbed Tom's shirt, yanked him down into the chair.

"What do you mean she killed herself?" The sheriff sighted over the shotgun still aimed at Tom.

Buck kept a tight hold on the back of Tom's shirt. "Those bastards had her locked up in a dugout where they held her to get the cooperation of the stockyard manager."

"I'm sorry, men," The sheriff laid down his gun, shook his head, "I meant to hit that bunch for several days already, but I knew they had Mrs. O'Brien. Her husband confided in me the day Donovan got shot."

For a long moment they sat in silence. Finally Buck stood. "Think I'll check on the coffee." The room so quiet even the soft leather of his moccasin boots shuffling across the floor sounded like rain pounding on a wooden roof. "Hey, looks ready to drink." He poured three cups.

He kept one, handed one to Sheriff Zeller and sat the other by Tom. "Where do we go from here?"

The sheriff took a long slow sip. "Tell me about the incident at Bar 7."

Tom seemed to regain his footing and spoke first. "Shorty and Farley are dead, so are a handful of their men."

"You two took on Farley, and cleaned out the nest?"

"Yep," Buck said.

It became obvious that sheriff Zeller was fast gaining respect for Tom and Buck. Alternately they told the tale of the gunfight at the Bar 7 ranch house. The mood stayed somber and when the sheriff was satisfied with the details and the coffee gone, he rose. "I'll ask you to take Mrs. O'Brien to the undertaker. I reckon I should go see Mr. O'Brien."

The sun had already awakened, bringing light to a new day, and the prisoner in the back howled about breakfast as their get-together adjourned. Sheriff Zeller paid no attention to the hungry prisoner. He pointed his shotgun to the undertaker's building four doors down, then pivoted on his heels and marched down the center of the street, toward the stockyards.

"Sure am glad he didn't ask us to go along, Tom," Buck sighed a long breath.

Tom took the horse's bridle and simply walked alongside the horse the distance of a few hundred feet to the undertaker's building. Buck knocked on the door. Most undertakers that Buck had ever met smelled of formaldehyde, wore black clothes, had sunken eyes, and just looked spooky. The man who opened the door fit that description perfectly.

"Sheriff Zeller asked us to deliver Mrs. O'Brien to you," Buck said with uneasiness evident in his voice.

"Mrs. O'Brien?" The undertaker squeaked. "My Lord, has she passed on?"

Following the direction of Buck's outstretched arm, the undertaker walked to the rear of the wagon and pulled the corner of the blanket from Mrs. O'Brien's face. "My Lord."

Buck and Tom carried Mrs. O'Brien into the undertaker's office.

"Last night we killed the men that did this to her," Tom said, his icy eyes freezing the undertaker. "If you let Mr. O'Brien see her before you have her looking beautiful I'll pay you a visit." He turned to Mrs. O'Brien and removed his bandanna from her neck and pointed to her throat. "He better never see this, and never know how she died."

"Certainly, sir," The undertaker guaranteed in his sad, soft voice.

CHAPTER EIGHTEEN

Freshly mounted, Tom and Buck set out for the Donovan ranch.

"Should've asked him about Buster Kelly," Buck said.

"I don't know, I'm kinda interested in Poke's whereabouts. I figured to see him out at the Bar 7. He's mixed up in this somehow."

"Yep, indeed he is. But I don't think he's mixed up with them old boys we danced with yesterday."

"You don't?"

"Sure don't. I believe there are two outfits going on. I believe Bar 7, Shorty and Farley have nothing to do with the outfit you tangled with up on the plateau."

"Could be you have something there, Buck. I had a real good chance to look around that camp before they trussed me to the wheel. I can guarantee I never saw a Shorty or Farley. Never saw Poke either."

"Yeah, but you followed him there."

"I did, till I got shot off Thunder," Tom rubbed the second bullet wound on his left thigh.

"Think about it, as far as Donovan can figure there's a 1,000 head missing in the valley. How many head did Bar 7 say they shipped? Three hundred or so? There were no more cattle out at their ranch. How many were up on the plateau, five or six hundred head. See where I'm going?"

"Beginning to," Tom pulled his horse up, took a second to gaze out over the grasslands. It had taken him a long time to get used to having a home, but now he had one. Looking out over the grasslands here a few miles outside of Denver City made him long for his own ranch. He was ready to head home. He was ready to go home and spend a loving night in bed with his wife in his own house. "I think you're saying those cattle that Buster Kelly pulled from the stockyard to return to their proper owners ended up on the plateau."

"Makes sense doesn't it?"

"How would Poke get the cattle away from Buster Kelly and up to the plateau?"

"How many wranglers did you see up there? Fifteen or so cowboys and another half dozen Cheyenne? He sure would have plenty of help, especially if Buster Kelly assigned Poke to return the stolen cattle."

"Seems like we need to find Poke to get this sorted out."

They picked up the pace and loped across the grasslands in a direct line for the Donovan ranch, choosing a straight shot over the prairie rather than the indirect route of the dusty roads. "Poke wanted to be a big man and stuck to Buster like a tick in a hound's ear. The operation needed to move quickly though, before word got 'round the returning stock never made it back to their proper owners." Tom heard Buck, but his thoughts tugged him home. He wanted to go home and build a new house for Soft Cloud. He was anxious to see his friend Cole marry Hannah Miller. And he was eager to take Iron Shell and the boys out gatherin' horses for the ranch. He planned to wrap this up quickly.

"Yo, Tom, look yonder," Buck pointed east. "A single rider heading toward the plateau!"

Even from that distance Tom recognized the lone rider as Poke. "That's Poke. I'd know that crooked sittin' dirty thief anywhere. Let's run 'im down!"

They dug heels and demanded top speed. Their horses bolted through the tall grass. Buck's hat danced like a kite on its hat string. Tom rode the bigger horse with longer legs and soon outdistanced Buck. When they closed to within half the distance, Poke realized his peril and kicked his horse into a gallop.

Tom still managed to gain on Poke but Buck faded farther behind. The ground lay level, the grass as high as a horse's chest. But further ahead Tom saw the terrain dropped to a small line of trees most likely along a stream bed. Tom wanted to catch Poke before he could slip into cover. His horse found more speed and closed rapidly.

Tom dropped his reins, cupped his mouth and yelled, "Poke

stop or I'll shoot your horse!"

Poke turned in the saddle to look at his pursuer and after a moment slowed his horse. Tom galloped beside him, revolver in hand. "Down."

Poke stepped from his winded horse and dropped one rein to the ground. Buck came to a sliding stop beside them. They stood in a small circle. The only sound was that of the horses blowing hard, trying to catch their wind.

"Where are you going, Poke?" Buck sized him up.

Poke stared at his captors but said nothing. He pulled off his hat, dragged his sleeve across his forehead, then jammed his hat back. "Why don't we walk over to those trees and I'll tell you boys a story."

"Sounds reasonable, but I'll take your horse," Tom took Poke's reins.

They walked slow through the hot grass, three abreast, Poke in the middle.

Buck stopped and turned to unlash his canteen only a few yards from the wood line. Poke gagged then staggered against Tom at the same instant the rifle report reached them. Poke tore at his chest then grabbed for Tom. Another shot split the air between Buck and Tom.

Tom fell to the ground, "Grab your rifle, Buck!"

Buck held fast to his horse, tossed Tom his Big 50 and saddle bags and dropped, firing his Winchester toward the trees. His horse tore free and bolted.

They hugged the ground while bullets kicked up dust around them. "Why don't you charge 'em, Tom? Worked last time we danced with this outfit."

"Grass is too tall," Tom dumped the saddlebag. One box half full of rifle shells and six rounds for the Sharps. One way or another this wasn't gonna last all that long. The men in the trees maintained steady fire keeping them pinned. "We can't charge 'em head on. Start crawling through the grass to that clump of trees over there." He took a shell, slapped it in the rifle and waited for a target. Buck slithered toward the aspens. Tom stuffed the ammunition back in the leather saddlebag and was about to follow Buck when he realized he could see just the top of someone's head in the trees.

Tom sighted and fired. The head disappeared. He yanked open the breech, pulled the spent casing and slapped in a new shell.

He sighted on what he figured was the shoulder of another man behind a crooked tree. He aimed a little bit off the shoulder into the edge of the tree confident that from that distance the Big 50 would bore through the tree and find a home in the man's chest rather than a shoulder. He fired again. His calculations proved correct and he watched a man lurch from the tree clawing his chest.

Buck opened fire from the aspens, and using his covering fire Tom scrambled to him. "Cozy spot you picked out Tom, all we're lacking for a picnic is a basket of food and a few gals."

Tom was busy surveying the lay of the land from their position hidden in the grove of twiggy aspens. A slight depression ran from their aspens to the treeline where the outlaws hid.

They crawled low in the depression until they reached the woods and realized there was no shooting. For a second Tom and Buck looked at each other. Then they heard galloping hooves running away from them.

"What's a man's got to do to get an all-night dance around here?" Buck tossed his arms in the air.

Tom crossed his legs and sat. He held Buck's Big 50 with the butt on the ground at his toes, the barrel standing straight up, his hands around the grip. He rested his head on his arms. "We lost our big lead."

Buck wadded through the waist-high grass to Poke, dropped down and rolled Poke over. "We didn't lose our lead just yet Tom. This fella's not dead!" Buck hollered.

Tom ran to grab Buck's canteen, propped Poke on Buck's knee and carefully dripped water on the dying man's lips. Poke feebly raised his hand, pushed away the canteen and tried to talk.

"I wasn't dirty," he whispered, barely audible.

Tom and Buck looked at each other. Whatever he was trying to say seemed as though it might be convincing, since somebody wanted him dead. They were close enough to the wood line that whoever gunned downed Poke knew who they were shooting.

"Poke, you're gonna die, you know, so keep trying. Who's dirty?" Buck steadied Poke's head.

Poke whistled, gurgled and tried hard to breathe. He opened his mouth and started to say a word and gave a loud garbled rattle and went limp. Tom stood and raised his arms to his sides, palms up. "What the hell?"

"Let's take a look at those fellas you shot, see if we can find anything on them," Buck suggested.

They left Poke lying in the grass. Silently they walked to the dead man. Tom searched his pockets and found four silver dollars. In his saddlebag he found ammunition, jerky and a worn, crumbled envelope. He threw the saddlebag over his shoulder picked up the Winchester and started for other man.

Buck had already gone to him. "Get over here Tom, this fella's still breathing."

Tom hurried to the wounded man. After studying him for several seconds Tom stood up. "Tell me who you work for." The man did not respond. Tom grabbed the man's hair and jerked him upright. "Tell me who you work for."

"I don't believe he can talk Tom," Buck said.

"Sure he can, he just needs to hear me asking." Tom held the man's hair, shook him violently and when he stopped, in a very gentle voice he asked, "Who did you work for?"

"Let him go, the poor bastard's almost gone," Buck pleaded.

"Well then, I can't hurt him. Who did you work for?"

The man chocked on his own blood but made eye contact with Tom. It was a begging kind of look. Tom could see the pain in the man's eyes. He grabbed his hair with both hands and shook him even harder. And then again in a gentle voice he said, "Tell me who you work for and I'll slit your throat and this will be over."

Tom's brutal cold-heartedness sometimes caught Buck off guard. He looked at Tom's icy stare fixed on the dying man's face. At times like this, Buck didn't recognize his friend. Buck would just let the poor fellow pass in peace, but Tom was getting his answer.

Tom shook the man another time, and then looked at the fistful of hair that pulled out of the man's head, and shook it free. "Tell me who you work for." The man reached up with his one good arm and laid his hand on top of Tom's arm and with the saddest of begging eyes he looked at Tom. He knew the man was sucking down his own blood and it would make it hard to talk but he shook him again.

Just before the man's eyes rolled back in he gargled. "The sheriff."

"Holy cow! I never thought it. The sheriff's dirty." Buck turned and paced.

"This thing's a mighty mess," Tom said, "I don't think Poke was dirty. I'll tell you who's dirty. Buster Kelly, that's who's dirty. Buster Kelly and that damned sheriff, that's the outfit."

"I believe you're right, Tom. Yes sir, I do believe you've got 'er nailed. We gotta find a couple of horses. We should take Poke and hustle back to the ranch and give Donovan a head's up."

It took an hour to find the horses grazing in the shade by the stream about a mile away. They tied Poke to Buck's horse then gathered rocks from the stream and piled them on the bodies of the two dead cattle thieves. "At least the wolves will have to work a little," Buck said. Satisfied they had done all they could, they set out for the Donovan house.

Twilight had begun to settle in when they rode up to the Donovan house. Donovan sat on the porch enjoying a cigar in the early evening shadows, Mrs. Donovan by his side. Soft Cloud and Hawk were also on the porch. Although difficult for him to do so, Donovan rose to his feet and pointed to Poke's body. "That Poke?"

"It is," Buck said. "But he's not your man."

"What do you mean he's not my man?"

Tom and Buck stepped down and the same young man who had walked Thunder to cool him came from the barn to take their tired horses. "What should I do with Poke?" The young man asked Buck in a very timid voice.

"Take him to the barn and lay him on a bed of straw for tonight," Buck said.

Tom went directly to Soft Cloud and Hawk, leaving explanations to Buck.

"Things didn't go as planned at Bar 7. We ended up killing Shorty and Farley and a few of their boys. Turns out they'd kidnapped the stockyard manager's wife and were holding her there and well, you know Tom when a woman's in danger. He just jumped up and shot Farley and Shorty dead on in the face. 'Course that started a whole ruckus. Tom found the woman in the dugout, but she'd already killed herself.

"We took her to the new sheriff you folks have, Bo Zeller. Got to Denver in the middle of the night and must've interrupted one of his poker games, 'cause he was sure unfriendly at the start."

"I know Bo Zeller. Don't know that I care for him. The saloons are sure prospering, but I don't see he's done much else for the town," Donovan said, "How's Mr. O'Brien?"

"We never did get to see Mr. O'Brien and you're gonna like Bo Zeller a whole lot less when I'm through talking. We took Mrs. O'Brien to the undertaker, got those horses from the livery and started back here. That's when we run across Poke. We caught him and were just about to get him to talk when we were bushwhacked and he got shot. He lived long enough to tell us he wasn't dirty. We killed a few of them that ambushed us, but most of 'em got away. One of them told us before he died he worked for the sheriff."

Mrs. Donovan gave a short gasp, Donovan shook his head, Soft Cloud continued to smother Tom with kisses.

"I knew I didn't like that fancy son of a bitch," Donovan said and he bit the end from his cigar and spit it over the porch rail. The night air grew heavy and quiet. Stars shone bright and the moon was just a sliver in the sky. Tom, Hawk, and Soft Cloud excused themselves and went inside.

Buck took off his hat and ran his fingers around the brim, something he often did when deep in thought or wrestling with a sour situation. He struggled with the fact that he and Tom were certain Buster Kelly was dirty, not Poke. The only unanswered question in Buck's mind was why did Poke kill Buster Kelly? If he did. Well he might as well jump in with both feet he reasoned.

"Sheriff Zeller wasn't working alone. He had a partner," Buck started in a slow, deep, quiet voice. "Now Tom and I don't have the proof yet—but we think Buster Kelly was working with the sheriff." Buck blurted the last few words and leveled soft eyes directly at Donovan.

Mrs. Donovan looked about to faint. Donovan threw his cigar over the rail and jumped up so fast the pain in his gut sat him back down in his chair with a thump, where he sat slamming his fist into his palm. "Buster ... Buster, you could've had whatever you wanted. Why didn't you talk to me, Buster? How long have you been scheming against me?" Chester Donovan pivoted on his chair and laid his big hands on Buck's knees. "Get the proof, Buck ... Get the damn proof!" Leaning on his cane, Donovan rose, took both of Mrs. Donovan's hands in one of his, and led her through the door, leaving Buck on the porch alone.

CHAPTER NINETEEN

"Our first stop will be Mr. O'Brien," Tom said as they rode away from the ranch in the morning. "I want to know all he knows before we hear Sheriff Zeller's lies." Tom no longer wore Donovan's oversized clothes. Today he wore his own deerskin leggings, and moccasin boots. He wore no shirt beneath his open leather vest that Soft Cloud had made him. Only the bone and claw necklace Red Cloud had given him danced beneath the vest. On his head sat the black wide-brimmed hat he bought that day in Ogallala four years ago. Dressed as he was, Buck reasoned Tom looked as much like any Sioux warrior he had ever seen mount a horse. Today the horse Tom rode was Thunder.

Buck did not answer right away. His thoughts were about the cattle on the high plateau. He wondered how many came from the Donovan ranch. How many of the cowboys they saw up there came from the Donovan ranch? Tom and he had killed a number of men in the battle on the plateau and Donovan had nothing to say about missing men, but earlier he said he had sent two hands to town to look for help. Could be none of the cowboys up there belong to any of the local spreads.

Buck saddled Diablo today and both men wore their gun belts, each carried a 44. They had their Winchesters and buffalo rifles as well, and saddlebags heavy with shells. Buck knew Tom had had enough and was ready to go home and hoped Mr. O'Brien would have useful information. But he was most eager to confront Sheriff Bo Zeller. Both he and Tom had little use for liars and fakes.

They entered town from the east end and rode directly to the corrals at the rail yard, tied their horses to the hitching rail and took a quick assessment. Buck recognized Smokey on the plank boardwalk at the top rail, carrying his tablet and counting cattle. "Howdy, Smokey."

"Hello there, Buck ... pretty busy today. We're sending 750 head to the cars in Kit Carson. These just came in yesterday, but Mr. O'Brien said send them first. How can I help you, if you make it quick."

"Can you point us to Mr. O'Brien's house?"

"Sure can, it's that green house on the end of the block yonder, but you won't find him there. He quit his job this morning and left town."

"Boy that's not going to help us at all," Buck beat his hat against his thigh, and built a small dust cloud that floated away in the light breeze.

Tom looked at the green house allowing his disappointment to show. "How long ago did he leave?"

"Can't say. 'Bout eight this morning he told me he'd done quit and I was in charge of all the cattle shippin' till someone told me otherwise."

"Did he have horses and maybe a carriage at the livery? Can we find him there?" Tom squinted in the sun to look at Smokey.

"I think he left on the 10 o'clock stage. Seems to me he told me once he had family in Cheyenne."

"Who's shipping all these cattle today?" Buck waved a hand toward the full corrals.

"Doggone if I know. Mr. O'Brien said they're good to send along and that boys would be here 'round noon to trail 'em to Carson. Every head in these first six corrals. There's Donovan brands, Hollister brands, some of Johnny Kirk's too. Mighty strange to me but I reckon Mr. O'Brien had it all sorted out before he quit."

Tom and Buck hopped up on the plank next to Smokey and examined the cattle in the pen below. It was easy to see the mixed brands. "Smokey, you know these are stolen cattle." Tom shot a hard look of disbelief Smokey's way.

"I know nothing about 'em ... I was told to ship 'em and by god that's what I aim to do."

"Well I'm telling you as top hand of the Donovan spread you'd better not send a single head with the Donovan brand on it." Buck pointed to the Donovan cattle with his dusty hat.

"I quit! I ain't risking my neck so some highfalutin' Sheriff and damned crooked mayor can get rich selling other folks' cattle!" Smokey threw his dirty tablet in the pen. "I've kept quiet long enough. I'll be movin' on. Maybe I'll see you fellas out on the prairie!"

"Hold on, Smokey! What'd you just say?" Buck shot a wide-eyed glance Tom's way.

"Oh boy ... I guess I did it now." Smokey sat on the plank and threw his stubby pencil in the corral.

"Why don't we wander over to Mr. O'Brien's house, see if we can find some coffee and you tell us everything you know about one highfalutin' Sheriff and one damned crooked mayor?" Buck suggested with his hand on Smokey's shoulder.

Mr. O'Brien must have left with only the clothes on his back for they found the house fully furnished, with food in the pantry and coffee just waiting to be boiled. Tom started a fire in the kitchen stove and set the coffee on to boil, then the three men took seats around the long kitchen table.

Buck rolled his hat around in his hands, running the brim between his thumb and fingers in his usual fashion when pondering a situation. Tom used the quiet moment to size up Smokey. He figured he was probably in his early forties and wore clothes at least one size too big, making his long lanky frame look spindly and weak. Tom noticed his hands were the hands of a hard-working man; long fingers dark tanned, and calloused where they should be. Beneath his gray felt hat that looked to be as old as the man was a weather-beaten leathery face with uninteresting brown eyes.

"Have you got family?" Tom asked.

"Naw never got around to gettin' married. Last year, I finally figured I'd settle down here in Denver City. I was only in town three days when Mr. O'Brien offered me the job of loading cattle for the Denver Pacific Railroad. Ain't a real railroad yet, but I was tired of buffalo huntin'. Tired of sleeping in the rain ... So I took the job."

That got Buck's attention. "So you're a buffalo hunter?"

"Not no more, I ain't."

"Been in some tough scrapes, have you?" Buck surveyed Smokey.

"Nothin' so tough I couldn't handle. A few scrapes with some Sioux and renegade hide thieves, but nothing me an old Betsy couldn't handle." Smokey let slip a faint smile of pride.

"Tom here grew up on the prairie hunting buffalo. Cut his baby teeth chewing hides, and I shot a few myself. Sort of a shame though the way the big hider teams are heading out there. Soon won't be any big shaggys left," Buck said.

"Well it looks like I might be goin' back to hidin' since I quit this outfit. Didn't really care for the Circle Y either."

"Don't be so quick," Tom said, "Might just be if you throw in with us, and help toss some water on this cattle stealing fire, the Denver Pacific Railroad may see you as pretty important to them."

"Naw, I ain't looking to fight," Smokey lifted his hat from his head and laid flat it on the table, kicking up a small dust cloud, "I thought we came in here for coffee."

"That's right, we did," Buck hustled to the stove and served up three cups of boiling hot coffee.

"Tell us about the mayor," Tom leaned in, his bone and claw necklace rattled on the table edge, the startling racket caused Smokey to take too big a gulp of the very hot coffee.

"Whoa," Smokey coughed out, waving his hand over his mouth, "that's hot stuff." He wore the look of a man who wanted to be trusted, and wanted to help. "I'd feel safer if I had my Betsy here with me." He rubbed his palms on his thighs. Buck yanked his .44 from its holster, pulled the hammer back and laid it on the table in front of Smokey. "Nice Colt." Smokey picked it up.

Buck showed Smokey his one of a kind smile and said. "There you go."

"The mayor's been in town about ten months. I'm not sure how he got to be mayor but a few days after Mayor Evans died in his sleep this fella Jack Martin became mayor. He's the one that brought in Sheriff Zeller." Smokey went to the stove to top off his coffee. He carried the Colt with him. He walked the few steps from the stove to the kitchen sink took a quick glance out the window into the rear yard and a sip of hot coffee, then turned around and leaned against the sink facing Tom and Buck.

"I never heard about any kind of investigation into Mayor Evans' death. My bet is it wasn't a peaceful death," Smokey went on.

"You figure this new fella Jack Martin had something to do with it?" Buck prodded.

"You ever been asleep on the prairie under your wagon and

get up in the middle of the night 'cause you knew something weren't right and sure enough see a pack of dirty rotten hide thieves crawlin' your way? I'm tellin' you I got that same feelin'."

"Have you ever met this Jack Martin?" Tom asked.

"Several times, mostly in the last couple months. He'd come down here with Sheriff Zeller and they even knew I was listening when they would tell Mr. O'Brien what cattle he was to send. Brand or no brand. That's how come I was gonna let all them cattle go today. I didn't have the stomach to stand up to them alone, but if we're throwin' in together, that's a fair bit different."

"We're throwing in together," Buck said, "how's Buster Kelley fit in all this?"

"Well, first off it weren't Poke who killed Buster Kelley," Smokey said.

Tom watched Smokey talk and found he had no problem believing him. Smokey was the kind of man you felt pretty quick you could trust.

"Had to be, I went out with Poke to get Buster's body, and the next day Tom and I went out to the spot where he got it, and there wasn't any other horse tracks there. So it was only Poke and Buster Kelley, and Buster Kelley was shot dead on in the face."

"Yeah he was shot plumb square in the face all right," Smokey said with a nod, "only thing is, that weren't where he was shot. Poke told me himself, Buster Kelley was shot up in the camp you boys discovered on the high plateau. Yeah, I know you boys were up there. I heard you gave 'em what for, there and at the Bar 7. That's why I'm willin' to throw in with you."

"Why didn't you just didn't hightail it out of here?"

"Might be I wanted to see how this story ends," Smokey smiled, "Might be I wanted to see if you boys just wanted to take over and kill Mr. and Mrs. Donovan, cause that's what the cattle thieves threatened Poke with. That's how come Poke disappeared for a few days. He was up on the high plateau waitin' for a chance to get a bead on Sheriff Zeller when they caught you, Tom. He was trying to figure a way to get you out of there when Buck showed up and you two shot the place to hell and stampeded their herd."

"Sort of did the same thing out at the Bar 7," Buck said.

"Was the Bar 7 part of this?" Tom asked.

"You bet. They figured on holdin' the cattle up on the plateau and once a month or so they'd move 'em down to the Bar 7, closer to the corrals and ship 'em out from there. That's why they had Mrs. O'Brien. But you boys know that."

Tom got his all too familiar feeling of rage, his cheeks boiled and he pounded the table spilling his and Buck's coffee. The tin cups rattled to the floor. He grabbed the table, flipped it across the room smashing it against the wall and kicked the nearest cup. He made a lunge for Smokey but Buck caught him in midair. "Tom, damn it! He's on our side. We'll get the rest of these bastards. You know that. Now sit down! 'Course we ain't got a table any more, but sit down and let's hear the rest of the story. I'll get us coffee … don't make me tie you to that chair."

"Mr. O'Brien was clean, right?" Buck filled the cup Tom held in his trembling hand. Buck knew he had to settle Tom and get that icy stare out of his eyes.

"Charlie O'Brien was clean. Musta been awful scared 'cause he never even told me they had his wife. I did ask him a question or two and he said as long as Buster Kelley approved the cattle they should go. But then in the last few weeks Buster Kelley would pull cattle out and say they were stole, and then him and hands from the Donovan spread would round 'em up and leave with 'em. The whole thing is more confusing than I could follow. Poke figured some of it though."

"Buster and some other dirty hands he hired for Donovan were doing a double cross, right?" Buck floated.

"Yep, Buster had just about took over the camp on the high plateau. He was running the cattle he pulled from the rail yard pens back up there. He was wanting to gather up a few thousand head then light out for Montana to start a spread of their own. I even heard him say with his own lips he was tired of being Donovan's second fiddle. He figured he spent ten years building that spread up. I think Buster just got evil, turned no good."

"Donovan would have given that man anything he wanted," Buck said. "All he had to do was ask."

"We figured Poke wasn't dirty," Tom said, noticeably cooled down, "his last words were 'I'm not dirty.' Dying men don't usually lie."

"So now that you had a chance to talk this through, I guess you'll agree those cattle in the pens out yonder came down from the high plateau," Buck said.

"I reckon so. Only one way to tell for sure. We gotta go up there."

"Yeah, but that'll have to wait. Where do you keep your things?"

"I got a room behind the livery. It ain't much but it's dry and cheap," Smokey showed them his first smile.

"Do you know where this Mayor Martin lives?" Buck's eyes twinkled.

"Sure do, he moved right into Mayor Evans House, the big brick house down by the courthouse yard. I'm to get my things and we're gonna to visit the Mayor?" Smokey said.

"You guessed right," Tom pitched his empty cup into the sink.

"Evening's not far off, what do you say to a good steak dinner over at the Denver Hotel?" Buck suggested.

"You two go on ahead. I've got to get those horses out of the sun but I sure want to keep 'em handy," Tom said.

"There's a carriage house in the back and there's a hand pump in the backyard," Smokey said, "I don't believe they'll let you in the Denver Hotel in that outfit, Tom."

"Might be a problem," Tom said with a grin, "I didn't dress for hotel visiting, I had other plans. I'll just go through the closet over here and find a shirt to borrow from Mr. O'Brien."

CHAPTER TWENTY

Tom watched Smokey and Buck head toward the Denver Hotel, then walked Thunder and Diablo from the rail yard corral to Mr. O'Brien's carriage house.

Inside the carriage house he found not only comfortable shade and a not too plain carriage but also a very dead Mr. O'Brien. The pitchfork still in his chest as he lay on his back on the dirt floor, both hands gripped the handle. His last efforts in this life obviously failed.

What an outfit this cattle stealing bunch must be. Mr. O'Brien lying in the dust looked as if he had been a gentle man. Probably worked hard at his job and never asked for any of this mess to come his way. Tom pulled the fork from his chest, then laid him across the seat in the carriage. "They'll pay for this," he promised.

He found hay stacked at the end of the barn, put Diablo and Thunder in stalls, threw them hay, and carried two wooden buckets of water. After Tom had loosened Thunder's cinch, he bent down to loosen Diablo's when he felt a terrific blow to the back of his head. His first instinct was to dive away thinking Diablo had kicked him but then he realized someone had struck him from behind.

He lunged across the stall and under the partition boards, Colt in hand. Tom knew the back of his head was caved in, he felt blood run down his neck, but he couldn't allow himself to pass out. The big man who slugged him spun and kicked him in the stomach. Tom didn't wait for another blow. He shot the man dead.

His head pounded something terrible as he staggered to the carriage and sat on the tongue. He yanked the tail of his shirt up, cut it off, dunked it in a water bucket and bathed his wound until he finally stopped the bleeding.

The only thing Tom could figure was he must've moved at exactly the right time to make the big man's blow miss slightly. The club, still in the big fellow's hand, was stout enough to bash in a bull's head. Tom checked the horses one last time and headed for the Denver Hotel.

"We were just beginning to worry about you," Buck greeted. "Looks like maybe we were right to worry."

"I could sure use that steak, but I'll start with coffee." Tom understood Buck and Smokey were curious but he didn't feel like talking right away, so he sipped coffee, his elbows propped on the table. He planned to enjoy this lull in the action for a few seconds, sipping hot coffee and looking across the room full of people talking and eating.

"One of the horses kick you?" Smokey asked.

"Feels like it." Tom gingerly felt the wound in the back of his skull. "Some big fella slugged me with a war club."

"Did you get even with him?" Buck grinned.

"Pretty much, he's dead ... as dead as Mr. O'Brien."

"How do you know Mr. O'Brien's dead?" Smokey sat up.

"Cause I pulled the pitchfork out of his chest. He's in his carriage shed with the fellow that jumped me."

"So Mr. O'Brien didn't make it out of town," Buck said.

"No, and I'm beginning to wonder if we will. We're gonna have to get right at it. If my guess is right, Sheriff Zeller is going to miss the fellow I shot. Someone must've seen me take our horses into the carriage house. Someone's probably watching you too, Smokey. Good thing you've got no family to worry about. As soon as I finish my dinner, we'll go together to get your rig."

They walked in darkness to the livery, then around to the rear. Inside Smokey lit the small kerosene lantern. A cot sat along the back wall, the table that held the lantern, some shirts and a coat hung on pegs, and his buffalo rifle and Winchester leaned against the wall by the cot. Smokey looked at them with a funny smile. "All a man needs fits in one room."

"Or in one bed roll," Buck nodded.

Smokey handed Buck his buffalo rifle and sack of shells, rolled his few belongings into a bed roll and tied it with leather strings. He made a loop with a piece of latigo and flung his bed roll over his shoulder, then picked up his Winchester. "Let's go."

Smokey led the way down dark back streets to the rear of the big brick house that Mayor Jack Martin called home. "We'll just give them a while to settle in for the night, and then we'll go calling," Buck said.

It took hours for the house to go dark, but finally only one window on the second floor had light. They waited another half hour but the light stayed on.

"You ever been in that house, Smokey?" Buck whispered.

"Never even been this close to it."

"We'll sneak up and figure it out as we go along." Tom led the way.

Choosing every step, and being careful to stay in the deepest shadows, they crept to the back door. Tom tried the door first and found it secure. He gave a glance to Buck, who shrugged his shoulders. Smokey had the solution. From out of somewhere neither Buck nor Tom saw, he produced a long hunting knife, so large Tom and Buck both raised eyebrows.

"I took it from a hide thief I killed one night." Smokey held it across both hands for them to examine. He slid the long blade in the door jam, gave it a slight twist and at the same time leaned on the door. The door swung inward without a sound. Smokey gave Tom and Buck a smile and a bow, then led the way into the house.

The back door opened to the kitchen; they tiptoed through it into the hall beyond. The hall led to the front of the house and the main stairs to the second floor. One by one they crept up the stairs, pausing for long moments after each occasional stair squeak. They knew they could be discovered by any number of Martin's cohorts.

After long, tense moments they climbed the last stair and started down the hall that led to bedrooms. Total darkness made even seeing doors a challenge. Tom walked his fingers along the wall, stopped at the first door and with a nod, he opened it. Little moonlight drifted in the single window, but enough for them to see the room sat empty, not even a bed.

They moved to the second door, Buck turned the knob, which gave a loud groan. The men froze, holding their collective breath. After a minute or so they decided no one heard, so Buck eased the door open. Another empty room greeted them.

About to move to the third door they held firm, a man

snored behind the door directly to their left. Smokey still had his hunting knife in his hand and held it up so Tom and Buck could see.

Buck grasped the doorknob and eased the door open. Silence held them. Tom and Smokey crept across the room. "Is that Jack Martin?" Tom whispered. Smokey nodded and Tom slammed his hand down on Jack's mouth. Smokey poked the tip of his huge knife up Jack Martin's nose. Jack didn't move but his eyes bulged wide open and darted back and forth from Tom to Smokey.

"Let's go for a walk," Tom whispered, his lips nearly touched Jack Martin's ears.

Jack Martin pulled his feet from under the blankets, swung them to the floor and stood up mindful of the knife point in his nose.

"He got no clothes on," Smokey stated the obvious.

"Where do you think you're taking me? I'm the damned Mayor!"

"You're damned, alright, you're damned out of luck," Tom said. "Keep your mouth shut."

CHAPTER TWENTY ONE

"I will not shut my mouth!" Jack Martin mumbled through Tom's hand and he tried to struggle free. Tom gave Smokey a nod and Smokey yanked his knife from Jack's nose, bashed the handle down on top of his head and Jack Martin went limp. Tom caught the naked man and flung him over his shoulder like a sack of flour.

"Grab his pants and shirt," Tom moved toward the door. They crept through the hall and down the stairs a little more quickly this time. Tom carried Jack Martin, Smokey carried his Winchester with a shell levered in the chamber, and Buck had his .44 cocked and ready.

They did not bother to close the door as they left and quickened their pace through the yard to the dark alley. Mayor Martin began to stir but only for an instant. Smokey was quick to level another blow on the mayor's head with his rifle barrel.

"Cooperative isn't he though," Smokey said, and Tom noticed with a chuckle that Smokey had mastered Buck's smile.

At the end of the alley, they paused. "Where are we going to take him?" Tom shifted his load.

"O'Brien's house," Buck answered and led the way down the street.

Keeping to the shadows, the trio slinked down the main street toward O'Brien's house at the far end of town. They were careful to dodge light streaming from saloon doors and windows and felt quite good about their progress as they sneaked past the sheriff's office.

Thunder from a shotgun got their attention. "I got one shell left, boys! Stand where you are!" Sheriff Bo Zeller ordered. "What the hell do you think you're doin'?"

Buck yelled, "Leaving town!"

"Not yet, you're not. What's that you're carrying?"

Before he answered Buck whispered to Tom and Smokey. "I'll confuse the sheriff—you make a dash for the jail house." Then he turned toward the direction of the sheriff. "Nothin' worth worrying about." And he fired into the shadow where the sheriff's voice came from.

Smokey and Tom ran for the jail and found the door unlocked. Smokey kicked the door open and dove through first. Buck, still in the street, fired two more cover shots toward the sheriff. The sheriff returned fire, the force of the blast knocked Tom forward and he fell on the brick floor with Jack Martin on top of him. Buck sped through the door, slammed it shut and dropped the bar across it.

"Get those shutters closed," Buck yelled.

Tom rolled from under the still unconscious Jack Martin. Smokey and Buck closed and latched the shutters on the two front windows. The three men looked around and decided it was as good a place as any to have a standoff. "Well, at least we have plenty of firepower." Tom pointed to the Winchesters and shotguns on the gun rack behind the sheriff's desk.

"I knew I tucked ol' Betsy up in my bed roll for one reason or another." Smokey dropped his bed roll on the sheriff's desk. Tom and Buck watched as the large wool blanket unrolled to reveal an old Sharps, a leather sack of bullets and primers, and a neatly bundled assortment of fleshing and skinning knives.

"Holy cow, I imagine Sheriff Bo Zeller better get some help," Buck gave Smokey a smart slap on the back.

"I reckon that might be true enough. Me and ol' Betsy been in enough scrapes to know how to hold out."

"You in the jail open that damn door! Let me in!" Sheriff Zeller stayed in the shadows.

"That don't sound friendly," Buck responded.

"I ain't being friendly! Open that damn door!"

"Give us a minute, Sheriff, let us get our thoughts together," Buck used his sure to be polite voice.

"I'll give you one damn minute!" Two rounds from a shotgun slammed the front door.

"He just can't be reasoned with," Buck pulled his hat and ran his fingers through his sweaty hair.

"Look here, the mayor has an ass full of buckshot," Tom said.

"I'll be, we better take a look at that. Hoist him up on the desk here on Smokey's blanket," Buck said through a chuckle.

They hoisted the mayor onto the desk and examined his buttocks. He had been hit by more than a glancing shot, at least twenty pieces of buckshot in his left thigh and buttocks.

"Tie him down to the table before he comes around," Tom suggested and they quickly lashed him to the table face down, still nude.

"What's going on in here?" a voice from the rear called out.

"We're having a discussion with the sheriff, go back to sleep," Buck said.

"Well you tell him I've been in here two days and I ain't been fed yet!"

"Might be a new sheriff in town soon," Smokey said, "hang on a little longer."

Another round from the shotgun banged the front door. "I'll shoot my way in, you sons of bitches!" Sheriff Zeller hollered.

Smokey snatched Betsy, slapped a bullet into her breech and dashed to the firing slot in one of the front shutters. "Watch this." He told the others with a wink and let go a round that hit between the sheriff's feet. The 50-caliber shell slammed into the street, sending dirt and gravel flying high and into the sheriff's crotch, knocking him backwards to a sitting position in the dirt. He found his feet in a hurry and ran into a saloon a few doors down the street.

"That was sharp, but you know he's got to be gatherin' help to come back at us," Buck had to fight to hold in his laugh.

The mayor began to stir and tried to get up but the restraints held. "What's going on? My ass is on fire and why the hell am I tied to this desk!"

"Don't wiggle too much," Buck said, not trying to hide his amusement. "Your ass is full of buckshot, the sheriff shot you, but we'll keep you safe in here."

"What the hell do you mean the sheriff shot me?"

"He did. We just meant to take you for a stroll, but your sheriff shot you." Smokey laid Betsy's barrel next to Jack Martin's nose.

"Untie me!"

Tom sat on the edge of a chair by the stove, twirling a tin cup on his trigger finger. He found himself as amused as Buck, and in fact enjoyed the entire situation. He knew Sherriff Zeller posed little threat, and welcomed the chance to set things straight. "No, we can't untie you till we get a Doc to pull the pellets out. Buckshot festers fast you know."

"You got the mayor out there?" The man in the rear spoke up.

"You bet, we're having a town meeting, might be a new sheriff and a new mayor by the time this meeting is over," Tom said.

Smokey found the key for the door to the jail cells in the rear and went back to look in on the prisoner, and make sure the rear entrance was well barricaded. "Don't I know you?"

"Yeah, you know me Smokey. I ramrod for Johnny Kirk, What the hell's goin' on?"

"Billy, Billy Hart! What are you doin' in jail?"

"Oh, I shot one of the sheriff's men, guess I killed him. But I know he was part of this cattle stealing mess. And I'll tell you something else Smokey, it was him or me!"

Smokey unlocked the jail door and released Billy Hart and led him to the front room where Tom and Buck both had rifles stuck through the firing slots in the shutters. And the mayor was running his mouth demanding to be set free and that doctors see him immediately.

Tom spun around, leveled a frozen-eyed stare on the trussed, naked, bleeding man. "When everything else is done, we'll get you a doctor. I'll tell you right now you keep your mouth shut or you won't need a doctor."

Jack Martin laid his head down and closed his eyes.

"We really ought to dig that shot out of his ass Tom," Smokey warned.

No one answered. All eyes were on the street. At the moment no one was on the street but everyone in the jail knew Bo Zeller was rounding up a crew and there'd be some fine conversation sooner or later.

"Billy," Smokey said, "how long would it take you to get out to Johnny's ranch and back here with some boys? We're gonna need some help before too long."

"I don't know, Smokey. How many people do you want to get involved in this thing?" Tom said.

"Dang it fella, I'm already involved ... Bo Zeller wants me dead," Billy told them.

"Damn right you are involved! I just heard you confess to killing one of the sheriff's men. When this is over you'll hang! I'll pull the damn rope myself!" The mayor's cheeks glowed red with anger.

"I told you to keep your mouth shut," Tom voice rang eerie, cold, quiet. He took the piece of torn latigo from Smokey's bed roll and stuffed it into the mayor's mouth and with unnecessary roughness yanked it into a tight knot in the back of his neck. Tears dropped to the floor from the mayor's eyes.

Tom looked at the others. "Well, we can't keep knocking him out."

"I can be out to the ranch and back in less than an hour. Heck I can get ten men for sure," Billy said.

"What are you going to use for a horse?" Buck postulated.

Billy's eagerness faded a little. "That's a good question."

"Here take my gun belt," Tom held out the laden belt. "Sneak down to O'Brien's carriage house and take my horse, Thunder. He's the big black stallion. He's the fastest horse that ever left a track."

Buck turned from the window and pointed his finger directly at Tom and with a friendly laugh, he protested. "That ain't been decided yet, Tom."

"Billy, you ride Thunder out to the ranch and when you get back here you tell me if you ever rode a faster horse," Tom boasted.

"You want me to run him flat out both ways?"

"Well maybe not, don't leave the boys from the ranch too far behind."

"I think I'll sneak along down there with him, make sure he gets away alright," Smokey offerd.

Tom opened the rear door a bit to peek out. Seeing all was clear, he held the door for Billy and Smokey. He watched until they were out of sight, carefully pushed the door shut and dropped the barricade bar into its bracket. By Tom's guess they still had two or three hours of darkness left. So if Billy was right he could easily get to the ranch and back in the cover of night. Maybe Smokey should have gone along with him on the ride. But Tom had little doubt that on Thunder, Billy could outrun almost any trouble that came along.

"I wonder what's taking the sheriff so long to get back to us," Buck said.

"Could be he's a slow thinker." Tom took some kindling from the bucket next to the stove and started a fire. "Might as well have a little coffee, Buck. Could be a long night."

"Got a plan?"

"Yep, I'm gonna have some coffee."

Just as Tom sat the coffee on the stove to boil a light tap sounded at the back door. He hustled down the brick hallway to the back door. "Smokey?"

"Who'd you think it would be?"

Tom swung open the door and Smokey stepped in. "Might not have been a good idea to give that boy your horse. The way he was singing his praises he may keep right on goin' and forget about us being trapped in here."

"Inside the jail," the sheriff shouted from shadows across the street.

"We're in here," Buck answered, "step out from the shadows so we can get another crack at you."

"You have one hour, then we're coming in."

"That should be about right, we just put coffee on," Buck taunted.

"You won't think it's so funny in a little while."

"Just watch where you shoot. You wouldn't want to shoot the mayor again," Buck warned.

"The mayor's home in bed!"

"He was 'til we got him, and wait till we tell them it was you who shot him in the ass with scattershot." Buck hooted, and let go a cackle.

They watched Bo Zeller reenter the saloon. The coffee started to boil so Tom left the window and retrieved three tin cups from their pegs. With little concern for whatever mischief Bo Zeller might stir up, Tom served everyone a cup. He took his coffee and walked to the desk and examined the mayor's wounds. "That's got to be sore. Do you think we should send for a doc?"

Buck joined him gazing down at the mayor's bare, bloody rump. "Looks kind of funny doesn't it? I'll agree to send for a doc if

Mr. Mayor here clears a few things up for me."

Jack Martin turned his head and nodded. Tom squatted down on his knees. "I guess that means you're willing to clear a few things up." Jack nodded that he would. Tom untied the knot in the latigo and jerked it from Jack's mouth. Jack rolled his tongue around his lips and spit on the floor.

"Get me a doctor first or I won't tell you a thing!"

Tom shrugged and started to stuff a latigo back in.

"Okay, okay. What do you want to know?"

"Everything you know. Heck we may not even know all the questions," Buck said.

"The whole thing was Buster Kelly's idea. He met Shorty and Farley in the Laramie saloon about a year ago."

"And they were looking for just the right man to cut out a few cattle," Tom guessed.

"Yeah, before too long they had Buster Kelly convinced Donovan was using him and that Donovan owed him plenty."

"So Buster turns dirty, and he has the perfect hiding spot for a large herd up in the high plateau, a range on the very outfit he works for. But to send cattle to rail yards in Carson, you needed someone at the rail yard to ignore the brands," Buck surmised.

"Yes, that's when we bribed Charlie O'Brien."

"Bribed? You call kidnapping and suicide a bribe?" Tom shouted.

Before Buck could stop him, Tom kicked Jack in the face. Buck leaped across the floor and knocked Tom to the ground and held him there. "Settle down. You can't keep coming apart like this. He's gonna pay! He's gonna pay plenty."

"I didn't know anything about O'Brien's wife," Jack mumbled.

Tom grabbed his hair and yanked his back head. "I don't believe you," and released his grip of the hair. Martin's head dropped onto the desk with a thud and a stream of blood trickled to the floor from his nose.

"Better try again," Buck suggested.

"All I know, is I told Bo Zeller to make O'Brien play along. I didn't care how he did it, just so we could load cattle in Carson."

"Who killed Mayor Evans?" Buck asked.

"Nobody killed Mayor Evans. He died in his sleep."

"Want to try again? Or you want Tom to help you think it over?"

"I'm telling the truth, but I did have a hand in running his wife and kids out of town."

Tom grabbed Martin's hair again, pulled his head back even farther. "Had her sign the deed before they left, I reckon." As best he could, Jack Martin nodded his head. Tom slammed his face into the desk.

Smokey had been keeping watch of the street. "Here they come and it looks like Bo Zeller got him some help."

Tom and Buck left the mayor to peer onto the dark street. Sheriff Bo Zeller led a group of eight or ten men from the saloon across the street. For a moment, Tom watched as the men began to come together in a formation of sorts and started onto the street. There was just enough light for Tom to see the sheriff was careful to have several men in front of him but being the big man that he was, he stood a head taller.

"I had enough of him," Tom whispered.

Buck knew what that meant and tried his best to get to Tom before he could fire. In the time it took Buck to run three steps and shove Tom from the rifle slot Tom had fired three shots. One round into the sheriff's face, killing him instantly. One round each into the chests of the two men in front of him.

"Get off me, Buck ... " Tom whispered, his eyes icy and voice even colder. Tom pushed Buck aside hard enough to knock him off his feet. "I'm starting to get a little tired of you shoving me around."

Smokey saw and heard Tom's actions, so in a clever maneuver to redirect Tom's anger, he shouted out to the street. "The rest of you boys go on home now. This here's over. Sheriff Zeller's dead, two other boys might be, and we got the mayor in here on suspicion of murder. I'm making a citizen's arrest. Now get off the street, and go home."

Buck got to his feet and looked through a rifle slot. "There they go, you did good job, Smokey. Citizens arrest, huh?"

"Sorry, Buck, I shouldn't have said that."

Buck accepted the apology with a nod. But held onto the message Tom sent.

Smokey leaned on the table with ol' Betsy standing on the floor between his legs. "What's next?" No one had time to answer before a knock sounded on the rear door.

"Open up in there, it's me, Billy Hart."

Buck let Billy slip in. "I could only roust six men tonight. They're in the alley back here what do you want us to do?"

"I don't know our next play. Tom went and shot the sheriff!"

"I'll leave three men back here and send three around front," Billy made his own choice.

"Good thinkin'." Buck waited as Billy stuck his head out the door and told the men. They left the door un-barricaded and hustled to the front room. "Look here Tom. Billy made it back but I never asked him about your horse. How'd that big black stallion do for you?"

"Howdy! What a horse! Would you sell 'im?"

"Not for all the tea in China! Actually he was a gift from Buck. He stole him from the United States Cavalry," Tom said with a sly grin.

"I didn't exactly steal him. General Ferguson gave him to me to run a dispatch from Fort Kearny to Fort Laramie back in '65. It was mighty important and the General said I had to get to General Sturgis in less than a day. Did it in twenty hours. I took my two, Diablo, the paint in O'Brien's barn and my roan River, and I told the General to make the trip in less than a day I'd need a third. So he gave me Thunder. He says use him up and turn him loose. Well I did just that, but wouldn't you know, that horse followed me all the way to Fort Laramie! So I kept him! We do have about twenty of his sons and daughters on the ground back at the ranch, yearlings and two-year-olds. When the dust settles here in Denver City, why don't you take a trip and pick yourself out one or two."

Billy held out his hand and shook with Tom. "I'll see you in a few months—that's a guarantee!"

"Okay, okay, okay! Now that you're all done horse trading how about me?" wailed Jack Martin.

"Think we can send for the doc?" Tom floated.

"Smokey, take one of Billy's men from out front and go find Doc. Keep your head down," Buck said.

"My head'll be down and ol' Betsy'll be loaded," Smokey guaranteed. No one bothered to barricade the front door after him.

"Can you untie me now?" Jack Martin pleaded.

"You'll stay tied until I say. Open your mouth again without being asked a question and I'll stuff that latigo so far down your throat you'll feel it in your toes," Tom gave Buck a stern look.

"Billy, how did a man like Jack Martin become mayor of an up-and-coming town like Denver City?" Buck wanted to know.

"Jack here had been in town about six months before Mayor Evans died. He'd been spreadin' money around here and there. When the mayor died the city had an emergency election. He bragged he had an in with the governor of the territory and we would get two more stage lines and at least one more rail line. He promised all sorts of stuff. Of course, he wasn't in town long enough for people to really get to know him before the election. The election was held only thirty days after Mayor Evans passed on.

"After he was mayor, most of the town figured out pretty quick they'd made a mistake. But by then Bo Zeller was sheriff and he had his own special way of keeping complaints to a minimum." Billy explained.

"If you complained, you disappeared," Tom guessed.

Buck opened the door in response to Smokey's clamor. The doctor, an older gentleman wearing a well-aged black hat, coat and glasses, carried a black medical bag, and walked a little slow. Standing over the mayor, his attitude told everyone in the jailhouse he was pleased to see the mayor in such a predicament. He sat his bag in the middle of the mayor's back and when the mayor protested, he barked, "Now lie still, mayor. This is going to hurt." And after a moment's inspection added, "Yeah, this'll hurt."

"I demand you give me some ether!"

"Fresh out of ether, Mayor."

"I want something for the pain. You do something before you dig in my ass!"

Tom said, "Okay," and whacked him on the back of the head with the butt of his Winchester.

"Ow! You fool!"

"Darn, guess it takes another dose of anesthesia," Tom raised the rifle.

"Don't hit me again! Just give me something to bite on."

Tom crammed the latigo in the mayor's mouth. "Okay Doc you can get started but no hurry, we want the mayor to enjoy this."

Doc went to work on the pile of pellets in the mayor's rear. Smokey, Tom, Billy, and Buck all watched with some pleasure as the mayor squirmed, grunted and pissed himself.

"What did you see out there, Smokey?" Buck needed to know.

"Not a thing. Not a soul on the street and not much racket coming from any of the saloons, either. Of course the sheriff and those two other fellows are still lying on the street, but they ain't makin' any racket."

Buck turned to Doc. "Do you know any of the folks on the town council?"

With some effort Doc rose up from his work with a long handled tweezers in his right hand and a bloody rag in his left. "I do. I for one, then there is Mr. Ripley, who owns the general mercantile, Mr. Hill runs the Denver City Hotel, and Mr. Randolph is owner of the freight company in town. And, oh yes, Mr. O'Brien. He handles the rail yard business for the Denver Pacific. Why do you ask?"

"Because we're gonna hold a town council meeting right here in this jail as soon as Smokey and Billy can round them folks up. Well, except for Mr. O'Brien."

The doctor studied Buck with more than a little bewilderment showing in his face. "What are you getting at?"

"We made a citizen's arrest of your mayor here, soon as you're through, we're locking him up. Your sheriff is dead, so the town council needs to appoint replacements. And I nominate Smokey as sheriff, and Billy Hart as his deputy," Buck explained.

"Now hold on here, Buck!" Smokey protested. "I ain't sheriff material. I'm an old buffalo hunter who retired to countin' cows in a pen."

"This town needs you, Smokey, and you too, Billy," Tom joined in.

"Johnny Kirk needs me too," Billy Hart pointed out.

"You boys need to saddle up and ride this bronc. I have a feeling after tonight it'll get a bit more peaceful in Denver City," Buck said.

"I don't know. Sure tonight was fun, but I don't know. I'm gettin' old, Buck," Smokey rubbed his shoulder. "These old joints are gettin' stiff and cantankerous."

"I'm with Smokey, I have other plans," Billy added.

"What do you think Doc? Old Smokey don't have it in him anymore?" Buck teased.

Again Doc was slow to straighten up and before he could speak Smokey gave Buck a good hard look. "Don't got it in me? I reckon I got plenty left in me to handle the varmints that try to pester this town!" Then turned to Billy Hart. "Bring that Winchester young fellas, and let's go round us up a town council!"

Before their heavy footsteps faded on the plank sidewalk, Buck poked his head out the doorway and hollered, "Stop by and wake up that spooky old undertaker and have him get those bodies off the street."

CHAPTER TWENTY TWO

It took Smokey and Billy over an hour to return with Mr. Hill, Mr. Randolph, and Mr. Ripley. Doc took a break from his bloody job and greeted the three other members of the town council. "I'm just about done here and then we can get down to business."

"Conducting business in the middle of the night with the mayor slung across a desk like a side of beef is not why I volunteered my services," Mr. Randolph complained.

"I find the whole thing extraordinary," agreed Mr. Hill.

"I don't see Mr. O'Brien here," Mr. Ripley observed. "We can't have a town council meeting without Mr. O'Brien.

"Mr. O'Brien was killed tonight. I pulled the pitchfork from his chest myself," Tom watched for reactions, watched their faces pale.

"It's all his fault, it's all his fault!" Mr. Hill pointed a shaky finger at the unconscious mayor. "I knew supporting him would bring nothing but trouble to Denver City."

"Well then, why did you support him?" Mr. Randolph asked.

"Because you told me to."

Doc slowly straightened up. "I'm all done here. Perhaps we could move him to a cell."

Smokey jumped up. "Happy to oblige, Doc. Come on, Billy, grab an arm." Each took a shoulder and dragged the naked, bloodied Jack Martin to the first cell behind the door. The very one sheriff Bo Zeller had kept Billy in for two days. With a noticeable lack of tenderness, they deposited the mayor on the broken cot. Before locking the door Smokey tossed in a pair of britches and shirt.

"I see ... Well, let's call this meeting to order." Mr. Randolph's tone and demeanor suggested he lacked any level of bravery.

"Here, here, I agree! This meeting is now in order." Mr. Ripley swung an imaginary gavel. They looked to Doc for some guidance as to just exactly what the meeting should be about. Doc wiped blood from his hands on a white towel but was able to take charge, and did. "This meeting is to officially hire Smokey as sheriff and Billy Hart as his deputy and to remove the corrupt mayor Jack Martin from office."

"I nominate Smokey," And then Mr. Hill stopped and scratched his head. "What the hell is your name anyway Smokey?"

"Is that really important? Don't you all know me as Smokey?"

"We should use your real name to swear you in," Mr. Ripley suggested.

"Come on Smokey I always wondered about your name," Billy Hart chimed in.

"Well I ain't said it in a long time."

"Smokey, dang it, tell us your name. It's not like anybody's gonna care," Buck encouraged.

"If anybody uses this name or I find out anybody told anybody I'll introduce them to ol' Betsy." Smokey continued to stall.

"His name is Leslie Julius Rasmussen," Doc broadcasted with an audible chuckle.

"See! See! Everybody gotta laugh," Smokey howled and then advanced in Doc's direction, "Who told you my name? I need to thrash 'im."

"You had me do your paperwork when Mr. O'Brien hired you for the Denver Pacific, remember?" Doc answered.

"Leslie Julius Rasmussen! That is a mouthful!" Buck howled, slapped his leg and burst with gut deep laughs, which he cut off abruptly when he realized Smokey had the hammer back on ol' Betsy.

"Gentlemen, shall we proceed?" Mr. Randolph asked. Nods all around indicated that a more formal air should be adopted.

"Leslie Julius Rasmussen, raise your right hand. Do you agree from this day forward to represent the city of Denver City as its sheriff and enforce all laws and ordinances therein?" Mr. Randolph asked.

Smokey raised his right hand nodded in the affirmative and said aloud, "I do, sir, and you may call me Smokey."

"William, what's your middle name Billy?" Mr. Randolph

asked.

"Don't have one."

"Well then, William Hart, do you agree from this day forward to represent the city of Denver City as its deputy sheriff and enforce all laws and ordinances therein?" Mr. Randolph asked.

"I will, sir."

"By the authority vested in me by this committee and the city of Denver City, you two are now Sheriff and Deputy Sheriff of Denver City. You buy your own shells. We provide coffee, the jailhouse and $75 a month each."

Buck looked around after the ceremony and noticed Tom off to the side by the stove nursing a cup of old coffee. He didn't have to ask what Tom was thinking. He knew Tom wanted to make tracks for his ranch.

"Let's get to the Laramie saloon and run the rest of Zeller's men from town," Smokey said. "You fellas stay here and pass some kinda law or somethin' and make sure that mayor ain't mayor no more. Billy, tell those boys out back to just stay put and you stay here in the jail." Smokey took a look around and decided he wanted Tom and Buck at his side. "Buck, Tom, I'd sure be honored if you'd give me a hand in this, negotiation."

Tom strapped on his gun belt, loaded the Winchester and headed for the door without a word.

"Close the door behind us, Billy. Keep your rifle poked out this window and watch that saloon door," Smokey directed.

"What about us, is it safe for us in here?" Mr. Hill looked from face to face. "Maybe you should wait while we finish our legal duties and we can leave."

"I think you're safer in here," Buck said, "make a fresh pot. We'll be back before it's boiled.

"I don't know, I just don't know," Mr. Hill protested.

"You'll be all right. Start the coffee," Buck said.

Smokey, Tom, and Buck, armed and ready started out, Billy closed door behind them. Smokey gave orders to the three men on the front porch to stay sharp and explained they were going to Laramie saloon to run Zeller's men out of Denver City. One of the cowboys, Hank, insisted he go along.

As the four men moved from the shadows to light streaming from the swinging door of the Laramie saloon, they were noticed. A group of half a dozen tough looking men came outside and stood shoulder to shoulder on the rough board sidewalk, blocking the entrance to the saloon.

Smokey and his men stopped to size up the situation. Tom took one step forward just to test the water and as he levered a shell into his rifle's chamber. The men at the saloon door appeared unimpressed and stood firm.

"I'm sheriff here now," Smokey announced, "any of you connected with Bo Zeller, or Jack Martin and the outlawin' that's been going on no longer have any business here, and I'm inviting you to leave."

"Are you the big man that shot down Sheriff Zeller in cold blood?" One of the cowboys asked. Tom thought that fella was most likely planning on taking charge. He noticed the cowboy took a half a step out in front of the others. Tom watched the cowboy as he passed his Winchester to his left hand, and used his thumb and forefinger to slip the leather drawstring from the hammer of his revolver, making it ready to draw.

"I wouldn't jerk that gun, Mister," Tom warned in a gentle voice, "and I shot Bo Zeller."

"Well then, I guess I'm going to have to shoot you."

Buck stepped between them and raised both arms. He held his Winchester in his right hand high above his head. "You don't want to do that, fella. Tom's as fast and sure as I've ever seen."

"I'll bet he ain't so fast!" And the cowboy's hand went for his gun.

Tom lunged past Buck, yanked his Colt and dove to the ground. The other cowboys scattered. Buck pulled his Winchester down and began to fire at the retreating cowboys. Hank ran forward and followed two of them into the saloon without firing a shot. Smokey followed Hank into the saloon.

Tom's first round hit the cowboy's neck, knocking him back against the saloon wall. His second shot slammed into the cowboy's chest.

Buck watched Tom's deadly shooting and was troubled at Tom's viciousness. "I think he's dead, Tom."

"Big talker wasn't he," Tom stood up, brushed the street from his leggings.

"Hank and Smokey are in the saloon, two of those boys got

off down the street. Two or three ran in the saloon," Buck detailed.

Tom led the way through the bat-wing doors. At first he didn't see Smokey or Hank, then he saw Smokey sitting at a table his Winchester propped up on his thigh. Hank stood ready at the back door.

Tom surveyed the balcony that ran the length of the room on two sides. He could see doors upstairs but no one was on the balcony. Two bartenders stood behind the bar which sported a full-length mirror on which was painted a nude woman reclining. Eight or nine cowboys had their backs leaning against the bar facing the room filled with tables and chairs. Each table had one or two rough looking cowboys, some enjoying the company of a pretty saloon girl. At one table sat a well-dressed gentleman dealing cards to three cowboys hoping to beat a professional gambler. Tom could find no evidence of the men who ran into the saloon to avoid the gunfight. He and Buck joined Smokey at the roundtable.

Smokey banged the butt end of his Winchester on the table. He kept banging until finally the noise in the saloon subsided to the point where he could to speak. With Buck to his left and Tom to his right and Hank at the rear door, Smoky took charge of the saloon.

"Some of you folks know me, some don't," Smokey started in a loud voice that dripped authority. "I was just made sheriff of Denver City. I know some you boys in here are good as gold and I also know some of you ain't worth a broken spur. Cattle stealin' around here is over. Bo Zeller and a few of his boys died tonight. The mayor's in jail and I expect the town council to hold an election for a new mayor pretty quick. I'm giving you fair warning. If you're part of Bo Zeller's outfit, leave town. Hell, leave the territory! I won't tolerate any kind of low dealings. Spread the word I'll hire as many deputies as I need to clean up this mess. Enjoy the rest of your night, but keep it quiet."

Every eye in the place turned to Hank as he strode the center of the saloon toward the front door, tipping his hat to the ladies. Together they crossed the street to the jail as the sun began to burn its way through the night shadows.

A horse galloped toward them. All four men readied their arms. "That's Johnny Kirk," Hank lowered his rifle.

"Sorry I couldn't get here any sooner." Johnny swung from the saddle and draped a rein over the hitching rail.

"Come on inside, Johnny," Smokey invited "you missed all the fun."

Smokey had Hank and the other two Johnny Kirk hands stay on the porch and stand guard. Inside the jail they found the town council talking nervously to each other, except for Doc, who was back with Jack Martin.

"We have done our duty and removed Mayor Martin from office," Mr. Ripley informed them, and handed a handwritten document to Smokey. Smokey pulled open the middle desk drawer, dropped it in and pushed the drawer shut.

"I'll need my boys back," Johnny Kirk told Smokey.

"Hold on a minute, Johnny," Smokey protested, "let's just get through the rough spot."

"I have a ranch to run, Smokey. I want this outlawing stopped as bad as the next man, but we were just about to get to work on spring roundup. Doggone it, it's already June."

"Never been on a real cattle roundup," Buck intervened, "tell you what. Give us a hand for one day to clean up what's left of the outlaw's camp. Then me and Tom, and some Donovan hands will throw in and help with your mid-spring-summer roundup."

"Never been on a cow roundup either. Run down my share of horses though and since Buck taught me how to handle a rope, I just might come in handy," Tom toasted Johnny Kirk.

"I insist that our work is done here," Mr. Randolph moved to the door, "I am sure you gentleman will work this out." He turned and motioned to Mr. Hill and Mr. Ripley as he opened the door. "If there's anything you need contact Mr. Ripley."

"My work is done here as well. I suspect the ex-mayor will do a fair amount of complaining but the wounds are clean. He shouldn't have any trouble." Doc offered his goodbyes all-around.

Johnny Kirk sat on the sheriff's desk and sipped his coffee while he studied the faces of the men in the sheriff's office. The sun hung bright and the town struggled to come to life. Smokey opened the shutters and light jumped into the office, changing it from a dungeon to an almost cheery room.

"If we're going to do it, we should get right at it. Let's go close that camp today before they even have a chance to figure out what to do next." Johnny Kirk took the last swallow of his coffee.

CHAPTER TWENTY THREE

Smokey, Tom, Buck, Johnny Kirk and four of his men rode down the main street past the corrals and stockyard at the rail yard headed for the high plateau on the Donovan ranch. It would take the men half the day riding hard to reach the outlaw camp. They left Billy Hart and two more of Johnny Kirk's men behind to keep things under control in Denver City.

Each man rode well mounted, so keeping a hard fast pace was no problem. Tom soon took the lead on Thunder, setting a pace that covered ground at a speed lesser horses would have trouble maintaining. These were the moments Tom enjoyed, flying across the prairie on a strong, smart stallion. Tom's mind relaxed in peace, and while the high plateau sat in view some thirty miles away, he enjoyed the ride and would not allow himself to think of the confrontation to come. Rather he thought of the high fun the big round up promised, and he thought of going home, he longed to have his family home, safe.

Thunder's stride change jolted Tom back to the moment. Thunder's ears pinned tight, Tom glanced to the side. Buck and Diablo ran flat out, nearly overtaking him and Thunder. Buck wore an enormous silly grin and let go a "whoop." Tom snatched his hat from his head and crumbled it in his hand, his long dark hair flying free in the wind. Buck and Diablo had pulled almost even with Thunder. For a second Tom held Buck's eyes, then returned a grand smile of his own. In a blatantly taunting fashion he waved goodbye to Buck and shifted position on Thunder, which told the horse "give me what you got!" Already traveling at a speed most horses couldn't achieve, Thunder kicked it up a notch.

Tom peeked under his arm to see Diablo had dropped back, his head even with Thunder's streaming tail. He prodded for more speed, and Thunder gave it. But so did Diablo. Tom peeked back again and Diablo's nose was now even with Tom's knee. Neither man could do any more. The outcome of this race rested entirely in the horses' hearts.

Diablo pulled even. Tom whispered in Thunder's ear, "Burn the breeze, big boy."

The mighty horse obliged and with each exploding stride pulled away from Diablo. Tom wanted no question as to the fastest horse, and encouraged Thunder on. Diablo fell back. Tom watched under his arm as Diablo pounded the prairie soil with all he had, but he didn't have quite enough. Thunder continued to put more distance between him and Diablo.

Satisfied he had proved his point, Tom slowed Thunder. It took Thunder more than a dozen strides to come to a stop. Tom swung from the saddle, stood beside his magnificent horse, and smiled proudly at Buck when Diablo pulled up beside them.

Buck swung to the ground, offered his hand, "Congratulations to you both!"

They looked back at the rest of their group at least a mile behind, chuckled some, then walked their winded horses on for the high plateau. Both knew it was quite possible for one or both of them not to live out the day. All jocularity faded. As if they read each other's mind, they said at exactly the same time, "At least we answered that question."

CHAPTER TWENTY FOUR

Tom and Buck walked on in silence. A lone tree provided shade so they stopped to wait for the rest of the group. "Why do you figure those Cheyenne got mixed up with this bunch?" Buck wondered out loud.

"Can't figure it. But from what I heard in the camp they didn't have much love for Donavan."

"Kinda made it easy to recruit 'em, I imagine."

Johnny Kirk rode up first. His men followed close behind. Smokey rode in last.

"Nothin' like riding into a hornets' nest on spent horses, is there boys?" Smokey was the least impressed with Tom and Buck's exhibition.

"Nothin' like a sheriff's badge to take all the fun out of a man is there, boys?" Buck answered. Most of the men joined in and teased Smokey for his paternalistic comment.

"I'm just tellin' you, boys, if we need to skedaddle you're going to wish you had some of what you asked your horses to use up back there."

"I'm not figuring it's us that's going to be doing any skedaddlin'," Tom grabbed fistfuls of dried grass and rubbed Thunder's neck with firm long strokes.

"About an hour from the high plateau, I reckon," Johnny Kirk said. "You boys agree?"

"Maybe for the rest of us," One of Johnny's men said, "Tom and Buck can get there in ten minutes." Even Smokey had to chuckle at that one.

They rode on until the sun climbed about as high as it gets, then dismounted in the shade of the first trees on the timberline.

"Let's take a break here." Smokey passed around his sack of jerky. The mood somber now, they had no way of knowing how many of the cattle they would find in camp.

In quiet they led their horses through trees and brush. Smokey took lead in a direct ascent and twice they passed over the zigzag trail that led to the top and was far less steep. "Follow their trail and it could be we don't make it to the top," Smokey had explained. After an hour of tough climbing they reached their goal and peered from cover of brush onto the flat plateau on the high point.

Tom admired the beauty stretched out below them. Miles of wide, flat grassland, bordered by majestic towering trees ... A beautiful grass-rich pasture land about to become a battlefield.

They had climbed the plateau on the east. Two miles distant, on the west, sat the camp of tents and wagons. Over five hundred cattle grassed under the watch of a few riders on the southern slope. While they could see the tent camp, they could not judge any amount of men there.

"I make it six or seven cowboys riding herd," Johnny Kirk said.

"On this side of the herd, we can't see the other side," Buck advised.

Smokey yanked ol' Betsy from her custom leather scabbard and tied a sack of shells around his neck with a leather drawstring. "Even if there's six or seven on the other side of the herd, that's still only a dozen. Ready your rifles, we're about to say howdy to those boys."

They rode to open grass and started toward the herd. It seemed reasonable the men riding herd would have no cause for concern until they recognized the men approaching. Tom, Buck and the rest rode on in confidence until within a hundred yards of the nearest outlaw.

He broke lose and galloped toward them. "Who the hell are you?"

"Howdy, they call me Smokey. I'm the new sheriff," Smokey moved his leather vest to show his badge.

The young cowboy tried to wheel his horse to escape. But one of Johnny Kirk's men tossed a wide loop over the cowboy's shoulders. His horse bolted from under him and with a thud the surprised thief hit the ground.

The young outlaw scrambled to his feet and would've surely yanked his revolver, if he could just move his hand. He stood dumbfounded as a roped calf and looked at his captor who with a great smile turned to Johnny. "You wanna heel 'im?"

"I believe you have him," Johnny said, grinning.

"Party's on now," Tom pointed to cowboys racing their way.

Buck nudged Diablo to the roped cowboy and whacked him on the head with the butt of his Winchester. The man's legs folded and he dropped to the ground.

"Well, I didn't want to shoot him," Buck allowed.

"I believe you smashed his skull," Smokey said.

"We better get busy," Tom started Thunder at a fast trot.

Buck followed Tom's lead hustling to the outlaws' right flank. The others in Smokey's group split left. Eleven cowboys charged them, but before they had traveled fifty yards the cattle thieves found themselves surrounded.

Smokey fired ol' Betsy and one of the eleven lurched and dropped from his horse.

"Give it up, boys, you ain't surrounded by beginners," Smokey advised.

They weren't quite ready to follow Smokey's advice. The nearest cowboy to Tom tried to jerk his Winchester from its scabbard. "Don't do that," Tom warned. The fellow released his grip on the Winchester but dropped his hand to his revolver, yanked it from the holster. Without hesitation Tom shot him from his horse.

"You boys had enough lessons?" Smokey surveyed the confused group with Betsy making the finer points of cooperation easy to understand.

"I have," one cowboy tossed his rifle to the grass.

"Each of you get down, stand mighty still, and keep your hands where we can see them. These fellas have a lot of guns aimed at ya." Smokey cocked Betsy.

The outlaws dismounted without protest, their hands held high. Smokey told one of Johnny's hands to gather guns and horses. Buck and Tom stood them together, back to back and ran a rope around them until they stood tied like a bundle of kindling wood. A few men untacked the horses and turned them lose.

"Anybody else over there with the cows?" Smokey asked.

"We ain't saying nothin'!"

Smokey fired ol' Betsy, the round slammed the ground dangerously close to the feet of those poor fellows tied in a bundle. "Let's try again. Who else is over with the cows and how many?"

"Nobody. We're it."

"How many at the tent camp?" Smokey reloaded Betsy.

"Don't know. A few Indians, maybe the cook and most likely eight or ten other boys."

"See how easy that is?" Smokey gave a wink and nod. "You stay here and keep an eye on 'em," he told a Johnny Kirk man.

Smokey led the others in toward the tent camp. Tom reasoned those in camp heard the shots. "We can't just ride in there. It's a naked two miles, we'll be target practice."

"When we get within rifle range, you boys will stop. I aim to ride in alone."

"Can't let you do that, Smokey," Johnny protested.

"Got a better idea?"

"They might," Buck pointed to riders coming their way at a run.

The riders coming at them fast looked to number less than ten. To the north rode another ten or so, Cheyenne. The terrain lay flat and open, affording no suitable place to make a stand. Still a safe distance from the oncoming riders they had a moment to consider options.

The distance back to the tree line was too great, but Tom felt confident they could make it to the cattle, there they could create enough confusion and have a chance. Someone had to make a decision soon. Tom took another look toward the cattle, and then to the north where the Cheyenne sat their ponies, waiting for an opportunity. The plateau came to an abrupt end about two miles to their south at the sheer wall to the prairie floor below. If they could outrun the outlaws, there they would have cover.

"I think we should make for the drop-off over there," Tom told Buck and he pointed south.

"We could make it," Buck agreed, "but none of these other fellas would."

"Wanna charge 'em?"

"Not on Diablo, and not with Thunder."

Smokey made their decision. "I'll be riding out to meet them. When they get a little closer I'll hoist this flag. You boys hang back ... If it goes bad I don't expect ya let any of the bastards live."

He tore the tail from his shirt, tied it to Betsy, stood the rifle up, propped on his thigh, slapped a big shell in the chamber and sat his mount as proud as any military General ever sat a horse. The galloping riders continued to close the gap.

"I can't let ya go alone, Smokey," Johnny Kirk argued.

"I don't want to spook 'em." Smokey turned to Johnny but stayed focused on the oncoming riders.

"Everybody dismount," Tom took charge, "loop one rein through your gun belt. Have your rifle ready. When those bastards stop, pick a rider, our left to our right. If something goes wrong, I want to see six of those sons of bitches fall.

"And listen to me now. Fire your rifle, get on your horse and ride straight at 'em, like the devil himself had hold of your horse's tail. Fire as often as you can. Don't aim, just point. First one to Smokey picks 'im up."

"Thanks for the vote of confidence, Tom," Smokey said with a grin.

Tom's eyes flashed dead serious. "If it happens that way, those Cheyenne are gonna come at us. Pay them no attention. Shoot your way through the outlaws and high tail it for the camp. We'll be able to make a fine stand there."

The riders closed to within two hundred yards and slowed. Smokey kicked his horse forward at a slow walk and held his flag high. He portrayed the image of authority sitting tall in the saddle, holding ol' Betsy straight up, his shirt tail flag gently waved in the breeze. Tom, Buck, Johnny Kirk, and his three men stood by their horses, rifles ready. Smokey continued at a slow measured walk toward the cattle thieves.

Things seemed to be working out for Smokey and he stopped fifty feet from the riders. Then Tom noticed the cowboys riding flank inched their horses forward, one slow step at a time. They're gonna box him in, Tom thought.

Tom wasted no time. Through the high sight on his buffalo rifle he sighted the man's chest closest to Smokey, fired and watched him flip backwards from his horse. The deafening roar of his buffalo rifle caught everyone off guard, for just an instant. Then Buck fired.

Then Johnny Kirk and his men all fired. With talent gained from years in the saddle, each man swung up and galloped into the fight, rifles fired with every stride.

The cattle thieves' numbers were halved with the first volley. The remaining cowboys were so startled, Tom and the boys were nearly upon them before they realized things had gone bad for them. Betsy roared and Tom saw another cowboy blown from his horse.

Sticking to the plan, they made for the camp at a flat-out run. They charged directly through the confused outlaws, and were some two hundred yards beyond them before the cattle thieves could organize a chase. Tom and Buck led with Johnny and his men strung behind. The gunfire from the cattle thieves came rapid and reckless, and Tom worried for Johnny's men, he spun Thunder about, tossed his buffalo rifle in his left hand, and jerked his revolver.

He flew past Smokey and Johnny. Both wore bewildered looks. Reins flying free, urging Thunder on and guiding him with legs alone, Tom bore down on the outlaws. The last of Johnny's cowboys passed him on their way to the camp but Tom kept on pell-mell for the cattle thieves.

With some amusement, Tom noticed the Cheyenne stopped their attack. Most Indians enjoy watching a brave warrior pursue a coup. And pursue Tom did. He emptied his revolver and managed to drop one more cowboy. He dropped his buffalo rifle, yanked his Winchester and emptied it at the astonished outlaws.

As one, the cattle thieves turned to flee, the Cheyenne waved rifles and lances high, hooting and hollering at their cowardly brethren. And then Tom heard hooves pounding the ground behind him, Buck and Diablo raced to his aid. Buck fired as fast as he could lever the rifle's action.

The outlaws were on the run, but Tom didn't feel they could allow them to escape. They would surely find Johnny's man they had left behind with their trussed friends. Although only three outlaws remained, shooting them from their horses at a dead run was not a certain thing. And his revolver and Winchester were empty. He drifted close to Buck. "We have to get to Johnny's man before they do."

The cattle thieves settled into a flat-out run in a more northern direction. Tom slowed his pursuit just enough to load the Winchester as he galloped along. Glancing at Buck, he saw him doing the same. They closed the distance stride by stride, Tom was about to fire when suddenly the outlaws wheeled around, halted their horses and held up their hands.

"How about that, they plain give up," a note of disappointment rang in Buck's tone, "I'll herd these fellas to camp, you fetch the others."

CHAPTER TWENTY FIVE

Tom and Jonny Kirk's man rode into camp with ten horses and eleven outlaws about two hours after sunset. Buck, Johnny and the boys had coffee boiled and a beef slowly roasted.

"Looks as if you boys moved right in and made yourselves at home," Tom said.

Buck looked up from his beef-tending duties. "We were just about to send a search party out."

The outlaws had been led on foot over two miles with their hands tied in front and a rope tied around the waist of the next man. They were hot, tired, grouchy, sore, thirsty, and hungry.

"You can't keep us tied up like this," grumbled a man of miserable temperament.

"It's better than the way he had you tied up," Tom pointed to Johnny's man who had guarded them all afternoon. "And besides I can and will."

"You better give us somethin' to eat and drink," the same man demanded.

Tom wheeled about and stared at the complainer. "Open your mouth again without being asked question and I'll shut it, permanently."

He kept his mouth shut and so did the others as Smokey and Johnny led them to the wagon where the others Buck had drove in sat tied. They tied the first man to the front wagon wheel, wrapped a rope around the last man's waist and tied to the next wagon. This created a tight, secure picket line, with the men barely able to sit. Johnny put two of his men on guard with orders to shoot if somebody tried to chew the ropes, or in any other fashion tried to escape. He gave the order loud enough for all to hear.

Smokey carried a water bucket down the line of prisoners giving each a single dipperful. Then he returned with a large slab of roast beef and gave each a good-sized chunk. He warned them to keep their mouths shut and strongly cautioned them against making trouble, explaining he was the sheriff and would have to treat them fairly. Tom and Buck tended not to tolerate bullshit and if one of them should cause trouble he would have a hard time keeping Tom from shooting them.

The campfire burned high and hot. Tom, Buck, and Johnny rested, leaning on their saddles sipping coffee and chewing beef. Smokey pulled up a saddle, fashioned his own seat, grabbed the coffee pot, and filled his tin cup. With his Bowie knife he cut a sizable chunk of meat from the roasted quarter. For a while the men simply enjoyed the lively campfire, hot coffee and hot food.

"I put those two wounded fellows up in the small tent yonder." Smokey motioned to a tent that stood by itself near the wagons. "They won't make it out'a here though."

Tom studied the tents. Four wall tents set in a row and a number of A-tents, perhaps half a dozen. Tom, curious about the tents, had to investigate so he poured another cup and strolled across the camp. Inside the first wall tent he found six cots lined neatly along the wall and room enough for a table in the center. The second wall tent he found set up much the same way as the first.

In the third things were quite different. A bed on the end wall with a rug lying next to it. Along the side wall sat a very nice couch. It also had a rug. Against the opposing side wall, halfway between front and rear was a small table with one chair at either end. This tent must've been Sheriff Bo Zeller's home away from home, Tom thought.

The fourth tent held neatly arranged tools, equipment and weapons. Rifles, cases of ammunition, axes, shovels and ropes stacked and arranged neatly filled a third of the tent. There was even a brand-new forge. A pile of not yet rusted rod iron lay next to it. Unbelievable, Tom thought. They must have been so cozy with Buster Kelly that they thought they would never be discovered.

Tom left the last tent and walked through the darkness to the prisoners. For a moment he stood and looked at them. When he figured they had wondered what he wanted for long enough, he stepped closer.

"How many of you were hired on for the Donovan ranch?"

Three cowboys raised their hands.

"How long ago did you hire on?"

The three cowboys looked at each other and were reluctant to speak. Tom pulled his revolver, broke it open and slowly turned the cylinder. Then he folded the revolver closed and twirled it on his finger. He had all the prisoners' attention now, but none of the three cowboys who raised their hand were willing to talk, yet.

"How long ago did you hire on?" He asked again, but this time he had his .44 aimed at the middle one of the three cowboys.

"I hired on in the spring, about two months ago."

"See fellas? I'm easy to talk to, now I don't have to shoot you," Tom pointed his Colt at the second of the three cowboys, "and you?"

"Same as Todd two months ago."

"So your name is Todd?"

"Yeah that's my name. Mean somethin' to ya?

"I always feel better if I know someone's name before I kill 'im."

"I answered your damn question, you son of a bitch."

"What if that's not my last question? And you're right I'm a real son of a bitch, so watch it. Now you." Tom directed his attention to the remaining of the three. "When did you hire on?"

"Just last week." The youngest of the three looked at the ground when he answered.

"How much time did Buster Kelly spend up here?"

None of the cowboys volunteered an answer, so without a second's hesitation Tom fired between Todd's feet. The young cowboy next to Todd began to cry and Tom could see his pants get wet.

"How much time did Buster Kelly spend up here?"

"Kiss my ass, you big feelin' bastard," Todd answered.

Tom fired again, but this time it didn't hit dirt. Todd's body lurched back against the ropes, twitched a few times, then went limp. The shot brought Buck and Smokey running to Tom's side.

"What the hell are you doin'?" Smokey demanded. "You can't shoot them. Damn you, Tom, they're prisoners!"

"They're low-life women-killing cattle thieves! I'd be in my right by any law to hang every damned one of them. Besides you only have four jail cells. Where would ya put 'em all? Seems to me I need to whittle their numbers down some.""

"Dammit, Tom, don't you shoot anybody else!" Smokey ordered.

"What if they don't answer my questions?"

"Well doggone it ... just wound 'em then!"

Smokey walked away, shaking his head and declaring he really didn't want to watch this. And he tossed back over his shoulder that Tom should just tell him what he found out. When he finds it out. Buck grabbed a wooden bucket and sat down, saying he wouldn't miss it, but could Smokey bring him another cup of coffee.

"I guess it's your turn again," Buck told Tom.

Tom broke open his revolver and replaced two spent shells and closed it again. "How much time did Buster Kelly spend up here? And anybody can answer that one."

"Coupla days a week," one of the prisoners volunteered.

"Did he hire you?"

"No, Bo Zeller brought me in."

"The rest of you come with Bo Zeller?" Tom looked the men over.

"Naw, we work for Hollister." The cowboy nodded toward the two men next to him.

Tom looked at Buck who held his hat in his hands, rubbing his hair. "Anybody else work for any other ranchers?"

"Nobody alive anymore," the outlaw that worked for the Donovan ranch said.

"All right, Smokey can sort the rest of that out," Tom said, "Anybody here know Poke?"

"Yeah I know'im?" The same outlaw said. "He was a pain in Buster Kelly's ass."

"He knew about your mountaintop ranch didn't he?"

"Yeah, he knew too much. Buster had it worked so old man Donovan would be sure to blame Poke."

"Who killed Buster?" Tom needed to know.

The Donovan ranch hand spit between his feet. "Bo Zeller. That damn Buster was starting to double cross us all. He was trying to build a herd of his own right up here. Why he'd pull cattle out of the stockyard and tell the Association he was running them back to the rightful owners and then bring 'em back up here. It was me that told Bo he was gonna get double crossed."

"Big man," Tom said, "why didn't Bo kill Poke?"

"Bo figured if Poke told Donovan about cattle thieves killing Buster it would make Poke look guiltier."

"It did that." Tom figured he'd leave the rest of the questions for Smokey and the law and was about to walk away and then he thought of one more question.

Who killed Poke?"

The Donovan hand that had been doing most of the talking had nothing to say and no one else spoke up. Tom stepped in front of him and slapped him on the side of his face with his revolver. "You were a part of that weren't you?"

Still he had nothing to say. Tom gave him another rap with the revolver but the man kept quiet. He was about to strike him again when Buck grabbed his hand. "Well dang it, Tom, I have a question."

"Ask it then," Tom wiped the blood from his revolver on the cowboy's shirt.

"What can we expect from those Cheyenne?"

"I don't think anybody can tell you," a Hollister hand offered. "They just started drifting into camp. They would help out a little bit, mostly Bo just left them hang around for kicks."

"Guess that explains why they helped you so much today," Buck said.

"Yeah, they helped all right," The Hollister hand said.

They left the prisoners and Tom gave Buck a tour of the four wall tents. "Living high on the hog, weren't they?" Buck commented.

"I think I'm gonna load these up and take them home to the ranch," Tom said.

"What in tarnation do you want with four wall tents?"

"Who knows, but I like them. So I'm going to take 'em."

****

The next morning, under guard, the prisoners buried their dead friends. Buck had selected a place where they could rest with a view of the prairie below. After all, they would be dead a long time, he explained. Only one marker was displayed, "DEAD CATTLE THIEVES."

They tore down the tents and loaded them on a wagon. Their contents filled a second wagon and Tom was as excited as Buck had ever seen him.

Johnny Kirk rode by the loaded wagons. "Well, I reckon we're ready to roll." His light hearted chuckle rang out over the creaking wagon wheels.

They started east, traveling across the high plateau squinting into the clear bright sun, having decided the night before Johnny Kirk's men would stay with the cattle, until more men could come help drive them down from the plateau. Smokey and Johnny headed for Denver City with their prisoners all on horseback, but still tied together. Buck and Tom, each drove a wagon pulled by two saddle horses. Thunder and Diablo tied to the rear.

"Have Donovan bring you to my ranch in three days." Johnny Kirk called as they parted ways. "We'll start that roundup then, and I'm looking forward to meeting Soft Cloud and Hawk."

"See you in three days!" Tom shouted. "I'm anxious to learn the cattle business."

CHAPTER TWENTY SIX

Donovan had recovered enough to drive a team, and three days later he led the parade of wagons and riders down the dusty road with the fancy two-seater carriage he had given Tom. Mrs. Donovan had spent the past days finessing the roundup into a neighborhood gathering and festival. "It's been months since we've seen Beverly Kirk, and I think we should adopt Soft Cloud and Hawk," she'd told Chester.

Soft Cloud drove the Donovan chuckwagon pulled by four mules. Hawk sat with her on the open seat. Her reputation as the prairie's finest open range cook won her the duties as vittles wrangler. She had spent nearly the entire day before supervising Newly as he stocked the chuckwagon; two 100-pound bags of flour, one 100-pound bag of corn meal, four 50-pound bags of dried beans, 200 pounds of bacon, and a 100-pound sack of coffee beans. In the rear section, or kitchen, she had assembled the cooking utensils and plates and cups and such. Three cast-iron Dutch ovens made the trip, and a ten-gallon black kettle hung from a hook under the rear of the wagon. Two 50-gallon water barrels hung strapped to the side.

Following the chuck wagon came two heavy wagons, each pulled by four mules. One wagon was loaded down with branding equipment, blacksmithing tools and supplies. The other carried bed rolls, blankets, slickers, extra rope, miscellaneous toiletries and whatever else might be necessary to spend a week or so chasing cows. It also carried one large wall tent including riggings, ropes and poles.

Tom rode Thunder and Buck Diablo, although Donavan had provided each of them six horses in the remuda, all twelve coming originally from Tom's ranch. They rode together on the high side of the ranch road, and Tom rambled on telling Buck his plans for the house they would build later this summer.

Five Donovan hands had set out earlier in the morning, driving a string of eighty horses to the meeting place on the range between the Donovan ranch and Johnny Kirk's outfit. It had been established that some of Johnny's men were to trail the collected herd from the high plateau to the same spot for sorting.

Smokey had arranged for the cattle at the stockyards to be sorted there, and all Kirk and Donovan cattle would be trailed to the meeting place. It was not the first time the Kirk and Donavon outfits had worked together on a roundup. Until two seasons ago they had been good friends. But there came a time when Buster Kelly convinced Donovan that Johnny was no good.

The morning before, when they buried Poke, Donovan had been so embarrassed he could barely speak. For a year or more, he had harbored distrust and dislike for the poor man. Now it turned out Poke had been looking out for the ranch's best interests all along. He felt like digging up Buster Kelly and hauling him to Denver's Boot Hill … He claimed he just might yet.

A ranch this size needs a ramrod who can be trusted. More than half Donavan's men announced their support for Luke Mason. So he'd put Luke in charge of the roundup. *One step at a time.* He was grateful that Johnny Kirk was so willing to patch things up and forget the last couple of years. Sometimes old men do foolish things, he'd told Johnny.

Donovan hadn't been out to the roundup area for the past two seasons. But Luke had gone out ahead of them with ten men to make any repairs that might be necessary on the corrals. With a chuckle Donovan recalled the many light-hearted discussions he had with Johnny Kirk every season as to just whose land the corrals sat on. He had engaged Mrs. Donovan last evening to create a deed, in her lovely penmanship, clearly assigning the corrals and 200 acres surrounding them to Johnny Kirk. With the stipulation that each year the two ranches held their spring roundup together. It would be the Donovan ranch's responsibility to maintain the corrals and provide the cook and food. Thinking over the amusing qualities of the deed and its intent made Donovan feel a little better. He felt a comfortable smile creep over his face.

Donovan gathered all four reins in his left hand and put his right hand on Mrs. Donovan's thigh. "I think we're going to have a good time at this roundup. I expect it will be more of a festival than a roundup, what with Tom's insistence that we bring that big tent."

"He sure is excited about those tents!" Mrs. Donovan said.

By midmorning the caravan rolled into the roundup grounds. Donovan guided his carriage to the top of a small knoll so he could pause a moment and enjoy the scenery. Five years ago, he and Buster Kelly had selected this spot as home base for spring roundup. For several years prior to that, as the Donovan herd grew, spring roundup had become difficult. Donovan had always liked this spot, with its nice flat solid footing bordered on two sides by branches of Buffalo Creek. A large stand of old cottonwoods, willows oak and aspen along the north bank of the stream provided ample wood supply to build corrals and firewood.

His mind wandered back to that summer when he and Buster built the first corrals. Donovan only had a few thousand head at the time. That was the year he had purchased one 100 Shorthorn cows and 35 bulls of the same breed, from a man in Iowa, and today a great many of his cattle displayed characteristics of the blended breeds. Chester Donovan was one of the first in the Colorado territory to mix breeds, and his current stock boasted it. Prior to that, his herd was made up mostly of Longhorns he and Buster had trailed up from Texas in '59. His herd had long been free of the Texas Tick by the time the Shorthorns were purchased.

"Good morning Donovan, and good morning to you Mrs. Donovan." Luke tipped his hat when he stopped alongside the Donovan carriage sitting a tall buckskin. One thing Donovan liked about Luke, he always made a good appearance. Luke spoke like a gentleman, displayed good manners, and always treated his men fair.

"Good morning to you, Luke," Donovan replied, "everything you've done looks right as rain."

"The corrals are ready, sir. I'll have the boys run the remuda on the flat over by the north branch of the creek," he said, pointing to a level, thick-grassed pasture. Then he added with a polite laugh, "We even had time to gather a supply of firewood. I sure hope Soft Cloud is ready to start using it."

Soft Cloud drove the chuckwagon to the very edge of the cottonwood stand and Tom rode to the wagon, hopped down, and draped a rein over the rear wagon wheel. He gave Soft Cloud a hug, and a long kiss. A few of the boys, who were taking a break from putting the finishing touches on the last corral, gave a lively cheer. Tom scooped up Soft Cloud, grabbed Hawk and ran a short distance to a soft spot in the grass where they could watch the camp come together.

Several of the boys had the remuda comfortably grazing on the north side of the creek. Buck helped Donovan from the carriage, and Mrs. Donovan headed their way.

"I volunteer as your kitchen assistant," Mrs. Donovan said, "and that way I may learn your biscuit secrets."

Soft Cloud brushed bits of dried grass from her knee-length deerskin skirt, looked around at the gathering men, "And I your roast beef secrets. Let's go cook!"

Tom joined them at the wagon kitchen, just to help "get things set up." He unhitched the mules and led them and Thunder to the remuda. Walking back he stopped to sit on a fallen log in cool shade. He figured he would enjoy watching the horses for awhile, and was just about to drift off to sleep when Buck gave him a sharp kick on the soles of his feet.

"Let's go tackle that big old tent before things get too busy around here." Buck's excitement glistened on his face.

"There ya go!" Tom shook off the drowsies and with spring in his step led the way. Buck's excitement turned nearly to giddiness. Tom laughed out loud, remembering the convincing it took to talk Buck into hauling the tent in the first place.

The mules grazed in the remuda. The boys not busy with stock either sat in the shade cleaning their saddles or in general tending to business that can only be done at times like this. Both wagons had been parked under the same shade tree Soft Cloud had set up the chuck wagon kitchen. Tom and Buck stood side-by-side with their forearms leaning on the side of the heavy wagon studying their next move. "Sure is a big old thing, isn't it?" Buck said.

"Fills half the wagon."

"Think any of the boys would like to help?"

"Let's not bother them. Open the tailgate and take a hold of the son of a gun."

Buck pulled the pin and chains on the tailgate and let it flip down. The tent had been loaded on the back half of the wagon, but it had required six men to drag it on. "I don't believe we can yank this thing down alone," Buck took his hat off and dragged a gloved hand over his sweated blonde hair.

"I reckon we're just a little tougher than a couple of cow hands. Now take hold of that corner and pull," Tom directed.

They each took one corner of the tent and pulled for all they were worth. It moved about an inch. They repositioned their grip and gave it another try and succeeded only in pulling the wagon back. Buck stood up, wiped his hands together in a clapping motion, turned around and leaned his back against the wagon. "We got to ask those boys for some help."

"I don't think so. Let's show 'em how a couple of Indian fighters drag tents off wagons." It was plain to see the cowboys sitting in the shade were ready to watch a show. Tom figured he'd give 'em one.

"I'll be right back," Tom said, and walked with swagger toward the remuda. As he passed by the other wagon, he snatched a harness collar and a set of driving reins.

"What are you up to, Tom?" One of the fellows in the shade asked as he hustled by.

"Gonna get a mule to yank that tent off the wagon."

"Take the tall black one with the white sock," the cowboy advised, pointing out the largest mule in the remuda.

"Thanks."

"You're welcome," replied the cowboy, but Tom could not see the devilish grin he wore on his face. Nor did he notice the other cowboys gather to watch the show. All had the look of fighting hard to suppress laughter. "Let me know if ya need a hand, Tom," yelped the helpful cowboy.

"Thanks, but I reckon I can handle this little detail."

The big black mule took a few quick steps to avoid capture, but finally allowed Tom to slip the collar over its head and then the bridle. He didn't feel it necessary for such a little job to put on the harness, or buckle the throat latch on the bridle. Tom swung up on the mule's back and rode back to the wagon. At first Tom thought the mule would trot right past the wagon, but finally he got him stopped.

"Got a little pep, does he?" Buck observerd.

"Sure does, hope he has enough to yank this tent down."

Buck tied the tongue of the wagon to a nearby tree, and then he and Tom tied one end of a rope to the pile of tent canvas. Everyone stopped whatever they were doing to watch Tom and Buck. Tom took the other end of the rope and secured to the collar on the mule's neck. Feeling just a bit cocky Tom put one hand on the mule's rump and hopped. He gathered the reins and asked the mule to step on, which he did until the rope tightened and the collar without the harness flipped up and whacked the mule in the jaw.

Buck saw the mule's head jerk and rushed to help, but the mule jumped straight up and lunged forward, yanking the tent from the wagon. The flying tent swept Buck's legs out from under him, he landed flat on his back on the pile of canvas and the mule took off at a gallop.

The cowboys stomped, clapped, cheered and hooted. This was a good show, and bound to get better. They all knew that mule. They all knew that mule was not going to stop until it was good and ready. And no man born of a mother would change that mule's mind!

Tom stayed on for the ride and gathered reins to gain control. The mule had another idea. He dipped his head, kicked both hind feet at the tent, and did a mule's best imitation of a bucking bronc's sunfish. When his feet touched ground Tom had the reins in his hand, but the head stall flew in the air. Tom dropped the bridle and grabbed a fistful of mane, such as there was. The mule bucked and twisted and then suddenly, it turned around and charged the tent.

"Ride 'im, Tom!" The cowboys hollered. "Ride that tent, Buck—you got it under control now!"

The tent swung wide as the mule circled, Buck nearly rolled free but got tangled in tent ropes dragged along flailing, hollering and cussing.

"Damn you, Tom! Stop this mule!" Buck hollered.

Tom was too busy to give a reply. The mule saw the tent fly out to the side and whirled to attack it again. Tom grabbed the collar which spun to the bottom and left him hanging on the side of the mule as it galloped, bucked and spun. Somehow he managed to hang on to the side of the mule who then decided it could outrun the tent, and took off in a flat-out gallop.

The front half of Buck had come off the tent but his legs were tangled in the ropes and he dragged along backwards as the mule made a wide arc and ran for the remuda.

The cowboys knew exactly what was going to happen. But even Donovan could not persuade them to intervene. Luke started off at a run to catch the mule, but one of the cowboys tackled him, "Hang on now, Luke, let 'er play out." Luke sat with his legs crossed in the dirt, shrugged his shoulders and started to cheer with the rest of them.

Tom hung on the side of the mule by a few skimpy mane hairs, while Buck dragged half on, half off the tent as the mule galloped at top speed for the remuda. What Tom and Buck were unable to see at that moment, but the cowboys and everyone else knew, was the creek they needed to cross to reach the remuda.

The mule never slowed, it brayed and bucked for all it was worth when it hit the stream bank. It fell on its side and went crashing into the water but recovered its feet instantly and lunged up the other bank. Tom fell and sat chest deep in mud and water. Buck dragged on by one foot behind the tent, through water, mud and dust, and into the remuda.

The mule brayed, kicked and danced into the herd, and started a grand stampede. Nearly a 100 horses, 20 mules, one tent, and a retired Army Scout went flying across the prairie. The cowboys riding herd on the Remuda struggled to stop the runaway herd for a mile. One of the boys ran his horse alongside the mule and sliced the rope, setting free the tent. The mule slowed to a walk as soon as he realized the tent no longer persued him.

Buck took some time to unravel the ropes and get his feet under him. A rider came and hoisted him on his horse behind him. Another one of the fellas took hold of the rope on the tent and dragged it back to camp.

The cowboys in the shade stopped their laughter and leg slapping only after Tom climbed out of the stream bank and yanked his .44. No one could ever guess, and Tom would never tell if he would have shot anyone had the laughter not ceased.

"Doggone, Tom. I'm sure sorry," the cowboy that recommended the mule offered, "I sure never expected nothin' like that."

"I think I'll see if Soft Cloud has any coffee ready," Tom holstered his revolver.

Soft Cloud had the cook fire going and coffee ready. He parked on a pile of firewood and sipped the hot coffee to keep from laughing. He knew the boys pulled a good one on him and he couldn't help but like the mule's spirit.

"Well, we gonna to rig that tent up?" Buck stepped up to the fire.

"Soon as I finished my coffee."

CHAPTER TWENTY SEVEN

The boys all pitched in and by the time Soft Cloud had beans, biscuits, bacon and coffee ready for supper the 20-foot long wall tent stood erected. The long wall facing the chuck wagon they left open, so in effect it was a three-sided tent but better sleeping was never had on a roundup. They used the canvas from that wall to make a partition wall along the one end for the ladies to sleep in privacy.

Johnny and his boys rolled into camp just in time to dig in. Johnny brought his wife, Beverly, six hands and 40 horses.

"Good to see you, Johnny," Donovan said. "How are you doing, Beverly?"

"Very well, thank you and happy to have been invited to the roundup ... or is it a festival?" She pointed to the three-sided tent.

"Well ma'am," Luke said with a broad grin, "you missed the opening show."

"They'll be others," Tom said with a nod.

"That's what worries me," Bob, the cowboy who had suggested the black mule, wore a timid grin.

The men passed through the chow line and found seats here and there in the shade to toss down groceries, and mop their tin plates clean with Soft Cloud's light cornbread biscuits.

"Keep them biscuit kettles full, if you don't mind, ma'am," one of the hands requested.

The sideboards had been rigged into a makeshift table. The Donovans and Kirks, Tom, Buck and Luke gathered around the table. Soft Cloud did not sit until every hand was fed and well supplied with hot coffee.

"My boys will be arriving at first light with the cattle from the high plateau and the stockyards," Kirk said. "I understand that herd will total just under a 1,000 head. Might be a good idea if tomorrow we sort them and put yours on your side and mine on my side and then hit the range the day after."

"I'm good with that," Donovan said. "But first we have a little paperwork that needs attention."

Johnny got a look of surprise, "what are you getting at?"

"Oh, just a little something I'd like to clear up between the two of us."

No one but the Donovans knew what was up and most of the expressions told of uncertainty, and apprehension. Donovan asked his wife for the envelope.

"They'll be no roundup until this is settled," Donovan slid the envelope across the table.

Johnny took the envelope, tapped it on the table a few times, obviously displeased. He looked at his wife. He tapped the envelope on the table a few more times and then opened it.

"You old son of a gun!" Johnny blurted after he read it, "you old son of a gun!" He handed the paper to his wife, who, after she read it ran around the table and hugged the Donovan's.

"Had you going a bit there, didn't I?" Donovan said.

"That you did. But you know this was certainly not necessary."

"Of course, it wasn't, but there you have it."

"Well you can sure count on the Kirk outfit to pull its weight each roundup."

The evening shadows crept over camp. Soft Cloud, Mrs. Donovan, and Beverly arranged their sleeping quarters on the private side of the tent. Mrs. Donovan retired while Soft Cloud, Beverly and Hawk joined the men around campfires.

One of the Kirk men played harmonica and another a fiddle. Well into the night, foot tapping tunes floated up from the light of the fire, carried by ascending hot air into the treetops, on its way to the stars.

Tom left Hawk in the charge of Beverly, took his wife by the hand, and led her away from the campfires. Hand in hand they walked into the shadows and soon disappeared in a quiet place thick with grass on the stream bank behind low brush.

CHAPTER TWENTY EIGHT

True to Johnny Kirk's word, by the time Soft Cloud had coffee boiling and biscuits baking the next morning, the sounds of cowboys moving cattle drifted into camp. A great dust cloud followed the herd for the grass had already begun to dry this last week of June.

For the first time ever, Tom heard the whistles, shouts and hoots of cowboys trailing cattle. Mixed with the cattle mooing, he found the strange serenade inviting.

"Looks like I'd better mix up more biscuit dough," Soft Cloud pulled a sack from the back of her kitchen wagon.

The men filed through the breakfast line for close to an hour already and those who had finished made their way to the remuda to rope their mounts for the morning.

"Probably be a good idea," Buck said, "no doubt those boys'll be hungry when they get here. They'll stop the herd about two miles out until we sort 'em. Some of these boys are going to ride out and spell 'em, so keep biscuits, bacon and coffee hot would be my advice." He stuffed two biscuits in his mouth and dodged a swat from Soft Cloud.

Tom rode to the wagon, Hawk held onto the mane giggling as he rode double with his father. "I take it today is the day you'll introduce Hawk to working cattle," Soft Cloud looked up briefly from stirring another batch of biscuit dough.

"Well I don't know how much working we'll do. But I figured on taking a spin out there and at least get close enough to get Hawk's hair dusty."

"Try to stay clear of any new adventures."

"Why don't you introduce him to a big black mule while you're at it?" teased Buck.

"Reckon we'll do that tomorrow," Tom smiled back, "truth be told, I figure on acquiring that tall mule. Had spunk, didn't he?"

The herd plodded toward camp, and already some of the boys from camp headed out to spell the men that trailed the herd in. Johnny broke from the herd and made a dash for the chuckwagon. "Handsome horse," he told Tom. "Chester said this was one of yours. I'll take 30 soon as you can get them here."

"I don't guess there's 30 back at the ranch ready to go, maybe 18 or 20," Tom said. "What do you think, Buck?"

"Reckon you're right. But when we get home we'll sort it out, and I'll turn around and bring 'em back, fifty dollars a head."

"I can live with that," Johnny said, "Now if Soft Cloud would fill a plate, I'll have a bite." He snared a tin plate from the top of the wooden crate beside the wagon, "I'll take three biscuits, a slab of bacon and a cup of hot coffee please."

Buck lingered by the fire and occasionally swiped additional biscuits when Soft Cloud had her back turned, but he was really interested in cow talk with Johnny. In a few moments, Mr. and Mrs. Donovan joined them and the small group moved to the long table. Buck looked out over the camp and marveled at the similarity it held to the many military campaigns he had been on as a scout. There was the main cook fire by the chuckwagon, with its black kettle hanging over the fire, the Dutch ovens in the coals, and hungry men gathered around it.

Scattered throughout the camp area were half a dozen other smaller campfires. Even though a hot June day, many of the boys cooked their own coffee when they weren't in the saddle. A few small one-man dog tents dotted the campgrounds and some of the men used logs to rig rustic saddle stands which sat in the center of their particular campsite. Some cowboys rested, stretched out on blankets, while others sat on their blankets stitching torn shirts, mending a piece of equipment, or cleaning rifles. The atmosphere was much more relaxed than the military encampment, but that same feeling of preparedness hung in the air. Each man here knew his job as well as any cavalry soldier.

"We'll see you folks later," Tom called as he and Hawk rode from camp and trotted toward the herd. Tom put Thunder in a

gentle lope and was pleased to see his son use both hands to grasp
the mane and kept his balance with the horse. As they traveled
through the tall prairie grass at a good speed, Hawk's hair blowing in
the wind brushed on Tom's naked belly. Today, Tom rode as a Sioux
horseman. He wore deerskin leggings fringed on the outside seam,
Iron Shell's deerskin vest and bone necklace. His own long black hair
streamed behind him in the wind. The beads sewn on his moccasin
boots with great care by Soft Cloud were in exactly the same pattern
as the beads on Hawk's moccasin boots, and together they glistened
in the sun. Tom had decided today he would ride not only dressed as
a Sioux, but in the manner and style of a Sioux warrior on a buffalo
hunt. He carried the war lance given him by Red Cloud on his
wedding day. As they approached the milling herd he leaned forward,
reached over Hawk, grasped the bridle, shook it loose. Still
maintaining a gentle lope, he untied one rein from the bridle,
dropped the bridle to the ground, and tied the single rein around
Thunder's neck in a wide loop.

He brought Thunder to a halt at the first cowboy about 20
yards from the herd. "Damn son," the old cowboy greeted, "I
thought we was getting attacked!"

"Sorry about that," Tom offered his hand, "here to learn how
you boys sort cattle."

"They call me Jules. You ain't goin' to be able to cut cattle on
that big square horse with no saddle and a young'n sittin' on its neck.
Why hell boy, you ain't even got a bit nor bridle!"

"Do I need one?"

"They come in handy."

"You ever watch Sioux hunt buffalo from horseback?"

"Never did. Fact is this is the closest I've ever come to a real
live Sioux."

"Let me introduce you, my son, Hawk." Hawk held his tiny
hand out to be completely consumed in Jules' big mitt.

"Howdy son, glad to meet ya."

"Now I understand there's two herds mixed together here.
Johnny Kirk's and Chester Donovan's. I believe I can see the
difference in brands, already."

"Easy enough," Jules said, "our brand is a JK back to back,
Chester's a CD."

The cowboys riding herd had wandered over to see why Jules

might be talking to an Indian. They'd all heard stories of the exploits of Tom and Buck. But nevertheless were all surprised to find Tom dressed like an Indian.

"So our job is to sort Johnny's cows from Donovan's?"

"That's our job for today," Jules answered.

"You go on, get some of Johnny's cows so Thunder and I can see how it's done," Tom said.

"Tobacco, Sandy, go cut one of Johnny's cows out for this man," Jules directed. "Pick one close to the side here so Tom and his horse can see how a hard workin' man earns his keep."

Two horses bolted from the bunch and charged to the herd. The herd backed away and the cowboys stopped their horses short of the first cows. They inched forward one slow step at a time. The wary cattle backed, but kept their eyes on the horsemen and as they backed a seam opened within the herd.

Even though he had never appreciated domestic cows, Tom noticed the differences in the Donovan and Kirk herd. The Donovan cattle showed the evidence of improved breeding that Chester had explained. While the Kirk stock were good looking, they displayed more of their original rangy Texas longhorn appearance. Tom believed he could accurately separate the two herds without relying on the brands.

The cowboys continued to inch forward and the cattle stepped away creating an ever widening gap in their ranks. "We'll take these first two on my left," Tobacco said.

Tom watched Sandy cue his smart looking mustang. Forward he dashed. The second of the two cows tried to turn and run back into the herd but Sandy's little horse was too quick. In a flash Sandy and his horse robbed the cow of its escape route and turned it further from the herd. At the same time Tobacco urged his horse to the opposite side of the two cows and like a precision cavalry drill team two cows and two horses exited the herd. As soon as Tobacco and Sandy had the cows cut from the herd, two other cowboys intercepted them and drove them farther away and held them, penning them with their horses.

Sandy and Tobacco whirled their horses about, dashed back to the herd and eyeballed two more cows. Tobacco ran his horse through the seam the cattle gave and turned both cows out. Sandy's horse backed him up and cut off their opposite side escape. Slick as can be, the two horses and second two cows were moved to the location of the first two.

As soon as the outside cowboys picked up these two, Sandy spun his mustang again and focused on two more cows. His little mustang knew what to do and cut them from the herd. Tobacco ran his horse to the offside and turned out. Quick as lightning, the second cow turned and ran straight for Sandy and his mustang. Head low and bellowing, she charged Sandy. Sandy's horse turned to the cow and cut her escape. But that cow had a calf in the herd and would not be denied. She ran headlong into Sandy's mustang nearly knocking it from its feet. Her long horn opened a nasty gash on the mustang's shoulder.

Tobacco dashed to his partner. "You better take this fella back to camp. Might need to sew this up."

"If he hadn't turned into that horn, that gash would be on my leg," Sandy praised his mustang.

"Good little horse," Jules said, "go on, take him back to camp and get that wound fixed."

Tobacco walked back to camp with his friend to tend to the injured horse. Before they were out of earshot Tom called after them, "Let Soft Cloud sew that horse up. She'll have a poultice."

"So in three tries they cut and penned five cows," Tom said.

"They sure did," Jules gave him a wink, "reckon you're up. Who do you want as your backup man?"

Tom gave Thunder a few pats on the neck, "this fella will do."

Tom had many times, while living with the drunken buffalo hunter, taken his horse into a buffalo herd and cut out buffalo cows. He knew all the secrets of quietly milling through a herd and stringing it out, to separate the ones he knew the old hider wanted.

"Hang on to his mane, and stay with the horse," he told Hawk.

Slowly and confidently he moved Thunder toward the herd. Other cowboys were drifting from camp toward the large herd and the story spread that Tom was going to cut cows, by himself, on a horse with no saddle. Even Donovan drove across the prairie and with him Beverly Kirk and Mrs. Donovan.

Tom moved Thunder into the herd and as he did he, examined the stock. He walked Thunder peacefully among the cows and steers but directed him in a line that sliced one third of the herd away from the others. He moved Thunder in a zigzag fashion so the swath he cut was 20 feet wide, carefully touching any cow that needed direction now and then with the lance. When he reached the herd's far side he turned Thunder to walk in a zigzag line through the sorted bunch. Thunder moved along slowly, his head low, and cut a second swath. In this fashion he cut his already small bunch in half again. Most of the cattle they cut stayed in the small group the pair had sorted. He turned Thunder and drove his small herd with the same crisscross walk a little farther from the large herd, directing them with his lance from time to time.

Being careful never to stop Thunder, for he wanted this to count as one try, he took inventory of his herd. He had separated approximately 100 head from the large herd and he maintained his zigzag walk and continued to move his herd farther and farther away.

Tom guided Thunder through the middle of his herd and once more cut it in half, with the same successful slow staggered walk. He looked up and saw Buck sitting Diablo with his right leg over the saddle, smiling as big as ever while he took in the exhibition. Not a sound floated in the calm air, not a voice, not a moo, nor whinny or snort.

Now Tom turned his attention to his small herd. All along he had carefully separated cows from the herd with calves by their side and now had a large group of Donovan cows, most with calves, slowly milling in an ever outward spiral. He circled Thunder and walked, a little quicker, back through the seam they had just made in the biggest meander walk they had done yet. He wanted the separation to be extra wide for in his group of Donovan cows there was eight or ten Johnny Kirk young steers. He hoped if he left this group mill for a little while the steers would cut themselves from the cows to get back to the big herd.

Tom kept his group of cows and calves moving in the direction of the corrals, but had Thunder walk along the seam a bit faster. The cows were content because they had their calves, but the steers had become anxious. One by one the steers darted from Tom's herd back to the big herd and before he was halfway to the corrals his herd consisted of 31 Donovan cows, most of them with calves by their side, and no Johnny Kirk steers or cows. He took Hawk's hands from Thunder's mane and put them on the rein tied around his neck, and taught him to guide Thunder and the cows toward the corrals.

Buck rode to Tom. "So that's how an Indian sorts cows?"

Tom looked at Buck and found it difficult to keep from laughing, so he quit trying. "I had no idea how this was going to turn out. Sure I'd cut buffalo cows out already, but as skittish as these critters are I had my doubts."

Tom, with Hawk and Buck, guided the cows and calves to the other side of the encampment, where Donovan wanted his herd. On the way many of the other cowboys caught up with them singing praise and congratulations to the winner of the first ever Colorado Stock Growers Association cattle penning.

When the cows and calves were safely deposited on their own pasture, Tom and Buck turned and galloped across the prairie to Jules. On the way they could not resist a short race. Tom put his arm around Hawk, snatched him up and held him under his arm, picked up the single rein and whispered, "Go, Thunder!"

Buck and Diablo had jumped to a head start, but Diablo's lead faded with each bound of the magnificent black stallion. Thunder overtook Diablo, and Tom slowed to a nice trot to avoid spooking the cattle.

"Never saw anything like that sortin' you did there, young fella," Jules said, "my hat's off to ya!"

CHAPTER TWENTY NINE

Tom spent the day with Soft Cloud at the camp kitchen. He carried water from the stream to refill the barrels and gathered great piles of firewood. The peacefulness of the camp among the trees convinced him he'd worked enough cattle for the day. His chores finished, he lay down with Hawk on a blanket by the chuckwagon and soon fell asleep.

Buck worked with the men sorting cattle and came into camp only twice for fresh biscuits and coffee. One of the boys had killed a young steer that had broken a leg that morning, and he and Soft Cloud had it on a spit. There would be quite a spread tonight.

Beverly and Mrs. Donovan helped Soft Cloud prepare for the evening meal, which had begun more and more to take on the air of a banquet. Donovan stayed busy driving his carriage and toting water, buckets of coffee and mountains of biscuits out to the boys sorting cattle.

By the end of the day they had cut three herds. Donovan's herd, mostly cows and calves, grazed on the high side of the encampment and numbered over 500. Johnny's herd, a little over 300 head and mostly steers, milled about on the camp's near side.

The third herd, about 150 head, held steers, cows and calves belonging to three other ranchers from the area. Johnny sent five boys to return the stolen cattle to their owners.

As evening insects began their chorus and shadows beneath the trees grew long, the men began to drift into camp. Soft Cloud had kept the Dutch ovens busy and hot all day and a mountain of cornbread biscuits towered on her table. Occasionally she would have to defend her small mound of biscuits from sneaky cowhands. Who, under the guise of refreshing their coffee cup, would sneak around the rim of the fire and risk the wrath of her long-handled black metal spoon? Not all escaped scot-free.

Beverly and Johnny had ultimately accepted the responsibility for roasting the steer. "You can start giving the boys their biscuits and beans, and send them down here for a chunk of beef. This steer is ready-to-eat!" Johnny beat a tune on a wooden bucket.

"Don't need to call me again," one of the fellas made a dash for Soft Cloud's fire.

One by one the men filed by Soft Cloud and Tom and had beans and a biscuit shoveled on their plate. Those that wanted it had a tin cup of hot coffee. Then through the camp to stop at the fire where Johnny tended the roasted steer, and carved out chunks, the size determined by the hungry cowhand.

It took less than 20 minutes for close to 40 hungry hands to pass through the two lines and fill their plates and decimate Soft Cloud's pile of biscuits. The boys out riding herd would have to wait until they were relieved. All through the camp around numerous small campfires, men sat on their blankets and enjoyed not only a good meal but each other's tall tales as well.

When the men were fed, Tom and Buck loaded their plates, then found Jules and Luke's campfire. Eight men sat around that fire and, when Tom and Buck sat down, their conversation stopped.

"Don't let us interrupt your conversation, boys," Buck squatted on a blanket.

"How in the devil did you get them cows to listen to you?" Jules had to know.

"Just lucky I guess," Tom said.

"Come on now, Tom," another fella insisted.

Tom never found it easy to talk about himself. He was always more of a doer than a talker. He chased his beans around his plate with his fork, hoping someone would take the conversation in a different direction. For the moment he was saved when Soft Cloud walked up behind him with Hawk in tow.

The men jumped to their feet. Those with hats tipped them. Johnny took her hand and helped her sit down.

"I didn't mean to break off your discussion," she apologized.

"Well, they were just pesterin' Tom," Buck said.

"Back to that," Jules said, "we'd like to hear how you did it."

Tom figured he had no way out. He didn't mind sorting cows, but talking about it would sure make him think of the old drunken hider. He reached for Hawk, sat him on his lap, played with his hair, and tickled his belly.

"I grew up with this old hider," he took a breath and looked at Soft Cloud, "he was a mean old bastard but he knew how to hunt buffalo. Back in those days the prairie wasn't loaded with buffalo hunters. Nowadays buffalo hunters go out in teams, maybe six, seven wagons to a team. I've seen them. A team today might have half a dozen or more skinners, usually one or two good shooters. They make a stand and in one day might shoot half a thousand buffalo. Back then we didn't kill that many in a year. And most hiders were one or two man outfits. Most days we'd just drive along 'til he found a small herd and we'd shoot a few. Maybe, five or six. When I got older mostly I'd have to skin. Most days, it took me all day. And then we'd stake the hides to the ground to dry."

"What does that all have to do with how you sorted cows today?" One of the boys asked, obviously not interested in extra details.

"In spring calving season," Tom went on, "the old hider taught me to ride our horse, I called him Tom Gray, into the herd, and work a few of the young bulls to the outer edge. Bull hides were almost always worth more. I learned I could move the cows into the herd by just walking Tom Gray back and forth and the bulls would drift out."

"Slick trick," Johnny said.

"How did you know you could do it with these cows? I've seen buffalo herds, too. They tend to just keep on walking in a straight line, nothing short of a stampede can get 'em going," Jules said.

Tom gave Jules a timid little grin, "I didn't."

"I'm sure glad I didn't bet money," Jules held his coffee cup high in a salute to Tom.

Soft Cloud sat quietly on the blanket next to Tom, her legs crossed, her knee touching his. As he spoke, she dragged Hawk to her lap. The little fellow had drifted to sleep. She watched her husband as he explained the hunting technique, but didn't pay attention for her mind wandered back to the first time she met him.

The day he saved Iron Shell's life and her mother brought

him into their lodge. What a quiet young man he was. Her first emotion for him had been pity. How her brothers had taunted this scared, out-of-place white man. She felt so sorry for him she had to follow when he ran from the lodge. She remembered her surprise the next day when he chose her as his "brave" to assist him, on that errand for Red Cloud. To kill the lone hider who had killed so many Sioux. She thought of the confusing emotions she felt for him in the first weeks they traveled together. In the following days, she had seen him kill four men, and one woman. But the man inside that she loved was tender and caring. He could be so kind, gentle and understanding. His ability to change in less than an instant, into that icy cold killer, was also part of her beloved husband. Even Bill Cody had commented to her that Tom's talents with rifles and revolvers at least equaled the skills of his friend, Bill Hickok—he had also warned Soft Cloud Tom's emotional trigger was touchier than Hickok's.

"I hear you rode Pony Express with Cody and Hickok," Johnny Kirk turned to Buck.

"That I did," Buck said.

"Cody was just in town," Johnny said, "on some Army business."

"He was, and crossed our trail a few weeks back just in time to save our bacon," Buck's silly grin showed spark. Not wanting to allow the conversation to take a turn toward the unpleasant business with Sidewinder, Buck tossed in a diversionary question. "How would you fellas like to hear a story about Hickok from those Pony Express days?"

"I think we would," Jules said, affirmed by nods all around.

"You may have heard of Jake McCandless. He ran a gang of desperados and outlaws along the Kansas border back in '61. Wild Bill was riding Pony Express in western Kansas at that time and killed old Jake in an awful fight with the gang.

"When riding Pony Express it was your duty to begin calling out to the stock tender at a quarter-mile from the station. That gave the stock man time to catch your change of horse and have it ready. The rider was to leap from his spent horse, onto the fresh and ready pony having to transfer only the mailbag. Most mount changes took merely a second or two. And we galloped away.

"This particular day, as Bill approached the Rock Creek Station for a change in horses, he called to the stock tender. The

162

stock tender at Rock Creek had just gotten married and his wife was living with him at the station. Bill shouted and hollered but the man failed to appear.

"Bill stormed into the station and instead of the stock tender standing with a fresh mount, Bill found him lying by the stable, shot dead.

"He jumped from his tired horse and from the corner of his eye he saw a man running from the house in his direction. Wild Bill is not one to ask a lot of questions and as the man fired at him Bill pulled his revolver and shot back, hitting the outlaw square in the head.

"At that instant he heard the screams of the stock tender's wife calling for help from the house. Bill raced to the house and kicked in the door and discovered two men beating the terrified woman. One of them was just about to hit the poor woman's face with the butt end of his revolver. Bill fired, hitting the man in the back of his head and killing him instantly, his arm still in the air. All of a sudden two more men appeared from the next room. Like I said, Bill doesn't ask many questions and he leapt to a corner and began firing at the two. One of them dropped dead just four feet from Bill. The other two managed to reach Bill and one of them attacked him with his Bowie knife, which Bill wrestled free, and with it stabbed to death the useless varmint.

"The remaining outlaw got his hands around Bill's throat. Now I need to tell you folks Bill is a big strong man, and when he gets riled he's more than a handful. Well, this fellow had a hold of Bill's throat and when Bill swung his own right arm striking the outlaws left arm with all his force, why that man's arm just broke. But he did manage to bolt through the door, jump on his horse and escape. The only survivor of the Jake McCandless gang."

Tom always enjoyed when Buck told his stories and from the looks of the faces of the men gathered around the dying campfire, they did too. A few more yarns were spun, as the fire continued to dwindle. Soft Cloud excused herself and carried Hawk to their bed in the wall tent.

"Let's all get some sleep," Johnny Kirk suggested, "we've got a few long days ahead of us."

Just as Tom moved to join Soft Cloud, a rider burst into camp in a reckless fashion. The man unable to stop his horse crashed over several men sleeping snugly in their bed rolls. All manner of hoots and hollers arose from the trampled men and still the horse and rider continued through the camp.

"Stop that horse!" Johnny Kirk yelled.

Half a dozen men scrambled and ran to for the horse. Finally one of the boys was able to grab hold of the terrified horse's bridle. Tom and Buck ran with Johnny to the prancing, snorting and lathered horse.

"Hold on there fella," Tom stroked his sweat-caked neck.

"Land Sakes! He's been shot!" The cowboy holding the bridle shouted. "He's been shot by a damned Indian, the arrow's still in his leg."

Two boys grabbed the wounded man and as they tried to help him from the nervous horse, the reason for the horse's panic became evident. The arrow had gone clear through the man's leg and was embedded in the horse's side.

"Let me go! Let me go! Your killin' me," the rider howled. They slid him back in the saddle. "Pull the damn arrow out first!"

Two men held the horse as still as possible, while Buck used his Bowie knife to cut the arrow in two, between the rider's leg and the horse's ribs. Four men slid him from the saddle, "you men carry him to the tent and make him comfortable. I'll be right there and we'll get that arrow out of you, Dusty." Johnny looked at Tom and Buck, "what do you make of that?"

"Cheyenne. Cheyenne dog soldiers," Buck said, "my guess is they hit the boys you sent to return the stolen cattle pretty hard."

Johnny threw his hands in the air, "We almost never have trouble with Indians anymore."

"You did tonight," Tom said.

"Somebody shoot this horse," Johnny said in a broken whisper.

"Whoa! Hold on a minute, Johnny!" Tom yelled. "No need to kill that animal. You tend to your man, I'll tend the horse." He grabbed Buck's knife, snatched the reins from the two men and led the horse to the cool waters in the stream. He walked the horse to the center and stood a moment examining the saddle fender and the arrow shaft pierced it. The excited horse quivered as Tom conducted his examination.

He carefully cut a hole in the fender and slipped it over the arrow shaft, loosened the cinch, and slid the saddle from the horse. The horse was a fine, tall stallion with long strong legs, a wide chest and massive rump. Tom recognized the intelligence of the animal in his clear black eyes. While blood streamed from the wound, this horse had gallantly brought his rider home to safety running who knows how many miles with an arrow between his ribs.

Rotated by the horse's movements, the arrow shaft had torn a large hole in the hide. But the metal tip, slowed by Dusty's leg and the saddle fender, stopped its penetration and wedged between two rib bones. Just enough light reflected up from the still water from the failing moon to guide the sharp tip of Buck's knife.

The horse stood perfectly still with the exception of an uncontrollable shiver as Tom worked. His left hand spread the wound on the hide open, while his right hand sliced just a shard of the horse's rib. The arrow felt loose enough now to yank free. He worked the knife's tip between rib and arrow tip and popped it out. The horse gave a quick snort and jump, but nothing else.

Soft Cloud had heard and brought fresh poultice. She waded into the water and when Tom had finished flushing the wound she packed the hole with poultice. Together they stood in the water, Tom whispered to the horse and Soft Cloud held her hand over the wound applying pressure to stop the bleeding. For half an hour they stood this way and in the east the horizon began to brighten with the light of another day.

Throughout the camp all the men had bed rolls folded, and ready for the new day. Many had already made it to the cook fire which was absent Soft Cloud, but Beverly had boiled coffee and all set for the men.

When Tom and Soft Cloud had stopped the bleeding, she applied another lump of poultice on the wound. To keep the poultice in place they cut a long strip of canvas and wrapped it around his belly and tied as tight as they dare.

Tom studied his wife and the bandaged horse, and with great satisfaction and a pleasant look he told her, "That should do him just fine." They led the horse into camp past several admiring cowboys and tied him to a short picket by the big wall tent. As they walked through camp they could hear the men commenting on Tom's ability to do "doctorin'" on the horse standing free in a stream.

It took about that long for Mrs. Donovan to complete the

surgery on Dusty as well. Buck had yanked the arrow from his calf, and after being cleansed with liberal doses of whiskey, she had packed it full of Soft Cloud's poultice and tied a bandage around his leg.

Although exhausted, in pain and scared, Dusty was just beginning to tell the tale of the night's events when Soft Cloud and Tom entered the tent.

CHAPTER THIRTY

Pile of Bones sat quietly on the hidden ridge and watched the white man chase his tiny beef cows for most of the day. Lone Bear and the others had wanted to move on for they knew the white soldiers had been in search of their camp for many days. Pile of Bones understood they had much to fear, for this time they came with many, and were helped by Pawnee scouts, enemy of the Cheyenne, and the one the Sioux called "Pa-he-haska" (Long Hair), Bill Cody … But his people hungered. The white man had killed nearly all the buffalo that once roamed the Sioux and Cheyenne hunting grounds. Most days of this summer the white soldiers harassed Pile of Bones, Tall Bull and their people. They had not been able to camp or hunt and the women and children cried with bellies empty.

Pile of Bones would not leave this place without food for his village. He would wait for a chance to scare away a few of the white man's cows. He would not go back to the lodges of his people, who were sick and hungry, with no food. He, Powder Face, and the 15 Dog Soldiers who rode with him this day would take the cows that eat the grass the Great Spirit had planted in the earth for the buffalo.

"Their numbers are too many," Powder Face protested. "They have many rifles and these men that chase cows on our hunting grounds are strong warriors. We should leave. We can look for buffalo."

"The buffalo have been driven far and those that have not walked away have been killed," Pile of Bones reminded his friend. "It is better today to take some boney cows and feed our women and feed our old people and children. So long has the white man Army and the Pawnee cowards chased us, our women and children are eating insects and grass. No, Powder Face, tomorrow they will have full stomachs of white man cow."

As if the Great Spirit watched as he spoke, Pile of Bones saw a small herd of cows being driven by only five white men away from the big herd. He watched from the safety of the tall grass and excitement caused his heart to pound in his scarred chest. These would be the cows that would feed his hungry people.

"We will follow that small group until they are far from their friends. Then we will kill them and we will take those cows. And Tall Bull will feed his people. We must get on our ponies and ride behind this hill and follow."

The Cheyenne braves gathered their ponies and rode in the deep ravine following Johnny Kirk's men as they drove the herd across the prairie in the gathering twilight.

Pile of Bones kept one brave on foot near the top of the hill to watch the white men below and make sure they did not slip away. When the time was right and the ravine began to flatten, Pile of Bones thrust his arm high in the air and with a shrill whoop demanded top speed of his war pony.

The others in his party followed and in seconds raced pell-mell down the hill through the tall grass shouting and whooping shrill cries of braves on the attack.

The cowboys had no warning and were surrounded by the time they realized they were under attack. Two men pushed the herd into a stampede and tried to save them. They managed to drive the cattle a short distance before the Cheyenne braves turned them. The other three cowboys leapt from their horses to make a stand in a shallow ditch.

The Cheyenne rode hard after the cowboys running the cattle; one fell from his horse, an arrow between his shoulders. The other cowboy, though wounded, managed to turn his horse and gallop into a small stand of trees.

The Cheyenne were more interested in pursuing the cattle than one wounded cowboy, and allowed him to escape.

"Gather as many of these cows as you can," Pile of Bones directed his braves. "Chase them as fast as they will go! Take them to our village. Feed our people with these white man's cows. We will follow soon."

Five of Pile of Bones' braves managed to turn a quarter of the herd and with it rode into the night toward their lodges near the gullies of Summit Springs. He and his remaining eleven braves turned to attack the three white men hiding in the dry bed.

****

"They're gonna hit us hard," Windy said, "Soon as they sort them cows they'll come back for us." The three men huddled in relative safety in the narrow dry creek bed. All three were armed with Winchesters and revolvers and had plenty of ammunition in the saddle bags they had managed to yank from their horses before hunkering down.

"Guess we're not gonna make it to the Hollister spread tonight," Jack Pike complained, "I was looking forward to a big piece of Mrs. Hollister's apple pie."

"Think she'll give us some pie anyway," Harry Miles wondered, "if them Cheyenne took all their cows?"

"You ready, boys? They're comin' back at us," Windy aimed his rifle.

Some of the Cheyenne rode armed with Henry repeaters and hung low on the side of their ponies and fired under their ponies' neck. Those armed with only bows, however, proved just as deadly. The braves cut a path across the ground in front of the trapped cowboys firing and yelling. Bullets and arrows slammed into the bank, but none found their mark in any of the men.

"Pour it on, boys, let 'em have it," Windy hollered. The cowboys slid low and fired their Winchesters as fast as they could lever shells. On the first attack two Cheyenne ponies fell. The braves landed on their feet and were scooped up by their comrades. They retreated out of rifle range.

"I sure hope someone back in camp heard our little tussle," Harry said.

"I don't know. We're a good ten miles from camp," Windy stuffed shells in his empty rifle.

"Here they come again…." Harry didn't finish, an arrow pierced his throat.

"God damn you heathen sons of bitches!" Windy stood straight up and emptied his rifle, firing one round after another, never lowering the rifle from his shoulder, sending spent cartridges flying in the air. A bullet punched his leg and knocked him back, but he stood straight up, yanked his revolver and with careful aim he shot one brave from his pony.

Windy fell back and crammed more shells into the rifle, "they killed Harry, dammit, Jack!"

"They aim to kill us too!"

The braves withdrew again to a safe distance. A misleading quiet settled over the little valley, but burnt gunpowder hung in the air and darkness crept in.

"I thought Indians didn't fight after dark," Jack said, "I heard it was against their religion or something."

"Well maybe this bunch ain't religious," Windy used the quiet moment to stuff a piece of bandanna in the bullet hole in his thigh. "This son of a bitch hurts."

"Well don't stand up and let 'em shoot at ya."

"Yeah that was dumb, but the bastards killed Harry."

"Well don't let them kill you too. I don't want to walk all the back to camp alone … I never told you, but I'm afraid of the dark."

Windy looked at Jack, unable to hold his laugh. "If those Cheyenne out there have anything to say about it, that won't be a problem tonight."

"I'm not kidding Windy ... I get downright skittish when it's dark. That's why mostly I sing so loud on night herd. Helps me forget how dark it is."

"I'm not kidding either, Jack. Those boys on the hill out there want our hair."

Pile of Bones led his braves on another charge. Down the hill they galloped straight toward the trapped cowboys. Screeching and howling and firing their Henrys as they attacked their treed quarry. Jack and Windy fought back fearlessly and turned the braves another time. All except one mounted Cheyenne Dog Soldier. When his fellow braves turned back he kept his charge. Hanging low on his pony's neck he reached the two men. Jack and Windy threw the lead into the war pony. It fell dead with a scream and a thud. But the brave hit his feet running and swung his massive war club. A round from Windy's rifle crashed into the brave's chest, but still his war club smashed Jack's skull. The dead Cheyenne brave fell on the dead cowboy.

Windy grabbed the dead brave and pulled him off Jack. He was staring at the smashed face of his good friend when Pile of Bones led another charge. His rifle was empty so he grabbed Jack's and with the seven rounds left in Jack's rifle he knocked three braves from their horses.

When the Winchester clicked on an empty chamber he charged the braves swinging the rifle and knocked one more brave from his pony. An arrow cut into his good leg and spun him. He fell face down in the grass and another arrow plunged into his back, piercing his body through, and pinning him to the dirt.

****

Johnny Kirk, Buck, and ten men rode out at a gallop for the little valley where Dusty had described. Tom chose to stay behind with his wife and son. He needed to be with Soft Cloud if defense of the camp became necessary. The men not riding herd or on guard sat at their fires mindlessly examining equipment, but their minds raced as fast as the horses of those who were on their way to rescue their friends. Most of the men in camp had never seen a hostile Indian.

"I'm sure glad Windy was with them," one of the boys at the chuckwagon said.

"Yeah, he's one knows what to do in an Indian skirmish for sure," agreed another.

It seems Windy had been one of Beecher's scouts last September along the Republican River when they were attacked by more than a thousand Cheyenne, Arapaho and Sioux.

One of the younger cowboys, called Speck in honor of his heavily freckled face spoke up, "Windy was in Indian battles?"

"He was in one of the worst ever," the cowboy known as 'Lippy' went on. "Now, understand I wasn't there, but as best I can, I'll tell you boys a true story told to me by Windy himself that'll stand your hair on end."

A small crowd gathered at the wagon as word spread that Lippy was about to tell a tale. Lippy had won fame on the Donavan ranch for his unmatched ability to spin yarns.

"It seems there was this Indian uprising," Lippy began, "in Kansas along the Solomon and Saline Rivers where a band of renegades were raiding and killin' settlers last summer. Well I guess

Windy was one of those settlers who was raided. You know, they killed his wife, all his livestock, and his little boy. You folks didn't know that about Windy cause he wouldn't talk about it too much.

"Come a day when a Colonel Forsyth was asked by General Sheridan to put together a company of experienced ex-soldiers, buffalo hunters and frontiersmen. Word went out that such men as was in the area should meet at Fort Harker where a Lt. Beecher would organize the company."

Tom was a veteran of too many battles with the tribes of the Plains. He and Buck had been pulled into some of the most fearsome fighting the Plains had seen. Last winter he and Buck had heard first-hand from their friend Comanche Jack of the nine-day siege at Arickaree Creek. He did not need to hear it again. Many good men, both white and Indian alike, died there. Including Red Cloud's friend Dull Knife. Tom knew as well as Soft Cloud, and hell, even Red Cloud knew these wars and battles would continue. They knew too, the eventual outcome.

Red Cloud had explained it was for that reason he tried so hard for fifteen years to live in peace with the white man. He had chosen to fight the white man the past two summers, not in the belief the great tribes of the Plains could win. Rather he chose to lead his braves into those horrible conflicts because the white man was such a liar and so dishonest. Never would such liars be allowed the position of Chief among the Sioux, Cheyenne, Arapaho, or Kiowa. Even the Crow, their enemy, never had such liars. Only the Pawnee who love the white man's gifts and pleasures could lie like the white man.

Tom quietly took Soft Cloud by the hand and they walked from the group by the fire. It was best he thought. He knew what the men with Buck would find. He knew that tomorrow there would be too much talk of hatred and vengeance.

"Well, you see, Windy, he was one of those ex-Army that went to meet Beecher at the Fort. They set out with 50 men thinkin' they was trackin' 250 Indians. They followed them to the Republican River and there they discovered sign that the Indians they were chasing had camped by the river only days before, problem was there were signs of over 600 lodges. Well, those 50 men followed the trail and later the next night they camped by the north bank of the Arickaree Creek.

"The very next morning trouble started. In the dark of night

Indians had crept to their camp through the tall grass and before the sun was up they jumped from the grass and stampeded most of mules and horses away from the scouts.

"Mounted braves, naked and painted for battle, charged shouting and whooping. The Colonel yells for every man to retreat a small island in the middle of the creek bed. The Arickaree Creek ran dry this time of year but they hoped the wide open streambed would stop the Indians.

"But they attacked. Finally The Colonel gave the order to fire and the roar of their rifles drowned out the savages' yells. Warriors fell from their horses bleeding and dying on the sand only yards from the men hidden in the trees on the tiny island. Volley after volley they fired into the charging Indians. They were turned back, leaving many braves and horses lying dead or dying in the sandy creek bottom.

"All the horses and mules they had saved were killed in the first attack. Before the second attack those men not wounded dug trenches, and positioned the dead horses and mules as best they could for protection.

"Chief Roman Nose soon launched a second attack. They turned this attack back as well and even killed Roman Nose. Until two o'clock that day the Indians charged the island, charge after charge, leaving many dead braves in the hot sand of dry Arickaree. And then sometime in the early afternoon Roman Nose was replaced by another Chief known as Dull Knife. Windy said he was an old Chief whose war bonnet was so long from his many battle victories that it dragged on the ground from horseback. Dull Knife led well organized charges at the scouts, who each time beat back the Indians. By the end of the first day Chief Dull Knife was dead too. By now half of the scouts were killed or wounded. Colonel Forsyth was shot in the leg and was commanding from his back in a ditch. Lt. Beecher died that day too. So did the only doctor.

"Comanche Jack and his friend were selected to slip through the Indian lines and try to reach Fort Wallace to bring help. They made it to Fort Wallace and returned with help eight days later. Those poor bastards lay in the sun for eight days with no food and almost no water. They were eating the dead animals to stay alive, but after the second day they were eating stinking rotten meat.

"I, for one, would rather push cows," Lippy finished his story.

Speck sat closest to Lippy, sweat beaded on his forehead. He had watched every word leave Lippy's mouth. "They're dead, aren't they? Windy and the others."

None of the boys by the fire had an answer. None were willing to give an answer, if they had one. The small group just began to break apart as one by one they filed away. Some going to take their turn riding herd, others simply headed to their bed roll. Each of them slept that night with a loaded rifle on their stomach.

CHAPTER THIRTY ONE

The morning sun had just begun to cast its tender rays on the bloodied bodies of men and horses when Buck and the men found the battle site. Buck had seen it all before, dead men scalped and stripped of their clothing, dead horses, their bodies punctuated with arrows, and ground covered with blood and spent shell casings. To Buck it was nothing new. But to the men who rode with Johnny Kirk, what they found ripped open their guts. Some sat their horses staring, mouths agape. Others slid from their saddles and stumbled mindlessly among the trampled and bloodied grass speechless, making meaningless motions with their arms. Others collapsed to their knees sobbing.

The beauty of the June morning made an incomprehensible contrast to the evidence that lay about them of their friends' final struggle. Light dew glistened on grass tips. Early morning songbirds performed at their finest, mixing nature's own with the cursing and damning of the overwhelmed troop.

"They didn't kill a god damn Indian," shouted one of the boys. He kicked the dirt and yanked the arrow from Windy's back.

"I reckon they gave 'em hell boys," Buck said, "Indians remove their dead from a battlefield so they can give 'em proper burial."

"I'll give 'em a god damn burial," Strayhorn let go a string of guttural cuss words. Strayhorn was a tough hombre. He had signed on with Johnny Kirk right before the trouble with Buster Kelly had started. He came up from Texas with a herd of longhorns soon after the Civil War and never went back. Story was he killed a man, son of a Judge, and had a price on his head. He'd never been known to lose a fight—fist or gun. A little over six feet tall, he usually stood out.

"Hold on, Strayhorn," Johnny said, "let's bury these boys first."

Not another word challenged the morning's stillness. They performed the solemn task of digging four graves in silence, save for the scratching sound of shovel against dirt and the early morning tune of a nearby songbird.

They gathered their friends, wrapped them in saddle blankets and placed them in the graves. No saddles remained to be buried with them. The Indians had stripped the horses as well as the men. They filled the graves then stumbled about gathering a few rocks for markers.

Johnny spoke a few words, remembering each man by name, then for each he told a short tale in a humorous vein. Windy was the hardest for Johnny, his voice broke often. Windy had told Johnny in detail of the day he lost his family in the Valley of the Saline River only a year earlier. Johnny had been trying hard to help Windy to forget and go on. "Perhaps," he said, "Windy is with his wife and son now."

Johnny turned to Strayhorn. "Take the boys and finish the job these men started. Gather the cows you can and return them. Buck and I will follow this trail. They didn't kill the herd. They stole cows. That means there's a village nearby. I aim to find it."

"I'm going with you John," Strayhorn protested.

"No, you're not. You'll do as I say or draw your pay. Gather that herd and return it and see that no more of my men get killed."

"I'll do it, but when the fighting starts you'll see I'm part of it."

Johnny sent a man back to camp to tell Luke Mason to start the roundup. It was best, he said, for everybody to get to work. It would be better to chase cows than to chase hate. He told him to have Luke make sure the men knew the Indians who did this would pay sorely. Finally Johnny Kirk and Buck Hawkins rode up the hill, following the trail of Indian ponies and a few cows.

The two made good time, the trail was simple. Buck was an experienced scout, and Johnny Kirk was "born in a saddle." From sign along the trail, Johnny estimated the Cheyenne pushed about 20 cows. Along the way, after following the trail for several hours, the two occasionally overtook a cow that had managed to slip away from the Cheyenne. On one occasion Johnny made a remark that he would be sure never to sign on any Cheyenne drovers.

Shortly after noon they crossed a wide, shallow stream. "They left the cows water here," Buck said, "they sure are taking their good old time. They have to know someone would come after 'em."

"Maybe not. Maybe they figure there's no one left to worry about."

"They didn't water the cows here. They left the cows! Look yonder, the whole damn bunch is right over there!" Buck pointed with his hat.

"I'll be. We must be worrying 'em more than I thought. Look here, they dropped the saddles too!"

"You bet. Most likely they had a rear scout. They're gonna hightail it for their village. Seems like they're headin' northeast of Denver City, up on the Platte most likely. Let's give these horses a drink and short break."

Buck was sure of himself and he knew it would be a long ride to the South Platte on horses already winded. He also knew they followed as few as five or six braves. After the horses rested a bit, Buck and Johnny pushed on. Even without the cows, the trail remained easy to follow. The Indians made no attempt to cover their tracks or in any way confuse their trackers. From all signs they were simply interested in reaching the safety of their village before being overtaken. All through the afternoon they pushed on, covering ground in a rapid trot.

Johnny pulled his horse to a stop. "Over there in the grass," he pointed to a rocky ravine, "I see something in there."

Buck searched the direction Johnny pointed. Sure enough, something or someone was hiding in the rocks. What didn't make sense to Buck was the lack of arrows flying their way.

"Get off your horse. Keep the horses between you and that ravine," Buck handed Johnny his horse and jerked his rifle. Johnny did as he was told and Buck dropped and crawled through the grass toward ravine. He was just about to level his sites on what he thought was a Cheyenne brave, when he realized it was in fact a brave. A dead brave.

"Come on over here Johnny, these boys are done killin'."

Wedged between the large rocks they found the bodies of five dead braves hastily covered with dried prairie grass. "They'll leave their dead behind if they're pushed hard enough," Buck explained. "They look for a crevice like this in rock to stuff them in. A lot of times they come back for them."

"I guess we're pushing hard enough."

"You bet, and we still have daylight, let's keep pushin'."

After a final look at the dead braves they mounted their weary horses, and urged them back into a steady trot. They trotted their horses as fast as they might, but now the trail proved more difficult.

Buck stopped and studied sign. "We have 'em worried alright, they're trying to hide their trail. Must be dragging blankets behind. See how most of the tracks are gone?"

"I do, and we're losing the sun. Let's stop for the night. Start out in the morning again, rather than lose the trail."

Buck agreed after some thought, subduing a well of anxiety over losing their quarry. They had traveled well past Denver City toward the South Platte. Buck felt certain he was correct and the Cheyenne village would be on the Platte. He was so certain he almost suggested they ride through the night, the hell with the trail. But the horses required rest. Better, he figured, to let them rest a few hours and push on in the morning with somewhat rested mounts.

They ran a cold camp, not that they had anything to burn anyway. They were in a totally treeless area of the plain, and buffalo were long gone from these parts so there were no chips. Just as well, Buck thought, even a small campfire could be seen for 50 miles. He hoped their quarry might stop for the night, and if they saw a fire they would not.

They took turns dozing through the night, resting on their saddle blankets using their saddles for pillows. They had no water for themselves or their horses. The only dinner was one very old piece of buffalo jerky Buck found deep in his saddlebag.

"I reckon the boys are having beef, biscuits, gravy and coffee at Soft Cloud's wagon by now," Buck said.

"Boy Howdy, a cup of coffee would do right now."

"Could be I have some in my saddlebag."

"As old as that jerky I'd believe."

"Ya know, I'm not sure that it was jerky. Maybe it was just an old piece of my saddlebag."

"Well, if it was I'll have another piece, I'm still hungry ... You and Tom been in your share of scrapes with Indians, I reckon."

"Been in a few, for sure."

"What was your plan for this bunch? By my calculation we might be outnumbered."

"Been outnumbered before. Couple of times."

"That's not much of a plan, Buck."

"Don't take much. You find 'em and fight 'em. Try not to get killed. But once we locate the village, if it's more than I figure we can handle, I'll make a run for Fort McPherson. My guess is it's less than a 100 miles."

"I don't believe that horse you're riding has a 100 miles left."

"I don't know, he's pretty stout. They have a way of surprisin' you sometimes ... when you need it most."

Saddling up while still almost too dark to see, they set out before it made sense. But they could no longer sit on their blankets and wait for the sun. At first they walked the horses, it was easier that way to follow the trail in the early morning shadows. Still on foot several hours later the trail led to trampled grass where their quarry must have spent the night.

"There's blood here. One must be wounded and slowing 'em down," Buck figured out loud. He examined the flattened grass and the small sheet of dried blood. He gazed out over the prairie, his eyes trained on the trail that led away from the campsite. The blood was not completely dry meaning they had recently set out. "Let's mount up. We're close now."

They put their horses in a slow lope, as the Cheyenne braves were no longer trying to hide their trail. Trailing became easy again so Buck pushed for speed. They continued for several hours at a good pace, following a trace that now headed due west. For over an hour the grade was steadily uphill and when they reached the summit they saw the Indians in the distance.

"Look out yonder, Johnny. Got a run in ya?"

"As much as you do, Army Scout!"

They took off at a hard gallop. The terrain between them and the Indians was level and their tired horses were up to the chase. The distance between the two parties lessened. Even though tired, it was obvious the horses from Johnny Kirk's ranch had more left than the Indian ponies.

The rear Indian scout soon saw them and the little band of Dog Soldiers pushed for more speed. But their weary ponies didn't have enough left to give, and the distance between them continued to shrink. The wounded brave fell from his mount, his horse ran with the others.

Buck pulled his horse to a rough stop, and flew from the saddle, buffalo rifle in hand, the butt of his rifle slammed into his shoulder, and the rifle thundered.

Johnny, caught off guard, flew by Buck. At the roar of the buffalo rifle Johnny's horse bolted, nearly unseating him. But he managed to regain control, turned his horse and was about to give Buck hell, when the rifle thundered again. Johnny looked toward the Indians in time to see a horse go down.

Before Johnny could react, or even comprehend, Buck fired again. Another Indian pony tumbled to the grass. Johnny froze, watching in amazement as Buck, back in the saddle, encouraged his horse with his reins.

It was not so much that Johnny asked his horse for speed as it was the horse itself, and he took after Buck like a shot, in hot pursuit of Buck's horse. The two braves still on horseback leaped from their ponies at a full gallop. Buck whipped his reins harder and faster screaming in his horse's ears, demanding the stout little horse find more speed. It did. But still the two Indians on foot managed to disappear.

Buck kept his horse at top speed in the direction where he last saw the two Cheyenne, before they vanished like dust on a breeze. When he passed their ponies, he slowed to look for a sign in the tall prairie grass that might betray the braves. But he found none. Nothing in the world is harder to do than to track a Cheyenne Dog Soldier on foot who wants to hide. For the moment he gave up the chase and trotted back to Johnny who was in the process of killing the two wounded horses.

"Two dead Indians here and one nearly dead," Johnny dropped his revolver back in its holster. "I'm guessing the first one to fall came this far with one of Windy's bullets in him, one of the others broke his neck in the fall, and I believe that fellow over there broke his back."

Buck went to the brave who crawled away using his arms alone. Johnny watched, somewhat taken back, as Buck kicked the brave over on his back. In addition to the war paint on the braves face, were the narrow eyes and clenched lips of hatred and rage.

Johnny heard Buck ask something of the brave, in what must have been Cheyenne. The Indian spit at Buck. Buck yanked his revolver and fired.

Johnny had seen men fight before; hell, he'd had his own share of gun battles with cattle thieves and other outlaws. But in all his life, he never witnessed a man so skilled and so cold-blooded before. With an apple sized lump in his throat he asked Buck what he wanted from the Indian.

"I asked him the location of his village."

CHAPTER THIRTY TWO

Johnny and Buck wasted an hour roaming through the prairie grass looking for sign of the two braves that had run away. They were unable to find a clear trail, but they did find enough sign to establish direction.

"I think we're on the southwest side of their village. Let's ride northeast and I'll wager we'll come over one of these summits and find a Cheyenne village tucked in the valley below."

"Let's ride then," Johnny said.

They started their weary but willing horses off at a fast trot but soon got off to walk the horses. Having no water and no promise of water until they reach the Platte, the horses needed a rest.

"We'll walk to the top of that summit, take a look around, and mount up again," Buck said.

The early afternoon sun beat on them and took its toll. Going without food or water for two days wore even the hardest man thin. They forced step after step and climbed ever upward for another hour, then Buck handed his horse to Johnny on a hunch, and crept to the crest. In the valley spread out before him lay a great village, nestled in the sand hills of the Platte. He slid back down to Johnny.

"The camp's over that ridge. Must be close to a 100 lodges, no wonder they wanted cows. There must be 400 or 500 Indians in that village. Probably close to 600 horses."

"Would this be one of those times you consider yourself outnumbered?" Johnny offered as much of a grin as his used-up body could give.

"Reckon so. My guess is Fort McPherson lays 60 miles east of here. Let's slip down to the bottom of the ravine and try to sneak out of here and get help. If they find us Johnny, we're in for a long day."

They led their horses to the bottom of the ravine they had just struggled to climb, their eyes on the ridge. At the bottom they mounted and started for the Fort. They forced their exhausted and lathered horses into a fast run.

For several hours they moved across the prairie in Fort McPherson's direction. Buck knew the area; he had scouted it in '66 with General Hancock. He knew the fort lay to their north. When he found a suitable gulch that traveled north-south he swung north.

"I think these boys are done in," Buck said. "We'd better walk."

"How far to the Fort? You Army Scouts sure seem to walk a lot more than cattlemen. I'm thinking I just might let the Indians kill me. I haven't walked this much in the last five years put together."

"Twenty-five miles give or take. If we're lucky we'll run into a patrol. And if we're real lucky they'll have water, and you might think about tradin' your boots for moccasin boots like these." Buck held his left leg high.

They walked head down, dead on their feet through the hottest part of the day, until Buck spotted half a dozen riders on the horizon. "Pretty small for a patrol, but I suppose we're about to find out. They've seen us! See 'em turning our direction?"

"Even if we start now, we don't have enough horse to outrun them. They're coming in an awful hurry aren't they?"

"Grab your horse, run after me." Buck turned and as fast as he could run and retraced their last steps. About a 100 yards back they had passed a rock ledge. They ran to the lowest side of the rock. Buck grabbed his Sharps, and Johnny his Winchester. They both slipped one rein through their gun belt. Through their sites they watched as the riders closed on them. It was a very long moment. Johnny heard Buck pull the hammer back on his Sharps, and he levered a shell into the chamber of his Winchester.

"When I give the word …" Buck said. But in the next instant he spun and pushed Johnny's Winchester up. "That's Cody, hold on."

Buck cupped his hands around his mouth, "Bill … Bill Cody … it's Buck Hawkins!"

Bill Cody and five Pawnee Army scouts pulled up.

"Buck Hawkins, my good man," Bill Cody shouted. "How is

it I might be of service to you this time?"

"We've been trailing a band of renegades for two days. They jumped some of Johnny's men and killed four on the prairie 60 or 70 miles south of Denver City, near Colorado Springs. Bill Cody, meet Johnny Kirk."

"Good to meet you sir," Cody greeted with a firm handshake. "You would be interested in settling the score I presume."

"As a matter of fact," Johnny said.

"I'm scouting this very moment for General Carr, who is leading the Fifth Cavalry. We are presently in pursuit of a large band of Cheyenne who have been causing havoc all summer. These are the very Cheyenne that massacred the settlers on the Saline. We have had a running battle with them for a number of weeks."

"We found 'em for you," Buck said, "Say, any of those Pawnee's have an extra water skin on them?"

Cody motioned to the Pawnee and two dismounted and offered their water skins. "Found them did you?"

"About 20 miles due west of here. Camped in the sands by the South Platte. Big village, Cody. Most of a 100 lodges, nearly 500 Cheyenne. Don't know how many braves."

"General Carr and the main body are five miles to our rear. Have your horses five miles left in them?"

"Most likely," Johnny said, ever proud of his horses.

General Carr and the Fifth Cavalry were not as far to the rear as Cody had expected. The General had pushed on in Cody's direction in a forced march. After racing back less than three miles they found the General and the Fifth. Cody led Buck and Johnny directly to General Carr.

"General, Sir, these gentlemen have found our quarry. Twenty miles to our west camped in the sands of the Platte. They say we shall find nearly 100 lodges and 500 Cheyenne."

"Thank you, gentlemen. Your names?"

"The tired looking cowboy there is a rancher named Johnny Kirk. The other fellow, whom you've never met but surely have heard of, is Army scout Buck Hawkins."

"Pleased to meet you Mr. Kirk. And Mr. Hawkins to what Regiment are you assigned at the moment?"

"Oh I'm afraid I'm retired from the scouting business," Buck explained. "You may have heard of my partner Tom Named by

Horse. We have a horse ranch about 60 miles south of Fort Laramie, 40 miles east of Cheyenne."

"I have heard of Tom Named by Horse. Quite a reputation you two enjoy. In fact, I believe Cody is mounted on one of your fine stallions at this very moment."

"I am, General, and he is half brother to the stallion I gave you when I returned from Denver City just a month ago."

"You breed fine horses, Mr. Hawkins. That stallion is my favorite mount. Give your tired horses to the boys in the rear. They'll lead them on. Select fresh mounts."

The column of nearly 250 cavalry troopers and fifty Pawnee scouts led by Bill Cody, and Buck Hawkins and Johnny Kirk departed for the sands south of the Platte.

At Cody's suggestion the General made a wide arc north. In that way the large column was least likely to be spotted by the Sioux that had been helping the Cheyenne evade General Carr for weeks already. The maneuver proved successful and they completely avoided detection.

A mile out of the village, the General called halt.

He ordered the men close ranks and when the buglers sounded charge the whole command shall attack. For just a moment the entire Fifth Cavalry sat atop the hill overlooking the village. Then General Carr barked "sound the charge." The Indians had gathered their horses and were apparently preparing to move the camp. Many of them were able to leap upon their ponies and flee the village, leaving behind all possessions.

Buck and Johnny charged down the hill alongside Cody. About 50 braves from the village charged the column on foot, only to be cut down.

In the dust and smoke Johnny lost sight of Buck, but managed to kill his share. Enough anyway to help take some of the sting out of Windy's and the other boys' deaths. He'd never seen anything like this mayhem, insanity. He and everyone else fired at anything that moved. And anything that didn't move they set on fire. Men, women and children were gunned down. Dogs, horses, and mules slaughtered.

So thick and black lay the smoke from powder and fire, targets were simply anything visible. Screaming and wailing of women mixed with crying children, yelping dogs, and screaming horses. War whoops from braves became less and less. Spinning his horse Johnny realized he was completely surrounded by young braves. None more than children armed with lances far too long for them. Nevertheless, they charged him, one managed to stab his horse in the chest. He shot the five dead, and fought his way to the edge of the village, shooting at such targets as presented themselves.

The most fierce and brutal fighting and killing was done by the Pawnee Scouts, hated enemies of the Cheyenne and the Sioux. The battle lasted less than an hour and the surviving Indians were chased miles away. General Carr ordered the Indian ponies gathered and driven back to his camp.

Some Sioux who had fled returned to the camp, and from the tree line fired at the soldiers. Johnny sat his horse, a changed man, and watched the battle. He had had his fill for one day.

Buck found Johnny and together they wandered a short distance from the camp where they dismounted and watched in silence as the soldiers gathered everything in the camp onto a great burn pile. Over a 100 lodges, hundreds of blankets, skins, buffalo robes, and over 100 dead Indians were set ablaze.

Small battles on the outskirts of camp began to die out. Soon only the sound of cracking and popping of the mountainous fire broke the eerie silence. Even the moans had ceased.

"Let's ride to the top," Buck told Johnny, "it stinks down here."

There they sat in the grass in the shade of their horses as the General's wagon train arrived. Troopers gathered more than two hundred prisoners including squaws and papooses and close to five hundred horses and mules and they started for the South Platte River, some eight miles away, to bivouac for the night.

In the morning, around a pleasant breakfast fire Buck and Johnny said their goodbyes to Bill Cody who promised to visit Tom and Buck before the year was out. By midmorning they left the camp behind, making tracks for a roundup south of Denver City, mounted on fresh Cavalry horses. They rode mostly in silence.

CHAPTER THIRTY THREE

When Jimmy returned to roundup camp with the news from Johnny Kirk, Luke Mason called all the boys together and sent word to bring the boys riding herd. He asked Soft Cloud to fix extra biscuits and boil plenty of coffee and sent word through camp they were to assemble near the chuckwagon and the long table. When everyone gathered Luke stood and called for quiet.

"Every man here knows something terrible has happened. Windy, Jack, Harry, and Pete were all killed by Cheyenne."

Everyone started talking at once; they knew it was true, they already knew it had happened. Word had raced through camp like water down a gully after a cloudburst. After several attempts to re-establish order, Luke fired his revolver.

"They were buried out there in the valley. We pray they're at peace."

Again the camp erupted in voice. Tom sat on an overturned bucket holding Soft Cloud and Hawk on his lap. He knew how she always wrestled with her emotions and fears at times like this. He knew, for her, with loyalties and love rooted on both sides of the battlefield, times like these tore at her heart. Tom also knew this time could be dangerous. He slid his revolver from its holster so gently, even though she sat on his lap, Soft Cloud never noticed.

"Jimmy brought word that Johnny and Buck took out after those that did it." Luke continued.

"What's them two gonna do against a whole tribe of murderin' Indians?"

Tom felt Soft Cloud harden at the question. He tightened his hold and kissed her cheek, and bounced his knee for Hawk.

"I reckon they'll figure out what to do," Luke went on. "Most of you got to meet Buck and you know he's an experienced Army scout. I'm sure he'll have a trick or two he can play on those Indians.

"Strayhorn and the others are working on gatherin' those cows again and will return 'em to their ranches. Should be back here in a day or two.

"The important thing today is Johnny wants us to get back to work. Now Soft Cloud and Tom have some chow ready. Get a plate, then saddle up."

"I ain't eatin' no food cooked by no Indian!" One fellow shouted. A sentiment soon echoed by several more.

"Yeah," another shouted, "we want us a white cook!"

Tom was about to react, but was headed off by Luke Mason who jumped atop the long table and fired. "Anybody feel that way, see Donovan and draw your pay."

As Luke stepped down he tipped his hat to Soft Cloud. But Tom watched as eight men walked to Donovan to draw their pay.

It didn't take long for those that stayed to get their beans, biscuits and coffee. Before long the camp grew nearly peaceful again, although the air of discomfort had not yet totally evaporated. Tom wanted to ride roundup but chose to stay close to Soft Cloud. He helped spoon beans, and watched as one by one they filed past Luke and were told what part of the range to work.

By the time Tom and Soft Cloud had all the tin plates washed and stacked to dry, the only ones to remain in camp were a few cowboys who had stayed behind to relieve those now on herd, and Luke, Mr. and Mrs. Donovan, Beverly and he and Soft Cloud.

Soft Cloud and Tom sat together at the long table discussing whether or not they should leave for home. Buck could follow later. Soft Cloud seemed to be holding up better than Tom. She told him how her life had been filled with times like these. As a child growing up she often watched her mother, the only white woman in a village of over 1,000 Sioux, suffer the stares of the many Sioux women who would not befriend her. Her brothers had grown to be two of the fiercest warriors in Red Cloud's village, honed that way by constantly defending their little sister.

"I have watched often," she said, "as you and Buck walked from the sod cabin to the horses in the corral so you could tell each other your stories and relive your many battles. Battles that were sometimes against my people.

"I know, dear husband, this troubles you deeply. It is simply who we are. It is who we are and what makes us love each other so."

They held hands across the table. Soft Cloud gazed lovingly into Tom's blue eyes. Those blue eyes that stung like fire pits as he felt tears fill the corners and dribble over to splash on the table. So entranced with each other were they, they never noticed Beverly and Hawk.

"I apologize for the actions of the men," Beverly said.

Tom turned her way but could not find his voice.

Soft Cloud patted Beverly's arm. "We understand. My grandfather and mother have explained many things to me. I … we understand things will always be difficult. My grandfather watched for many years as my mother and father endured the everyday hardships in our own village which come from Sioux marrying white.

"When Tom and I fell in love and Tom spoke to my grandfather for his blessing, he and other chiefs in the village counseled us for many days."

Tom recalled the day he knew he would take Soft Cloud as his wife. He had just returned from Ogallala. Buck lay in the sod cabin recovering from his wounds and Soft Cloud had been down by the stream. He remembered how the dogs knocked him to the ground and wanted to play and wrestle. But he tossed them aside and swept Soft Cloud from the ground and for the first time told her he loved her. He told her he loved her and would have her for his wife. "Yes! Yes I will be your wife!" She shouted in his ear. Tom had never been happier. He remembered now, sitting at this long table, looking at this lovely woman who bore him his fine son, how wonderful, powerful that feeling of love is.

"Oh Soft Cloud," Beverly blurted, "tell us of your wedding, how do Indians, I mean, I'm sorry. What are the customs of the Sioux, when they marry?"

Soft Cloud turned, gathered her son in her arms and pulled him onto her lap.

"Our people are Oglala Lakota Sioux," she began. "We are the proudest of all the Sioux. We have very strong customs and even though my mother was white, my father was the son of one of the greatest chiefs of all Sioux nations, Chief Red Cloud. My father was dead by the time we were to marry, so it was necessary for poor Tom to discuss his plans with my grandfather.

"Of all his grandchildren, Red Cloud has always loved me best. He knew my brothers, both strong warriors, would be able take care of themselves even though half white. But he worried so about me. When I was a child he spent as many evenings in my mother's lodge as he did his own. I remember many, many nights going to sleep in my mother's arms listening to tales of the old ones told as only Red Cloud could tell them. He has a wonderful way of speaking.

"Tom had already won great favor in my grandfather's eyes. He had done the challenging biddings of my grandfather with total success and had proved himself to be a brave and loyal friend of the Sioux. But nevertheless I was young and I was Red Cloud's only granddaughter."

Tom tried hard to control his thoughts. He trained his mind on thoughts of the wedding and the ceremonies. He would not allow thoughts of Tall Dog or Black Feather to steal his mind. Rather he watched Soft Cloud's delicate lips as she told the tale of those troubled and confusing, but wonderful days, of their wedding.

"Weren't you afraid to ask such a powerful man as Red Cloud for his only granddaughter to be your wife?" Mrs. Donovan's voice rang with anticipation. Soft Cloud's story had been so engrossing that until now, no one noticed Mr. and Mrs. Donovan had joined them at the table.

"No ... I never thought I should be afraid. I understood I must do the things Still Water told me if I wanted to wed her daughter."

"What did Red Cloud say the first time you went to him?" Donovan fought back a man-sized chuckle.

"He said nothing. He knocked me from the log I sat on and stood over me. I remember thinking he would to kill me right there in front of his lodge and no one could help me. I remember thinking that it would be wrong for me to strike out in my own defense. So, I closed my eyes and waited for his lance to pierce my heart. But as I lay there with my eyes closed, waiting, I heard Iron Shell laugh."

Everyone at the table heard the giggles Soft Cloud tried hard to suppress. But it was Donovan again that spoke, "Did Iron Shell save you?"

"Nope, just watched. I didn't know that it was wrong for me to fall from the log. Red Cloud had been so surprised by my question that he had struck me with his lance with all his power. I know now the blow was intended to be a mock blow, intended to inflict a little pain, but not break ribs like it did."

"Poor Tom," Soft Cloud laughed, "all during a mock battle the broken ribs hurt so much he could barely run. My uncles taunted him so. I remember them telling me they expected lots of nieces and nephews, because such a poor runner could never escape me."

"Mock battles?" Beverly's eyes danced.

"It is our custom that families of the wife to gather on a hillside, and the families of the husband must charge the hill and capture the bride. Since Tom had no family he was allowed to select braves from within the village. And Tom, being as timid as he was then, was afraid to ask advice."

Tom remembered that day, a very, very hot day. And the hill selected was very steep. His ribs hurt so badly he nearly had to be carried up the hill.

"While the braves he selected were young like him, few had the experience of my uncles. And since two of them were forced to assist Tom, they were outnumbered when they reached my blanket. They were quickly driven back. Even though the blows from unstrung bows were supposed to be light, several braves spent that night licking their wounds," Soft Cloud continued with the tale, pride glowing in her eyes.

"How did the wounded Tom capture his wife to be?" Mrs. Donovan only pretended to hide her amusement.

"Two of my braves made it to Soft Cloud's blanket carrying me the last 50 yards. As a boy I had become quite handy with the long bullwhip. I realized her uncles were dealing blows to my braves many times with all their force, so I used my long bullwhip to the best of my ability. When I reached Soft Cloud's blanket I jumped to my feet and I began to whip her uncles. For some, the scars of my whip have been badges of honor! Holding them off with stinging blows I wrapped Soft Cloud in her blanket and carried her from her hilltop to my waiting horses."

"And what did you do with the woman you captured that was not yet your wife?" Mrs. Donovan wanted to know.

Soft Cloud took up the tale. "The wife to be must be returned to her family's lodge where she will spend three days and three nights being counseled by her mother and other mothers chosen by a tribal elder. The husband to be must spend those days being counseled by his father, and three fathers chosen by tribal elders. Since Tom had no family, my grandfather served as his father.

"At the end of three days it is believed the young man and young woman have gained enough knowledge to begin their life's journey together. The marriage ceremony is planned for the morning after the third night."

"We must hear about your marriage ceremony," Beverly insisted.

"It is expected that when a man takes a woman for his wife that they remain married until separated by death," Soft Cloud began. "A Sioux marriage ceremony is attended by the entire village and often Lakota from other villages are welcomed. Because Red Cloud is my grandfather, and because Tom had such a reputation, our ceremony was attended by over 4,000 Sioux! It was the largest gathering of Lakota in many summers. I remember my mother telling me that braves had hunted for one week and killed more than 100 buffalo for our wedding feast."

"How I would have loved to see that," Beverly nearly swooned.

Tom chuckled. "Buck was so worried by the great numbers of Sioux gathering together, he took a dispatch to Fort Laramie to General Sturgis explaining it was a peaceful gathering."

"In one week our village grew from 500 lodges and 1,000 people, to over 1,000 lodges and 4,000 people. It took almost half a day to ride around the camp!" Soft Cloud waved her arms in a wide arc, indicating the grand scale.

Tom nodded and grinned. "The grasslands surrounding Red Cloud's village held more than 3,000 Sioux ponies. When General Sturgis and his wife, Bill Cody, Private Cole, Private Cooper, Smitty and the others, returned from Fort Laramie with Buck, General Sturgis said they could see the lodges and horses from over half a day away."

"All those people attended your marriage ceremony?" Mrs. Donovan searched Soft Cloud's face in awe.

"Almost every one. Tom and I were seated on a blanket-covered log. On either side of us sat two tribal elders. There was also a blanket-covered log before us, on which sat four more tribal elders. A circle of our closest friends and families surrounded us. More distant friends and family made the next circle. And circles keep going, on and on, until everyone who wishes to be part of the ceremony is standing in the circle. Our ceremony had 30 circles.

"When everyone is quiet the ceremony begins. One by one each elder is to ask up to four questions of each of us. If an elder's question is answered incorrectly the correct answer is given, and explained. If an elder has heard his question asked, he may ask less than four questions. But each elder must ask at least one question."

"What happens after all the questions are answered?" Luke Mason had joined the table.

"The Lakota wedding prayer is read," Soft Cloud said. "And when the selected elder has completed reading the wedding prayer, we are allowed to embrace. Then we hold the Sacred Pipe, and our hands are bound together in red cloth. We then address the circle and tell them we now belong to each other, and are bound together for life. A large crowd, as you may guess, followed Tom and me as we were led to our wedding lodge where we were left alone for the night. All that night and for three days after everyone feasted and celebrated our marriage."

"What a marvelous ceremony," Beverly said, "Johnny and I were married by a judge in a saloon in Denver City."

"So Bill Cody was at your wedding," Luke Mason said.

"It is possible had he not been, I would've never scaled the summit of Soft Cloud's hill. He helped to drag the braves who carried me over the top," Tom told a surprised Luke Mason.

"I thought Bill Cody was a scout for the Army and hated Indians," Luke questioned.

"He was and is," Tom said, "as I have been, and Buck, too. And none of us scorn the tribes of the plains. It may be hard to understand, Luke. It's hard for me to understand. Why do we fight each other? Why do the Sioux fight the Crow? Is it so different than fighting the dishonest sheriff? Is it so different than fighting cattle thieves? Is it so different than the War Between the States? I don't know these answers."

A heavy feeling began to settle over those at the table. All there suffered through several long seconds of silence. It was Donovan who asked a more lighthearted question: "I've always heard a brave must pay for his wife."

"Yes, sir," Tom said, "and Red Cloud's price was 200

horses."

Luke leaned to look squarely at Tom, and with a big grin on his face he said, "I suppose you went to the ceremony with your 200 horses."

"Not exactly. You can marry a Sioux woman before you pay for her. But she must stay in her mother's lodge until the debt is satisfied. But you see, I had a little secret even Red Cloud didn't know. Iron Shell had been to the sod cabin when Soft Cloud and I had first begun to fix it up, before we were married. Iron Shell brought us four dogs for protection and while he was there he promised he would bring enough braves to help with my first horse gathering."

"So Red Cloud's own braves helped you gather the horses to pay for his granddaughter?" Donovan asked.

Tom looked across the table, his head cocked and wearing a broad smile, "Sure enough."

"What a grand story," Mrs. Donovan clapped her hands. "I'm so glad you were willing to tell us. I only regret I wasn't part of it."

Luke left the table to check with the boys who rode in, and as he stepped away he turned to Tom, "I would've liked to help you up that hill."

"Just how large is your ranch, Tom?" Mrs. Donovan asked.

"I really couldn't say. I don't know how to measure such things. It covers a lot of territory though."

"We had our ranch surveyed by railroad engineers," Mrs. Donovan continued.

"Well," Tom squeezed Soft Cloud's hand. "We had ours laid out by Red Cloud himself. From the lands of the Lakota Sioux winter grounds."

"What does that mean?" Beverly asked.

"On the southern boundary of the Lakota Sioux territory lay some of the most beautiful land south of the Platte. Want the story of when Red Cloud gave us our ranch?"

Beverly leaned in on the table and her eyes danced, "PLEASE tell us!"

Luke had returned and took a seat across from Tom and Soft Cloud with the Donovan's. Beverly sat next to Tom along with several cowboys who had just come into camp.

"One week after our wedding ceremony," Tom began, "with

the help of Iron Shell and 30 braves, we had gathered close to 400 wild mustangs. It was necessary, Iron Shell had told me, to have more than the number Red Cloud had requested so he may choose the very finest of my ponies. Iron Shell sent a messenger to Red Cloud's village that we had the ponies gathered and he should come and select those he would have.

"The next morning Red Cloud, along with four other chiefs, all wearing their long headdresses, rode to our ranch. Spotted Tail, Big Mouth, Red Iron, and Low Dog rode with pride along with about 200 Sioux braves.

"The four chiefs rode a slow circle around our gathered ponies. They took a very long time. I watched from the yard of my sod cabin as the chiefs rode away from the herd to the top of a hill on the prairie. They had a long council. At the end of their council, I saw Red Cloud throw a signal to the braves.

"They kicked their ponies into a fast trot and soon circled the entire herd. I knew then the price for Soft Cloud had gone from 200 ponies to 400. I watched as the entire herd was driven away to Red Cloud's village.

"Lucky for me my own horses, including Thunder, were in the corral. Soon Red Cloud and the chiefs came back to my cabin and Red Cloud rode to me.

"He told me that he was honored for me to have Soft Cloud as my bride. He said, as he had told me weeks before, I would always be safe on the land at the mud lodge. This he had promised me for the things I had done, which he had asked of me. He told me he took 200 horses for Soft Cloud, and 200 more to pay the four chiefs for the right to give me the land and their word that Soft Cloud and her husband would always be safe from all Sioux and Cheyenne.

"He told me although the Sioux do not own land to give he knew the white man believed they could own the land. He knew the white man made marks on the earth and that these marks told other white men this was their land. He said I should gather a horse and such things as I would need for a journey and that he, Spotted Tail, Low Dog, Big Mouth, and Red Iron would take me to the boundaries of the land that they would give to Soft Cloud and her husband.

"I will never forget those important but troubling words, 'This land they do not give from the Sioux for the Sioux can own no land. Only the Grandfather Mystery owns the land. The marks we will make will prove to greedy white men this land belongs to you. I have promised these four chiefs we will continue to visit this land to hunt and perhaps make winter village. I have promised these four chiefs you will do nothing to bring harm to us on this land. But this land from the banks of Little Bear Creek to the Walls of Buffalo Ridge, along the banks of the powerful Squaw Run River, and all that lay between, shall belong to you and my granddaughter Soft Cloud. No Sioux, no Cheyenne, no Arapahoe, no Kiowa will drive you from this land. And when we have made our marks along Little Bear Creek and at the base of the Walls of Buffalo Ridge and along the banks of Squaw Run River, no white man will drive you from this land. For this is your land for as long as the moon moves through the sky.'"

"That sounds like an awful lot of territory," Luke said.

"What was it like to be all alone with four chiefs?" Mrs. Donovan asked.

Tom shot a quick glance toward Soft Cloud to see her reaction to the question, as he expected she was smiling a jolly smile for she knew what an uncomfortable time that trip had been. "It took us two weeks to ride the boundaries of the land Red Cloud gave us."

"Two weeks?" Luke blurted, "It must be thousands of acres!"

"Like I said, I don't know about such things. But the journey from the sod cabin, along Little Bear Creek to the Walls of Buffalo Ridge, took three days. The first night is when I realized I was the only hunter. Sioux Chiefs direct things such as battles and hunts, so the responsibility of providing game or other food fell only to me.

"We had set out with the ponies they rode and one pony dragging a travois loaded with a lodge and personal belongings of the chiefs. My belongings fit in the saddle bags on Thunder. Fortunately, I had taken my buffalo rifle and ammunition.

"Each night as we made camp, I built a fire. Next I'd build the lodge. Then I'd hunt, and finally cook."

"You poor thing," Beverly mused, "all by yourself?"

"Red Cloud would help set the lodge, but that was all. Each morning just before we broke camp Red Cloud himself would build a stone monument, marking the spot as the westernmost boundary of my ranch.

"The evening of the third day we were on the sandy banks of Little Bear Creek in the shadow of the Walls of Buffalo Ridge. We camped on the very ground that was the site of the Lieutenant Harris massacre just one year before. I could see the graves of the Lieutenant and his men from our campfire.

"Around the fire that evening, Red Cloud, whose English had been improving, told the tale of Walls of Buffalo Ridge. The story tells of a time long before white man, long before horses, when their Sioux ancestors hunted buffalo with dogs, women, children and braves young and old. Sometimes it would take days to gather a large number of buffalo. They formed a circle that sometimes stretched for miles around, and banging drums and shields, closed the circle ever tighter until finally the terrified buffalo went over the cliffs, crashing to their deaths on the very sands where we now camped. This was the only way they knew to gather enough food and robes for the winter.

"I remember as he spoke I looked up to the top of the 500-foot wall. It rose from the sands of Little Bear Creek straight as a tree trunk, but five times as high.

"When he finished his story of the old buffalo hunts, it was Red Iron who had a story to tell. He told us the story of White Buffalo Woman. Want to hear the story of White Buffalo Woman?"

"I think we would all like to hear it," Mrs. Donovan answered.

Tom looked to Soft Cloud, suggesting she tell the tale. "One day long, long ago," she began, "two young braves walked, out searching for food. There were no buffalo then. And they came upon a beautiful Sioux maiden. She stood on the trail ahead of them and one brave unable to control his thoughts had thoughts of what he would like to do with this girl. She called him toward her.

"The second brave watched in fear, as a great dust cloud spun up from the ground completely hiding the brave and the beautiful girl. When the dust cleared, only the beautiful girl remained, and a pile of bones that once was the brave who had the bad thoughts.

"To the second brave, who had behaved rightly, she said, 'I bring good and holy things to your nation. Go tell the people to prepare for my arrival. Build a Medicine Lodge of 24 poles for my coming.'

"When the terrified young brave told his Chief his story, something caused the Chief to believe right away it was true. So Chief Standing Hollow Horn demanded everything be made ready. The large medicine lodge was built, taking four days. On the fourth day

White Buffalo Woman approached, carrying a large bundle. The chief invited her into the medicine lodge. She was pleased and invited the people inside. She waited while a sacred altar of red earth was made in the center. She laid her bundle upon the altar and rolled it open. Then she removed "the Sacred Pipe". She held the pipe up so all could see, the stem in her right hand, the bowl in her left, and so the pipe has been held ever since.

"She filled the pipe with red willow bark tobacco and she lit it. She walked four times around the lodge. 'This represents life's circle without end,' she said. The smoke rising from the pipe was 'the living breath of the Great Grandfather Mystery' she told them.

"She then taught our ancestors how to pray. She taught them the correct words and correct gestures. She taught them to pray and sing her songs and to lift the pipe toward the Sky toward Grandfather and down toward the Earth toward Grandmother and then to all four directions of the Universe.

"With this holy pipe, you will pray with your feet resting upon the earth and the pipe smoke reaching into the sky,' she told them. Your body is the bridge between the Sacred Beneath and the Sacred Above, for with this pipe you are one with, the two-legged, the four-legged, the winged ones, the trees, and the grasses. Together all are related, all are one family, the pipe holds all together.

"The bowl of the pipe represents the buffalo, who you do not yet know. You will know him today. I will show him to you. You will find your brother the buffalo all over your lands. For me, he will give himself to you, so that you will have all that you need. Your brother, the Sacred Buffalo, will give to you food from his flesh and shelter and robes from his skin. And tools from his bones. The buffalo represents the universe and all four directions, for the buffalo stands on four legs. The Circle of Life, we call the Sacred Hoop, will end when all the hair and legs of the great buffalo are gone.

"The wooden stem of the pipe stands for all that grows on the earth. Twelve eagle Feathers hanging from the stem are from the Great Spirit's messenger.

"White Buffalo Woman told the women it was the work of their hands and the fruit of their bodies that kept the people alive. 'You are from Mother Earth.' she told them. 'It is the sacred pipe that binds men and women together in a circle of love. Men shall carve the bowl and men shall make the stem. Women are to decorate it with bands of colored porcupine quills. When a man takes a wife, they shall hold the pipe at the same time and allow a red cloth to be wound round their hands, tying them together for life.'

"Then she spoke to the children. She told them they were the coming generation and they were the precious ones and they must listen to their parents and one day they would hold this pipe and smoke it and pray with it.

"Then she spoke to all the people again, telling them to remember the pipe is very sacred. She said to respect it and it will take you to the end of the trail. She said the four ages of creation are in me; I am the four ages. I shall come back to you.

"They watched as she walked away in the same direction from which she had come. Walking into the red ball of the setting sun. She stopped and rolled over four times. The first time she turned into a black buffalo, the second into a brown one, the third into a red one, and finally, the fourth time she rolled over she turned into a white female buffalo calf. In this way she showed us she knows all races.

"The White Buffalo Woman disappeared over the horizon. Sometime she might come back. As soon as she had vanished, buffalo in great herds appeared, allowing themselves to be killed so that people might survive. And from that day on our relations, the buffalo, give us all that we need. Meat for our food, their hides for our clothes and our lodges and even their bones for many tools."

When Soft Cloud finished her story, no one could speak. Tom watched Beverly wipe the tears from her eyes, as did Mrs. Donovan. He noticed the cowhands seated around the table had listened intently to his wife speak. He noticed too, they also had wet eyes. Donovan had found Mrs. Donovan's hand and cradled it between his.

"That is such a marvelous story," Mrs. Donovan said, "I am simply overwhelmed. Perhaps more people should be told that story."

"It is the story that tells of our strongest beliefs," Soft Cloud explained.

"We sure are all getting quite an education," Mason said.

"Yes, we are, and I thank you for it, Soft Cloud," Donovan agreed.

"Just in case anyone is still interested in the rest of my story,"

Tom said, "the next morning after I had everything gathered and loaded on the travois we left Walls of Buffalo Ridge and started across the prairie for the river of Squaw Run.

"The distance between Walls of Buffalo Bridge and Squaw Run River was another three days. The next morning as we prepared to leave camp, Red Cloud made a monument of rock to create the Northern boundary of my ranch. He then led me the highest ridge overlooking a beautiful meadow. It was bordered on the north and west by the descending walls of Buffalo Ridge. To the east it touched the wide Squaw Run River. In the grassland below us grazed a herd of at least a 1,000 buffalo. 'Those buffalo are for you to watch over,' he told me, 'You must never let them disappear from this grazing land. You must allow no buffalo killers on this land.' I accepted the honor of protecting that herd and Red Cloud was satisfied so we moved on.

"On the morning of the seventh day we turned our direction south along Squaw Run River. We traveled along the river for four days and again each morning as we departed camp, Red Cloud made a stone monument indicating the most Eastern boundary of the ranch.

"On the twelfth day of our journey our direction became due west. It was the evening of the twelfth day that we had visitors. I had just finished erecting the lodge for the Chiefs and had an antelope roasting on the fire. Chief Big Mouth was taking his turn at storytelling. Chief Red Cloud was translating with bits of English and lots of sign. He was telling the tale of a battle against a band of Ute. Red Cloud had chased a Ute brave on a wounded horse into a river. When the Ute fell from his horse into the river, Red Cloud pushed his pony into the deep water and snatched up the warrior by his hair, removed his scalp with one swipe of his tomahawk, and let the yelping brave fall back into the water. His status as a brave and fearless warrior was gained that day at the age of 14!

"Big Mouth had just finished his story when we heard approaching horses. It turned out to be three scouts for the Union Pacific Railroad. When they rode into our camp they were very nervous. I jumped to my feet, hand on my revolver, not quite knowing whether or not I needed to defend myself and my troop.

"The Chiefs sat motionless and showed no interest in the three men. I went to greet them. The man on the lead horse asked me why there was such a gathering of Indian lodges not far from us in the west. I explained to him that they had gathered for the wedding of Red Cloud's granddaughter whom I married.

"He was a good man and offered me sincere congratulations; his two comrades were more interested in the small circle of Chiefs. I introduced them to Red Cloud, who did not rise from his blanket. They said there would be a line of the railroad coming through the territory in that general area.

"I further told them they were on my land and should the railroad have any further business they would need to seek me out at my house where they had seen the lodges. I made sure they knew my name and I watched as one of them recorded it and the general location in his notebook. I invited them to stay and have roast antelope, but they weren't the type of men that enjoyed the company of Indians.

"For two more days we followed along the ridge of a small plateau that ran East-West. On the morning of the sixteenth day we were back at the sod cabin. I noticed then Soft Cloud had moved from her mother's lodge to our sod cabin. Her mother had erected her lodge in the yard by the well.

"With very little ceremony, the four Chiefs said their goodbyes and departed for Red Cloud's village, some 20 miles to our south. Many of the visiting Sioux had already gone, as well as General Sturgis, Bill Cody and the others from the Fort."

After speaking for such a long time, Tom hugged Soft Cloud and said, "I have very fond memories of that night, our first wedding night in our little sod cabin."

"Have you ever calculated the size of your ranch?" Luke Mason asked.

"Later that month Soft Cloud and I retraced the journey I had made with the four Chiefs. I estimated the distance around our ranch to be more than one hundred miles."

"That is some ranch, Tom," Donovan said. "You've got room for some cattle on that ranch."

"Well, we work a horse ranch. Takes a lot of time to gather and train quality horses. Maybe in the future we can run some cows."

"If that day comes, be sure to let me stock you with some of my finest," Donovan offered.

CHAPTER THIRTY FOUR

Three days later Tom, Buck, Soft Cloud, and Hawk left the roundup camp and headed for home. Tom and Buck were able to stuff three of the large wall tents in their chuckwagon. Tom drove the stately carriage Donovan gave them pulled by the matching white mares while Buck drove the chuckwagon. Happy hearts and pleasant thoughts ruled that day. The goodbyes had been many and emotional as many new friendships had begun. Plans had been made to see each other soon and Buck promised to come back as soon as possible with 20 fine horses for Johnny Kirk. They had gathered over 2,000 cattle since the roundup began and Donovan guessed they had another week of work.

"See you all next year at the Denver City horse auction," Tom guaranteed.

As he drove the carriage across the dusty prairie following Buck and the chuckwagon, he pondered the times. What was to come, he wondered. He himself, along with his friend Buck, had fought against and killed many Sioux, Cheyenne, and Arapaho. They had even fought that long and horrible day on the Bozeman Trail against Red Cloud himself, his own wife's grandfather. And Soft Cloud's father, Tall Dog—he'd killed him as well. How many battles were yet to come?

There had been a few more uncomfortable moments for Tom and Soft Cloud when Johnny and Buck told of the battle of Summit Springs. Tom had met Dull Knife and Pile of Bones in Red Cloud's village. They had been killed at Summit Springs. Tom also knew Powder Face and Chief Tall Bull. They too died that day.

All Tom yearned for was to raise and sell horses. He wanted

to live peacefully on his ranch with Soft Cloud and bring up young Hawk. He wanted to teach him to become one of the very finest horsemen that ever sat a horse.

"Good place for camp, I reckon," Buck called out.

"I wasn't really thinking about camp," Tom said, "looks fine to me."

Tom stopped the carriage beside the stream and helped Soft Cloud and Hawk down. They had some fresh beef and in no time Soft Cloud had a fine fire, beef roasted and coffee boiling. Nearly a custom now, Hawk played on a blanket with his father. They watched Soft Cloud pour hot coffee into tin cups and slice generous portions of beef for each of them.

"You reckon ol' Cole is worried about getting married?" Buck stuffed his mouth with hot beef.

"I would hope he was excited," Soft Cloud said, "I know I can hardly wait."

"Reckon they'll be an awful lot of people at the Miller place," Buck said.

"I hope so, it should be a grand time."

They looked to Tom for comment, but found him and Hawk sound asleep.

"I reckon Tom don't have an opinion," Buck observed.

"Do you think we can get the new house built before winter weather?" Soft Cloud asked Buck.

"Fort Laramie's saw mill settlement isn't that far from the Miller's, I'll go straight there when we get back and place the lumber order. If we can have the timbers and boards by August's end, we'll have a true shot at beatin' winter."

"Oh, how I would love that ... a two-story board house with wood floors and real windows."

"Liked the Donovan house, did you?"

Soft Cloud could only smile.

"It'll take some time to have a house as fine as the Donovan house, but we'll sure get a start on it this year. I can promise you that."

****

After three days of easy driving, the small troop crossed the last rise on the prairie, and the little sod cabin, barn and corrals came into sight. "Ye haw!" bellowed Buck, "we're back home, and that little mud house looks great to me. You'll excuse me if I make a dash for the house!" That tired old chuckwagon bounced a jig as the startled mules took off at a gallop.

Tom and Soft Cloud smiled and laughed, Tom stood in the seat and waved his hat as Buck hurried the mules faster. Down the hill they dashed, great puffs of dust exploded with every stride. Tom was glad Thunder and Diablo were tied to the carriage and not the chuckwagon.

Still miles away, Tom saw Iron Shell grab a pony and head their way. Soon Lone Feather and Coop rode toward them. Tom hurried the mares and they bounced along down the hill. Hawk stood in the seat and hooted and hollered as loud as his little voice would allow while Soft Cloud clung to both him and the rail on the carriage.

Lone Feather overtook Iron Shell and flew by Buck and the chuckwagon. He charged toward the carriage and at the last second he veered by the mares. Using the skills he possessed as a Sioux warrior, he stormed the carriage, snatched Hawk from the clinging arms of his mother, and with a great war whoop, galloped away with his prisoner.

Tom tossed the reins to Soft Cloud, jumped from the carriage, and cut Thunder free from the rear, swung up on the black stallion's back and raced after the pretend abductor. Guiding Thunder with only the severed rope and his legs, he turned him loose. "Go, Thunder, Go!" Tom shouted and urged Thunder on. But Lone Feather and his little pony had too great a lead. And while Thunder gave a valiant chase, he could not overtake Lone Feather's tough little pony. Lone Feather had reached Still Water and handed her Hawk before Thunder came sliding to a dusty stop in the front yard.

Later that night as they sat around the campfire, Tom took Hawk's hand and pointed to the North Star. "When I was a boy, each night before I went to sleep on the prairie I would try to find the North Star. Tomorrow night, let's see if you can find it."

CHAPTER THIRTY FIVE

The morning of the wedding had arrived. The Miller farm had never seen so much activity. Mrs. Miller hurried about like a nervous hen looking for her chicks. Buck sat on the front porch, feet on the rail, chair rocked back, and puffed a cigar. It had been some time since he had been able to enjoy such a moment. It could not help but remind him of the mornings at Fort Laramie sitting on old Bedlam's porch watching the ladies on parade. Watching Mrs. Harris …

Tom found it necessary to bring "at least one large tent" and Buck thoroughly enjoyed watching the show as Tom, Chuck, and Sam struggled to set it up. The wind had not been as cooperative as it might be and several times he was sure the men would be blown away on the large canvas walls.

Nearly half the families from the saw mill settlement had made the journey to share in the festivities. The two ladies who operated the eating establishment known as "Good Eats" had insisted on preparing the food. They had a fine fire pit in operation, and a 200-pound hog had volunteered to be a key participant in the ceremonies.

"Keep your eyes on the prairie as you work, men," Mrs. Miller called. "I don't understand why Reverend White has not arrived."

Tables and chairs filled the yard between the porch and Tom's tent. Mrs. Miller, Soft Cloud and Hannah spent the day before stringing homemade garland from the porch to the trees.

Yessiree, Buck thought, this place looks ready for a wedding. He stole a glance in the direction of Mrs. Harris's grave. For just a brief instant he allowed his mind drift back to that winter night four years ago when he rode all night fighting four feet of blowing snow to bring her here to rest. The memories had faded, just a little, but the pain ... no the pain had not yet lost any of its brittle edge.

"Come on now, Buck," Tom hollered, "come out here and take hold of one of these ropes. We need an extra set of hands."

Jerked back into the present, Buck bounded down the steps, "I reckon I can tame that canvas for you boys!"

With Buck's extra hands they secured the tent in short order, and Mr. Miller, Tom, and Buck arranged tables under it. All sat ready ahead of schedule for the big moment.

"I wonder where Reverend White is," Mrs. Miller worried to Soft Cloud, "he should have been here hours ago."

"You don't reckon Cole paid him not to show, do ya?" Buck taunted.

"Speaking of Cole," Tom looked around, "anyone seen him in the last hour?"

"He was in the barn, 'bout an hour ago when I fed the cow," Chuck said.

"What was he doing in the barn?"

"I think he was hidin'," Chuck flashed a devious grin.

Tom and Buck tiptoed to the barn and peaked through the window. Sure enough in the dark shadows there sat Cole. He appeared to be whacking away at a chunk of wood with his long knife.

"What do you think he's making?" Tom wondered.

"Looks like a pile of shavings."

"Yeah that's about right. Think we should worry him?"

"I don't know, Tom. Looks mighty scared already, don't he?"

"Let's go give him a hand," Tom let go a wink.

"Hi, fellas," Cole said, "I guess it's almost time. Isn't it?"

"You're getting married, Cole," Buck said with a chuckle, "not executed."

"Guess I got myself into a good one, didn't I?" Cole continued to mercilessly chop away at the wood, sending chips flying. "I'm not worried about getting married, Buck. I'm worried about becoming a farmer. I never milked a cow. I never walked behind any plow horse. Hell I ain't ever picked beans!"

With a bewildered look and loud laugh, Buck tossed a smile

to Tom. "Is that all you're worried about?"

"No, that ain't all," Cole stopped whittling, "I'm right worried about that other thing."

Buck and Tom looked at each other, their teeth gleaming in the sunlight streaming through the window. Their mischievous looks gave away their intentions. They could read each other's mind. The only problem they had now was how to make the most of the situation Cole just handed them. Knowing full well what Cole meant, Buck asked, "What other thing?"

Poor Cole's terrified, pale look made it difficult for Tom and Buck not to explode. The barn door swung open and Chuck and Sam joined the party.

"You know ... that other thing ... you have to do." Cole stared at his feet. Tom thought he heard a whimper.

Buck marched to Cole. When he was scarcely a foot from Cole's nose he bent over. Their noses nearly touching, and sporting a smile so big and devilish Tom thought his face would tear, "You've been with a girl before, haven't you?"

Cole chopped at the wood with reckless swings. Chuck and Sam moved closer, not to miss a word. Cole looked up at the men, the color washed from his face.

"Holy cow," Buck laughed, "you never .... *ever?* "

Still Cole had no answer. He turned his knife over and over in his sweaty hands.

"Tell you what, Cole," Buck turned to Tom, "give me the word and I'll talk you through it. Yes sir, I'll sit right there on the edge of your bed and guide you along step by sweet, tender step."

The barn door swung open again, in the light stood Mrs. Miller, "I want someone to ride out after Reverend White. I fear something must have happened. His carriage may have a broken wheel, perhaps something with his horse. I don't know but he is too long overdue."

The men did their best to sober up as Mrs. Miller walked toward them. "Why Cole, why are you hiding in the barn?"

"Oh, he's got wedding-night jitters," Buck said with a huge grin followed by an outburst of laughter from all.

"Buck Hawkins," Mrs. Miller declared in a threateningly stern voice. "Have you men been tormenting this poor boy?" She jammed her fists on her hips, marched to Buck and stood toe to toe.

Chuck and Sam made a hasty exit, leaving Tom and Buck to endure the stern looks of Mrs. Miller.

"No, no ma'am we haven't," Buck said, but his voice cracked, "not too much anyway." And he slapped Cole on the back with such force he nearly knocked him to the ground.

"I want you and Tom to go find Reverend White," her hands still on her hips, "Right Now!" She poked Buck's chest with her finger hard enough to bruise.

They saddled Diablo and Thunder in record time and galloped from the barn heading out the farm road as fast as the two magnificent horses could run. They raced at full speed until the Miller house faded from sight. Eyes trained by years of prairie life, battles and scouting scanned the land around them. They rode at top speed until both horses needed a rest then slowed to a walk; still no sight of the Reverend or his carriage.

"Reckon he forgot?" Tom asked.

"Maybe Cole paid someone to ambush him."

"Sure enough has the jitters don't he? Wonder how he'd like to spend his wedding night in a teepee surrounded by a few thousand Sioux."

"Did I ever tell you where I was on your wedding night?"

"Never cared."

"You might," Buck eased Diablo a little distance from Tom, let go his best attempt at a girl's giggle.

"You were outside our wedding lodge?"

"Well let's just say, when my time comes I won't be as scared as Cole!" Buck howled and gigged Diablo into a gallop again.

Tom turned Thunder loose and took after Buck, but Buck had the advantage. Down into a small valley they flew and up the next rise, Tom began to gain on Buck.

As Buck crested the hill he reined up Diablo. "I think I found the Reverend, and it doesn't look good."

A short distance out, on its side, laid a black carriage. They pressed their horses back into a gallop. As they neared the upset carriage they saw a man propped against the carriage's belly.

They jumped down next to the Reverend. He had a large cut above his left eye, his jacket ripped from him, and his bare belly showed the ugly black bruises of a beating. He gingerly held his right arm in his left. "I believe my arm is broken, fellas," the Reverend said through a sheepish grin.

"What happened, Reverend?" Buck examined the Reverend's arm.

"I was heading to the Miller's for a wedding. I'm afraid I'll be late. Those poor young folks planned all this time only to have their Reverend get waylaid."

"Someone jumped you?"

"Two men ... when they found I had only two dollars they beat me, turned over my carriage and took my horse."

"How long ago?" Tom looked across the land, searching.

"About an hour I suppose. I was about to try walking ... I saw you two come over the rise. At first I thought they were coming back to finish me, but then I recognized Diablo."

"If you can stand we'll right this carriage, harness Diablo and get you to your wedding. Cole is anxious to see you." Buck reached out his hand and helped the weak but willing Reverend stand.

Tom and Buck each took a wheel and in a few rocks, pulled the carriage upright. They repaired enough harness to rig up Diablo then helped Reverend White into the seat.

"Two of them, you say," Tom said.

"Just two."

Buck knew better than to try to talk Tom from chasing them down. Rather he handed him his revolver. Not having expected this kind of trouble, neither man had carried their rifles. Tom took the revolver and stuffed it in his belt, giving him two. Without a word he turned Thunder and moved away in a fast trot, already on the trail. He watched the black-and-white horse pull the black carriage across the hilly grassland until it faded into the horizon.

The trail proved easy to follow through prairie grass and dust. Two men riding and one horse in tow. Tom put Thunder into a quick lope. Never once did he lose sight of the trail. As Buck had once remarked, Thunder tracks as good as any hound.

The mid-afternoon sun burned blistering hot but Tom kept Thunder moving out. He knew if he didn't stay on the trail whoever beat the Reverend would escape unpunished. These two would not escape their just sentence.

Twenty miles west the gentle rolling prairie turned to brush-covered foothills. He hoped to overtake his quarry in the open and pushed on with as much speed as possible without losing the trail.

Luck was with him. As he crested the next rise he saw riders, possibly five miles ahead.

Tom figured it would be a chase. Cowards don't stand and fight. He was certain Thunder could outrun anything the two outlaws rode. They soon realized they had been discovered and took off at a run. They turned loose the Reverend's horse in their panic, but Tom continued to close the distance.

The bandits made a dash for the cover of the foothill brush. Tom thought if he had his buffalo rifle this would already be over.

As Tom closed they turned in their saddles and fired recklessly. They had no way of knowing how that only served to stoke the fires in his belly. At first the distance between them was too great and Tom was in no danger of catching a round. But as he continued to close in he worried for Thunder's safety.

He yanked Buck's long barreled .44 Colt from his belt, but before he could fire the rider closest to him flipped back over his horse. In crazy desperate shooting the lead man had shot his own partner.

"You wait," Tom barked as he galloped past the fallen man, closing fast on the runaway who had tossed his empty gun and rode hard. Thunder pulled even and Tom slammed the Colt's long barrel across the rider's face knocking him from the saddle. Tom reached low, grabbed his arm before he realized he had fallen and dragged him back to the wounded man.

The outlaw tried to wiggle free as Tom dismounted, but another blow to his face sat him in the dirt. "Don't you make a move," Tom whispered and shoved him face down on his belly.

Tom examined the wounded man. "It's pretty bad," Tom told him, "I don't believe you're gonna make it."

"Who the hell are you?" The uninjured man demanded.

"Just a man who thinks it's wrong to rob a preacher."

"I said it was a bad idea," cried the wounded man, "now I'm gonna die."

"Yeah, I reckon you are," Tom said coldly. He knew there was nothing he could do to save him.

He had seen that before. That hot day trapped in the makeshift wagon box corral not far from Ft. Phil Kearney on the Bozeman road. That day he held a young man close as rifles roared around them and the young soldier's life drained into the dirt. Tom remembered how the poor fellow had cried for his mother as Tom tried to hold him in some comfort, and keep those damned flies away. At least until he died …

There was even nothing he could do to help ease the pain. He looked up from the stinking wound into the dying man's eyes. Only he wasn't a man! "You're just a kid!" The words exploded from Tom's mouth. "How old are you?"

"I'm fourteen … don't let me die, mister. Please don't let me die." Tom dropped to one knee and cradled the dying boy's head, "you're going to die son. Nothing I can do. Nothing anyone can do. Why the hell did you beat that preacher?"

"I didn't do nothin' … he done it all." With a bloody, shaky, white hand the boy pointed to the outlaw lying in the dust. Tom rolled the boy onto his lap and wrapped his arms around him. He held him tight, trying to give him comfort. The boy's tears and sobs soaked Tom's shirt, while his blood soaked his leggings. Ever so gently Tom rocked and whispered in the boy's ear.

The other outlaw saw this as a chance to escape. Cautiously he positioned his feet, careful not to allow Tom see or hear any movement. When he felt the time was right, he jumped and ran as fast as he could, charging Tom with a knife.

Tom looked up when he heard the outlaw scramble to his feet.

"Sit down!" Tom yelled.

"Go to hell!" He lunged for Tom.

While his left arm cradled the dying boy, his watery eyes sighted down his right arm at the charging outlaw. One shot barked from his gun. The outlaw crumbled in a heap.

Tom sat softly humming in the boy's ears and rocked him. "Mister, could you do me a favor?" The boy's whisper was barely audible.

"Sure … what is it?"

"Could you send a letter to my mother, she lives in St. Louis. Could you tell her… don't tell her I died this …" the boy gave a violent jerk, then Tom heard the breath rattle from his lifeless body.

"I didn't catch her name, boy." He held the boy for a while longer. He wondered how he happened to be in the company of a lazy outlaw. Someone so low he would beat the preacher for two bucks. He wished he could shoot him again.

With his knife he scratched a shallow grave in the sandy soil, rolled the boy into it, and covered him. He walked the short distance to the dead outlaw, fished through his pockets and found the two dollars he had taken from the preacher, and left the man where he had fallen.

He gathered the horses as darkness crept in, mounted Thunder and headed back. He found the preacher's horse and turned toward the Miller's. He rode slow.

****

The next day another large hog had volunteered to ride the spit, cared for by the two ladies in charge of feeding the guests. Tom sat with Hawk playing pickup sticks. Buck lounged on the porch, rocked back in his chair sipping coffee and working on a cigar. Soft Cloud and Mrs. Miller devoted themselves to Hannah. Mr. Miller spent the morning with Cole in the tent with Chuck and Sam where they discussed the newfangled philosophies of growing corn. Reverend White sat next to Buck on the porch, his arm in a sling, but otherwise undaunted by the previous day's events.

The screen door swung open and banged shut, "Reverend," Mrs. Miller gave him a nod and smile.

Reverend White stood at the porch rail. "Friends, the time has come for the blessed ceremony. Let's gather at the arbor."

Cole looked to Mr. Miller. Mr. Miller had to smile as Cole's face quickly turned chalky white. "Appears we're through talking about corn, Cole. I reckon my daughter would like to see you over by the arbor."

Buck dashed down the stairs nearly knocking the astonished Reverend White over. As fast as he could run he made it to the barn and returned carrying an anvil.

Tom looked up from his game of pickup sticks and shook his head. Buck granted no man any quarter. He watched Buck carefully position the big black anvil under the beautifully decorated arbor and led Hawk to a chair in the front row, not about to miss any of the ceremony, or Buck's play. The screen door banged again, and a hush swept over the gathering as Mr. Miller led a stunning Hannah down the steps. Tom had always considered Hannah the essence of beauty, and on this day she glowed with the magnificence of loveliness.

In a hurried but orderly fashion, the guests found seats in chairs surrounding the arbor, or at the long tables in the yard. Buck sat next to Tom grinning like a coyote with a chicken. They both watched in amusement as Reverend White took his position on the far side of the arbor and cast a puzzled look at the anvil, followed by a displeased stare in Buck's direction.

As Cole approached the arbor and saw the anvil, he too threw a look of scorn at Buck. Tom caught the returning glance of innocence Buck offered. Wait 'til Mrs. Miller sees that, Tom thought.

When Mr. Miller and Hannah reached the arbor he took her hand. No one in the crowd could miss the love in Cole's eyes as he looked up to Hannah.

Then came a moment of complete silence as the Reverend White positioned Hannah and Cole. In that silence the screen door banged once more and Soft Cloud and Mrs. Miller hurried down the steps to their seats, in the front row, next to Tom and Buck.

Just as Reverend White began to speak, Mrs. Miller saw the anvil. It appeared to Tom as if she was going to level Buck when Cole, with a wink and smile pitched Buck's way, stepped up onto the anvil making him exactly as tall as Hannah and causing everyone to explode in laughter. It was the first time Tom had seen anyone get the better of Buck. But Cole, making practical use of the anvil and showing no displeasure, sure took the punch out of Buck's prank.

It took Reverend White a bit to regain control. But without any further mischief from either Tom or Buck, Hannah Miller became Mrs. Peter Cole. Tom wondered if he was the only one that noticed Cole stood on the balls of his feet atop the anvil when the Reverend said he may kiss the bride. But, Tom thought, Hannah is a tall girl.

CHAPTER THIRTY SIX

"How do you think Cole's doin'?" Buck rested his foot on the fence rail.

Tom dropped the horse's foot and straightened his back. "Tomorrow makes it a week. We've been home five days and haven't heard anything. I reckon he's gonna stick it out."

"Somehow I always figured to marry Hannah myself."

Tom studied Buck with a look that told of his bewilderment. "You ever tell her?"

Buck lifted his hat and wiped the sweat from his forehead with his dusty shirtsleeve, "Time never seemed to be just right."

"You might be a little tall for her anyway. Can't wait for the right time, Buck. You find the girl for you, you need to speak right up."

"You ready for another horse?"

They had devoted the better part of the last five days readying 20 horses for Buck to trail to Johnny Kirk. After almost every hoof trim, Tom scanned the prairie hoping to see the wagons. He and Buck had worked every night by kerosene lantern perfecting drawings for the new two-story wood board house.

"I sure was hoping for the lumber to roll in today. It would be better if you were here to set the first timbers."

"Mr. Buchanan figured to bring five men and stay as long as you need. These 20 horses should finish payin' for the lumber."

They leaned on the corral fence admiring the horses. Tom looked to the large mound in the shade of the only cottonwood near the barn, the grave of the old horse, Tom Grey. He had returned from the trip to Denver City to the sad news that old Tom Grey had died while he was gone. That old horse had gotten him through some of the toughest moments of his life. Back when he was a boy living with the old drunken hider, that horse was his only friend. How many times had he cried in his mane after a lashing? He had many horses now. But Tom Grey. Yeah, Tom Grey, a very special horse. A special friend. Hard to say how he'd miss him. It was good that Still Water and Iron Shell buried him under the lone cottonwood the old horse liked so well. For the last year or so he had spent the hot afternoons in the shade of that big cottonwood … Somehow he didn't feel all that far away. Tom let loose a whistle—and was sure he heard Tom Grey nicker, as he always had.

"I thought you two might be ready for water." Soft Cloud offered the wooden bucket with a tin cup hooked on the edge.

Tom wiped the stinging moisture from his eyes, hoped no one noticed. But she had.

"That'll be just the ticket," Buck flashed his smile of approval.

The ranch had come a long way since Soft Cloud had first introduced Tom to the little sod cabin. After the house, he planned to build barns for hay storage. He was anxious to give the horse-drawn hay mower Buck purchased that spring at Fort Laramie a try. It would soon be time to cut hay and now with Cole gone, and Buck leaving—well, somehow things would get done. "I was just thinking if I built just the right seat on the hay mower I'll bet Iron Shell could learn to mow hay."

"You figure on turning a Sioux warrior into a hay mower, do ya?" Buck gave a chuckle.

"Think he won't do it?"

"Can't say, but do me a favor. Wait to ask him 'til I'm trailin' these horses."

Soft Cloud stood on the lower rail and pointed far away at a rising dust cloud.

"Howdy!" Buck shouted, "That'd be our lumber!"

They ran to the soddy and watched the dust cloud slowly turn into a train of wagons stacked high with lumber.

Two riders broke from the wagons and galloped flat-out toward them. "Holy cow, that's Bill Cody and Todd Harvey!" Buck hollered.

"Doggone if it isn't!" Tom leaned against the porch post to

watch them ride in.

"Holy cow, I can't believe it—Bill Cody and Todd Harvey!" Buck hustled to his chair, reared it back on two legs and grinned like a cat about to pounce on a mouse.

"Howdy folks. Promised we'd get here before the year was out." Cody tipped his hat to Soft Cloud.

"What in tarnation caused you fellas to ride escort on our lumber train?" Tom tossed an inquisitive look.

"We were at the saw mill and General Carr, who is temporarily stationed at Fort Laramie, sent Todd and me and a few others to handle a little business there. A small band of outlaws had been making a bit of trouble for the settlement. Didn't take us long and when Mr. Buchanan told us this was your shipment, I sent a dispatch back to the General. We are officially on 60 days' furlough, if the General agreed with my request."

"We aim to help ya get this house started!" Todd Harvey swung down, grabbed the cup and gulped down a slug of water.

"Well, I'll be doggone. You're sure welcome to all the ax swinging, beam dragging, nail banging, hole drilling, and board cuttin' you can take!" Tom shook Todd's hand.

"Still riding that young stallion of Thunder's, I see," Buck said to Cody. "Throws good blood doesn't he?"

Todd Harvey rode a son of Thunder and like his sire and Cody's stallion, was black as a mine shaft. "He does that, strongest, smartest stallion I've ever rode! Cody give one to General Carr. Just about only horse he'll ride these days!"

Bill Cody spun about, snatched Hawk from Still Water's hand and tossed him in the saddle atop his black stallion. "This young man learn how to handle a horse yet?" Cody kept hold of the reins and jogged away leading the stallion in a quick trot. Cody ran a wide circle picking up speed. Hawk sat the horse straight, soft, and true, never losing his perfect balance.

"Been working at this have you, Tom?"

Tom tossed a sheepish grin to Soft Cloud. "From time to time."

"Young man," Cody addressed Hawk as he lifted him from the saddle, "you have the makings of a marvelous horseman!"

The freight wagons began to roll into the yard. Six mules and three men per wagon. "Tom, Buck, everyone. Good to see you all again. Okay if we let the mules run loose?" Mr. Buchanan asked.

"You bet," Buck said. I'm sure they'll hook up with our mares out on the grass and won't wander far. Reckon their legs had enough for the day and their more thinking about their bellies."

The air felt light and full of excitement. They parked the wagons at the new homesite, beside the soddy. Tom planned to build the new house close to the tiny sod cabin. "This was my first house and I don't want to move too far from it," he had once told everyone. Still Water decided it could serve the rest of its days as her canning kitchen. She had learned the technique from the German families who lived a few miles to the north, on the west side of Little Bear Creek.

"Largest order we ever had for a civilian," Mr. Buchanan said.

Soft Cloud took Tom's hand, "it's going to be a large house."

"Funny how a girl can change, isn't it Tom?" Buck teased, "seems not all that long ago she was happy in a buffalo hide lodge."

"I have changed. And I have also studied the drawings of our new house and I could not help but notice the large area labeled 'Buck's place'. Are you not the same Buck Hawkins who so proudly declared all you needed in life was a good horse, a buffalo rifle, and a bedroll?"

"I may have said that," Buck admitted. "But it was probably before these old bones started talking to me every morning."

"Old bones?" Todd Harvey declared, "let me tell you about old bones you young pup! Why these old bones was scoutin' with the likes of Jim Bridger before you took your first tottering step!"

"Old you all are for sure, Todd," Bill Cody agreed, "I did notice you keep finding shorter and shorter horses."

"Why you ..." Todd Harvey started but was interrupted by a call from Still Water that biscuits were ready.

CHAPTER THIRTY SEVEN

Early June 1882

Buck leaned against the corral fence. The short cigar in his mouth had gone out moments ago, but he never noticed. Like the previous five, this had been a busy morning working the last horse of the 40 leaving for the Donovan ranch in two days.

The past 12 years had been good years for the ranch. Tom and Buck kept close to 25 men on payroll year-round. They ran a 1,000 horses and never less than 5,000 cattle. And a herd of more than a 1,000 buffalo. Buffalo had always been a part of Tom's life.

The herds of the big woolies had almost completely gone in the past decade. The prairie Tom loved so well was littered with bleached bones of the Sioux brethren left behind by too many thoughtless hunters. Whether for profit or sport, it mattered not to the buffalo. They paid the price. Tom and Buck had only one discussion. "These sacred hunting grounds of the Sioux will always have buffalo. I'll keep my promise to Red Cloud … and the buffalo. We have plenty of room to keep them clear from our cows and bulls."

Following Chester Donovan's advice, nine years ago they hired a team of railroad engineers to survey and legally record, with the land office, a deed to the ranch. Tom was finally able to answer Beverly Kirk's question, "How big is your ranch?" The engineers tracing Red Cloud's marking monuments found it to be 600 square miles, equaling 384,000 acres. Over 200,000 acres of grassland, good grassland, and slightly more than 100,000 acres of high-quality timber. More than 60 miles of rivers and streams flowed within its boundaries.

Tom Named by Horse had proven to be a good businessman. Their ranch boasted the finest house for hundreds of miles, two comfortable bunkhouses for the men, four hay sheds, and a water-powered sawmill. And corrals enough to hold 200 horses.

The only thing Buck found nearly impossible to tolerate was the more than 45 miles of five-strand barbed wire fence they had to build last year, running east from Walls of Buffalo Ridge to Squaw Run River ... damned emigrants!

Buck had insisted that nearly 60 line shacks be built two years ago. A man riding the ranch perimeter was never more than ten or twelve miles from shelter. Since the cattle thieves and squatters had begun to become a nuisance, Buck always had two or three men riding line. It was not uncommon for them to find one of the shacks occupied, sometimes by an entire family. So far they had been able to deal with encroaching squatters without bloodshed.

Buck watched Tom watching Hawk. Now 14, Hawk was one horse-ridin' son of a gun. Buck truly enjoyed his life here on the ranch. He got great joy out of watching Hawk grow up. The boy had a natural talent with horses, just like his father.

"If she does that again," Tom coached Hawk, "just give 'er her head and ride it out. Help her get the hang of it." Hawk nodded to his father and was ready when the mare was released from Tom's grip. Tom sprinted to the corral fence and stood next to Buck grinning like a little boy who just swiped an apple pie.

"Ride her smooth, Hawk," Buck advised, "she's gonna try ya!"

When the mare realized she was free she bolted. Hawk sat deep in the old McClellan saddle and let the mare have her head. The single rope Hawk held in one hand with plenty of slack, put no pressure the bosalillo. She raced for the fence where Tom and Buck stood. Tom grabbed the top rail and hopped over to land by Buck.

"Means business, doesn't she?" Tom's bright smile and sparkling eyes all the evidence Buck needed to know this was sport Tom enjoyed.

"Stay right with her, Hawk! Don't let 'er roll over on ya!" Buck hollered.

Hawk rode the wild wind from end to end of the corral, the mare offered a few crow hops, but Hawk stayed with her calling for her to take it easy.

"Ataboy, Hawk!" Buck encouraged.

"Looks good, doesn't he?" Tom bragged.

"You know she does have some size to her, she just looks a little short all stretched out like that."

Soft Cloud came with a tray of biscuits, a coffee pot, and a stern look for both of them.

The mare raced around the corral, showing no signs tiring. When she wheeled and cut through the center Buck hollered, "She's gonna jump the fence!"

The spotted mare cleared the corral fence by a foot and hit the ground at a flat-out gallop. Hawk was still in the saddle. Across the grass they traveled at breakneck speed. They splashed into Little Bear Creek. She never slowed. Up the far bank they clamored and out onto the prairie.

Tom cupped his hands around his mouth, "Don't come back without gathering a few horses!"

Soft Cloud whacked Tom in the back of the head with her tray. Biscuits flew everywhere.

"Holy cow!" Buck hooted, "She wasted a pile of good biscuits! I was just fixin' to polish them off!"

Quick as lightning, her left foot came up and settled in Bucks midsection. With a fierce push, she knocked him to the ground. He landed sitting on his bottom. "You go get my son!" Her outstretched finger poked Buck in the nose.

"He'll be all right," Tom said calmly, looking at his wife with a silly grin. This stoked the fire in her dark brown eyes even more.

"You go get our son!"

All three looked in the direction Hawk and the spotted mare had gone, already they were not much more than a tiny speck on the horizon. "He's a mile away already," Tom protested.

Soft Cloud raised the metal platter over her head and stepped toward Tom.

They knew any further delay on their part was dangerous, and ran for horses.

****

Red Cloud sat by his lodge in the early morning sun and with unusual contentment watched the goings on in the corral by the barn. He was pleased with his great-grandson. His hot Lakota blood made him a great horseman at a young age. He admired the spotted mare too, that had jumped the tall rail fence. In another time she would have made a fine war pony. She had the courage of a Sioux warrior. He knew she would run for many miles and his great-grandson would enjoy a good ride this day.

Red Cloud would, whenever it suited him, defy the orders of the Indian Agent and visit his granddaughter, Soft Cloud and son Iron Shell. Life at the Pine Ridge Agency was no life. Chief Spotted Tale had betrayed the Sioux Nations. Here on the land protected by Tom Named by Horse he could yet feel the hand of Grandfather Mystery. But even this tiny piece of Sioux hunting ground had to be defended. Red Cloud had listened the night before as Buck explained to him challenges they now face with new white people that rip at the earth. People Buck called sod busters.

As he enjoyed this fine morning sitting in the sun with Iron Shell, watching his great-grandson, he realized most sadly young Hawk would never know the pride and dignity of life as a Sioux warrior. He would never know the feeling of racing through a herd of stampeding buffalo on a trusted pony. His great-grandson would never feel heart-pounding excitement that is shared with your horse as you choose a magnificent bull to give its life to feed your people. The sacred buffalo are gone now. Where once great herds of shaggy brown rumps colored the plains, now only endless miles of white bones of their brother the buffalo shine in the sunlight. Red Cloud knew, as he had always known, the white man would take everything. In his visions as a young chief, Red Cloud had seen how the white man would take not only their most sacred hunting grounds but also destroy their very way of life. How could they not understand?

****

Tom beat Buck to the corral holding horses waiting to be trailed to the Donovan ranch. He slipped the rope halter over the nose of the first horse he could catch, and went through the gate leading the nervous horse followed closely by Buck who wrestled with a tall stallion.

"Better not take time for saddles. She's liable to come whack us with that tray again." Buck grabbed a fistful of mane and bolted from the corral.

They flew around the barn, between the two big corrals and plunged into Little Bear Creek at a full run. Tom looked back and saw Red Cloud rise to his feet. He knew the old chief would have enjoyed racing along with them. He wondered if he wasn't sending a message to the spotted mare that carried Hawk out on the prairie. "Run, gallant pony! This is your day!" He could hear Red Cloud call to her.

Through the tall grass they raced, until they crested the first rise miles from the barn and corrals.

"What do you make that out to be?" Buck pointed to a group of horses in the distance.

"A little far away to be sure. But it looks as if Hawk gathered horses. Let's go find out!" He surprised the mare with a good nudge, she surprised Tom with a blast of speed. As they lessened the distance between them, they realized Hawk had indeed gathered a few horses.

"Who's that with him?" Tom held his hat to shield the sun and strained for a look.

"Can't tell, let's find out!"

"Holy cow!" Buck hollered, "It's Bill Cody and Todd Harvey!" They reined up in front of the small herd.

"Gentlemen, I have come with a proposition!" Bill Cody called, "and by the way, young Hawk here is an impressive horseman."

"Gathered a few horses," Hawk beamed with more than a little air of pride.

"You sure did! Got that spotted mare acting respectable too, I see."

"She sure has the mind of her father, doesn't she?" Hawk grinned.

"Has Diablo's speed too," Buck boasted.

The riders grouped around the small band of horses and began the walk back.

"And what proposition were you thinking of, Bill?" Tom asked.

Todd Harvey moved his horse next to Hawk on the spotted mare while Cody, Tom, and Buck drifted to the rear. They had a few miles to listen to Cody's proposition.

"We had been enjoying a few months of rest at my Dismal River Ranch, the family altogether, and Todd Harvey here and a few others," Bill Cody began. "A few weeks back my old friend Dave Peary and our mutual friend Frank North made an appearance in my parlor. They shared with me a most interesting idea. They suggested I organize a grand Fourth of July celebration for the town of North Platte.

"I had intended to spend a few weeks with my family at our ranch. However the idea is so overwhelmingly intriguing I submitted. Though the details of such a celebration I have yet to solidify in my brain.

"I have, living presently at my ranch, 45 Pawnee Indians. These Indians are well civilized and have traveled widely with me performing on stage here and abroad."

Buck pulled up, shot a look to Tom. Then bewilderment painted on his face, turned to Cody, "You want me and Tom to come kill 'em?"

"No ... no, of course not, my good man. I have ideas of you and Tom Named by Horse performing in our show I've decided to call 'Old Glory Blowout'!" Cody let go one of his famous strings of laughter.

Now it was Tom's turn to pull his horse and display a look of bewilderment. "We're not actors, we're ... something else!"

"Don't be so quick, Tom. What did you figure we could do for you?" Buck's bewilderment flashed to excitement.

"I have thoughts on a grand scale boys. The Pawnees know their role. With them I have successfully staged buffalo hunts and vigorous battles. I want to entertain the people with such things as I can imagine. Stagecoach holdups, cowboys riding bucking broncs, perhaps some trick roping and shooting."

"Just how do you need our help, Bill?" Buck's excitement took the lead, always ready to put on a show, or battle.

"In the first order I have need of stock. As you know I have over the years purchased several of your fine horses. Each of them has performed splendidly. I will need to secure perhaps 20 seasoned mounts and perhaps as many as 30 green horses for the bucking displays and perhaps a horse roundup exhibition."

"Forty is all we have ready at the moment, and they're all

promised to Chester Donovan down Denver City way," Tom said.

"I'm sure if you send a rider to Donovan and explain your circumstances he would be happy to oblige," Cody suggested.

"Hate to short him like that, he buys 40 or 50 a year from us. Of course, there is the eleven we're bringing home right now. We can have these ready before too long, then Chester would only be ten light."

"Do I take it then; you boys are aboard?"

"Been a while since I had a chance to show off my fancy shootin'." Buck yanked his revolver and spun it on his finger.

"Old friend, it was more Tom's talents I'd hoped to exhibit," Cody apologized.

CHAPTER THIRTY EIGHT

As he closed the gate behind the last of the new horses, Todd Harvey noticed Red Cloud sitting by his lodge and handed his weary horse to Hawk. "I'll be visitin' with my old friend the rest of the day."

Hawk stretched his legs and decided he still had enough spit to work with a few horses. Being abandoned by his father, Buck, and Cody, he enlisted the help of his best friend, and top hand Jake Springer.

Cody and Buck gathered at Red Cloud's fire ring and settled down for coffee and Red Cloud's stories of time gone by.

Tom headed to the big house and as he expected, Soft Cloud had begun to lay out a spread for the noon meal. "Just about ready," she hustled about the table setting plates stacked high with biscuits, beef and fixings. "Want to gather the troops?"

"You know Red Cloud won't come to the table. He's never set foot in our house. Iron Shell won't come in as long as he's here either."

"Ask just the same."

Tom helped with the final settings, then hustled through the parlor, out the screen door, down the steps to the fire ring of Red Cloud's Lodge.

For first time in many years the memory of Red Cloud's fire ring in the winter village came to mind. For a moment, he stood and looked at the men gathered around the small fire. Iron Shell sat on his father's right side, just as he had the first day Tom entered the Sioux village. So much had changed since that day. Almost no Indians of any tribe hunted the Great Plains today. And far fewer buffalo than that could be seen. What can be seen are acres and acres of their bones bleaching, and railroads crisscrossing the plains. Towns and homesteads dot the grasslands like ticks on a hound's ear. He liked his ranch and was proud of the life he had built for his family. But he often wondered about the price paid by the Sioux and other tribes. As his own fortunes had improved at a steady pace, the fortunes of the plains Tribes and the buffalo had vanished. What's more he had played a role in the circumstances that created those changes. He wondered as his gaze fell heavily upon Red Cloud what the next ten years might mean to the proud Lakota Chief ... Today though was a day given them for friendship.

"Soft Cloud has a fine meal ready," Tom interrupted the conversation. "She would like us all to come in and enjoy it in her kitchen." Thinking quickly, he fixed his strong blue eyes on Red Cloud's own black eyes. "She is very proud of her house and wishes to share it with everyone."

Red Cloud was the first to rise. Extending his arms palms up, he made a sweeping motion upward and commanded everyone to their feet. Iron Shell grabbed the tired old crutch and followed his father's direction.

The small group lingered in their place to allow Red Cloud time to walk around the ring and lead them to the large oak plank porch steps. When he reached the first step, he turned back to those waiting at the fire ring. He beckoned them to follow. Iron Shell led them to the house and followed Red Cloud up the steps.

They entered the screen door and stopped in the parlor. No one spoke. No one had to. Everyone in the room knew this moment was for Red Cloud and his granddaughter. They stood for a few seconds more and watched Soft Cloud put the finishing touches on her preparations.

When her eyes chanced to look up from her work, she spied her grandfather standing in her parlor. Straight and tall he stood—the perfect specimen of a noble and proud chief of a noble people.

The tray of meat she held in her hands crashed to the floor. Never a downward glace, she raced to the parlor and flung herself into the arms of her grandfather. She nearly managed to knock him off balance. When she had enjoyed his embrace, she turned to the others, her wet cheeks glistening in the sunbeams streaming through the big windows.

"I'm sorry about the meat."

In long strides Todd Harvey marched to the fallen tray. "Nuthin' that can't be saved, ma'am. Besides, your lookin' at a room full of men that ate far worse than a dropped steak!"

"I can myself remember a time or two I would have given all I owned just eat a steak off Soft Cloud's floor!" Bill Cody declared.

At Soft Cloud's invitation, Red Cloud led the group to the long table and stood by the head chair until everyone sat. He offered thanks to Grandfather Mystery for this meal. With a tender look to Soft Cloud, and Still Water, he offered thanks for this "wood board lodge."

Bill Cody spoke first, "Young lady, this may be the very finest steak that ever melted in this old scout's mouth."

"Doggone it," Tom blurted, "no one bothered to roundup Hawk."

"Let 'im go," Buck mumbled through a mouthful of steak, "we need those horses he brought home today ready to go."

"If he doesn't come by the time we're through I'll take their meal out for him and Jake both," Still Water said.

"I have agreed to make this journey with Bill Cody. We should help him." Red Cloud said. All eyes turned his way, and with the exception of Todd Harvey everyone stopped eating. A look of discipline shot his way from Cody forced him to defend himself. "I'm glad he's comin', Bill," Todd Harvey said, "but I'm still hungry!"

Still Water gave a troubled look. "It would dangerous for you to be seen, Grandfather. Leaving Pine Ridge Agency to be here is far different from being among strangers in North Platte, someone will surely report you."

Cody intervened. "He will be safely in my custody. I have explained to Red Cloud I am an official Indian Agent at large, appointed so by the Secretary of Interior in the summer of '79. It was necessary that year that I become an agent for there was a devilish scoundrel doing his most to cause me difficulties and prevent my Pawnee actors from traveling the country with me. Fortune was on my side, however, as the Secretary was a close friend whom I had the pleasure of guiding on several hunting expeditions. I merely presented my situation to the Secretary and he immediately appointed me lifetime Indian Agent at large. I have since never again been troubled by any official of the government concerning these matters."

"Soft Cloud, you and I, Buck, Hawk, and some of the men are going too." Tom said matter-of-factly, "I want to help our friend and from the way he describes his plans, this is something we don't want to miss."

"Decided for us all, have you?" Buck teased.

"This time I did."

"Have you considered the difficulties of Cody's adventure?"

"Here ... here Buck," Bill Cody said, "I see very few difficulties ahead for us. The planned celebration is for July the fourth. Today being only the third of June you might say we have an entire month."

"Cody, the trip to your ranch takes practically two weeks. That's without driving horses." Buck pointed out.

"The horses shouldn't slow us down. It is a bit more difficult to trail the buffalo, however."

"Trail buffalo?" Buck yelled, "whose gonna trail buffalo?"

Tom tapped the edge of his plate with his fork and forced the biggest grin of his life. "I reckon you and me. We'll take a few of the boys and push 'em east while Jake and Hawk and anybody that wants to be part of the show in Platte city can trail the horses. We can travel nearly in sight of each other all the way."

"How many buffalo were you thinking would make this drive?" Buck stared in disbelief.

"I believe I can get by with his few as one hundred," Cody said.

"Trail one hundred wild buffalo over the Platte to perform in a show?"

"Now you understand, Buck," Tom fought back a laugh.

Darkness cloaked the house when breakfast was served. Buck continued to grumble about the insanity of driving wild buffalo across the prairie. He had tried to explain to Tom, and Cody too, that trailing buffalo just wasn't a thing a sane man did.

Cody argued that no white man alive knew more about buffalo than he did and if he wasn't in such a terrible big hurry to get back to North Platte, he would offer his knowledge to the effort. "Buffalo always move in a straight line. Just aim them as you would your Sharps, let them walk, that's all there is to it."

Buck gave in and hitched four mules to a wagon. Red Cloud's

Lodge and belongings he loaded on the wagon, as well as Still Water's and Iron Shell's things. They set out well before noon. Cody had explained he needed to return as quickly as possible as he was needed to organize the entire event. Tom and Buck should get the buffalo and horses to North Platte city in the best time as they could manage.

Hawk recruited five more men in addition to Jake Springer to trail the horses and compete in whatever events Bill Cody would stage. They too had set out before sunrise. Eager to be on the trail with 50 horses, with only 20 of them ready to ride. Everyone's excitement soared, except Buck's.

Soft Cloud would manage her chuckwagon as if they were headed for roundup. They planned to trail the herds close enough together to be able to feed everyone from her one wagon.

Buck and Stony led the way with four of the ranch's best drovers, handpicked by Buck for their ability to cut cows and ride herd, set out north to their buffalo herd. Tom rode the chuckwagon with Soft Cloud. "I want to start with one hundred buffalo, and I want to finish up with one hundred buffalo. And I'm not looking for anyone to get hurt on this crazy man's adventure," Buck formulated as they saddled up that morning. "I have to do this, Stony, what's your excuse?"

Stony Stead had ridden for Tom and Buck for close to five years now. Buck liked Stony an awful lot. Quick with a joke or to pitch in a hand, never shirked a duty, and always gave a good solid honest answer. He was new to the west when he started working on the ranch. But he sure knew his way around a horse.

"Well, I figured you needed all the help you can get, if you plan to push a hundred buffalo east to North Platte city, and get there alive. Besides Buck, in my entire life I have never been to a Fourth of July celebration. Talk is, this'll be a thing people will remember forever."

"I reckon no one in this outfit will ever forget this Fourth of July," Buck agreed.

The first sun rays bounced off dewy grass by the time they spotted the buffalo herd. These buffalo were as wild as any buffalo that ever lived. Since the day Red Cloud laid out the ranch they had been sheltered in their own vast and endless canyon. Not even Indians hunted these buffalo. Once a year Tom slipped up to the canyon and did his best at a head count. Over the last three years the herd had steadily grown and now numbered close to 2,000.

They stopped on the canyon ridge. Stony gave Buck a sly grin. "Have any ideas on how we're gonna sort out a hundred?"

"Yup. I intend to let Tom do it. A few years back he pulled a good one on Johnny Kirk. He got this way of zigzaggin' through a herd just as slick as can be. I watched him sort out thirty momma cows and calves from a big ol' herd, all by himself. We'll mosey down there and wait for him and Soft Cloud to roll in."

They stopped as near as they felt safe to the buffalo, dismounted and let their horses graze while they waited for the chuckwagon.

"I hear they're gonna have prizes for the best bronc rider at this celebration," Monty said. Monty, a tall weathered man, had ridden with Tom and Buck off and on over the years, and everyone who knew him trusted him.

"That's how Cody tells it. And we're supplying the broncs," Buck had to chuckle. Anticipating the big shindig at the end of this buffalo trail drive had Buck in high spirits.

"Hear tell Tom's gonna enter a shooting contest. That's gonna be something to see," Stewart said.

"I once watched Tom shoot six prairie dogs with six shots from close to a hundred yards," Monty continued. "Took 'im less than five seconds. Never saw anything like it."

"The only man I ever saw that might outshoot Tom was Bill Hickok. Ol' Bill's dead now... so I guess I'll never know."

"Well, I guarantee if Tom's shooting I'm betting my money on him for sure," Monty nodded, so did they all. The conversation centered on the coming festivities, with worries about driving a buffalo herd across the prairie. Finally, the chuckwagon rumbled up beside them.

Tom saddled Thunder and laid out his plan. "I'll peel off twenty or so at a time. You boys need to get between them and the herd. Just ride nice and easy, back and forth and they won't even quit grazing."

Tom started to the herd with Thunder at a slow walk. "Been a little while fella, but we'll get it." Thunder was working on turning twenty years old. Still Tom's favorite horse. He had lost some of his speed and stamina recently, but none of his smarts. There's no other horse Tom would trust to sort buffalo.

Carefully they walked into the herd and started their zigzagging walk, slicing about 25 head from the herd. Stony and the boys picked them up and worked them some distance away. Tom turned and sliced into the herd a second time. Again peeling off 25 or 30 head. The boys picked them up just as quick and drifted them into the other bunch. Two more times Tom cut the herd.

Buck had been counting. "That last bunch makes it one hundred and three!"

"Let's take 'em to North Platte City," Tom eased away from the herd.

Riders formed a horseshoe around the small herd and slowly moved them away. It was necessary to ride closer to the buffalo to keep them moving than the boys were used to when they worked cattle. But in a short time every man and horse was comfortable with the peculiar duty.

"Looks like we're on our way boys," Buck shouted.

"Fourth of July celebration here we come!" Stewart answered.

Tom stayed on Thunder and decided he would ride the rest of the day. By his calculations, it would take six or eight days to reach North Platte City. He was eager to get out of the canyon and be on their way. He wondered what it was going to be like to drive a herd of wild buffalo across Squaw Run River. Find out soon enough, he told himself.

Soft Cloud had the mules going straight and honest just like she always did. Tom had two more horses tied to the rear of the chuckwagon, both sons of Thunder, both five-year-olds and not for sale. He was pretty sure he would enter Storm in the horse races at the celebration. Over the past 12 or 13 years, Thunder had sired more than 100 foals. Storm was the first to look and think exactly like his sire. The other black horse following the chuckwagon came closest to duplicating Thunder. Cloudburst, however, did not have quite the speed. Faster and tougher than most horses, but not as fast as Thunder had been in his prime. And not as fast as his half brother Storm.

They pushed on through the early afternoon hours. Calmly and quietly the buffalo were nudged across the prairie. Tom had been careful not to sort any cows with calves. Not so much that he was not interested in losing the calves as the fact buffalo cows with calves were almost impossible to do anything with. Not like domestic cows, and they were bad enough.

Buck loped over to Tom, "Squaw Run River just ahead. Let's keep them moving nice and easy and maybe they'll walk right through."

"Have to give it a try that way, I reckon."

Buck and Stony rode ahead and found a good place to ford about two miles upstream. Working the buffalo north along the riverbank was easy. For thousands of years buffalo had drifted north and south on the plains. They found it natural to follow the riverbank in the north. When Stony signaled, the riders on the west moved in closer, drifting the herd into the water. Stony had picked an excellent place to cross, here the river had wide banks and shallow water with firm footing. It proved to be no challenge, and in less than an hour the entire herd was on the east side of the Squaw Run River plodding slowly along, continually grazing as they walked, totally uninterested in Buck and his men and seemingly unaware they were walking away from home.

CHAPTER THIRTY NINE

June 21, 1882

"Took a little longer than we planned. Right, boss?" Buck taunted Tom.

"Only seven or eight days longer, no stampedes, no buffalo thieves, no thunderstorms. I call this a good trip!"

"We left home with one hundred and three, we have North Platte in sight, and we're still pushin' one hundred and three woolies. Wonder if that's ever been done?"

"Of course not," Stony yelled, "who else but this bunch is crazy enough to trail a herd of buffalo from anywhere to somewhere else?"

"Let's hold them out here," Tom said, "Buck, you ride into town, find Cody and find out where he wants his livestock."

Buck left for town and called back over his shoulder, "If I find a hot bath you'll not see me anymore tonight!"

"Did he say a hot bath?" Stony yelled. "Better watch what you say, Buck. You just might start a workin' man stampede!"

"Monty, ride out there and see if you can find Hawk and Jake and the horses. Have them come over this way within eyesight."

Tom and the boys let the buffalo drift closer to town for the next few hours and then held them a safe distance. Soft Cloud began her evening routine a bit early since they were at trail's end.

Tom rode Storm and Cloudburst the last two days of the drive and found they did just fine. Getting to know Storm better, he was even more anxious to enter him in the five-mile race. Tom felt confident Storm would be hard to beat. He was less interested in entering the shooting contests. But he knew the boys were rooting for him, so he figured he would give a good show.

July 4, 1882

Tom and Buck's duties had been completely fulfilled two days prior. The 50 horses were in corrals at the "Rodeo Grounds," the words Cody used for the 50 acres he had set up for the celebration. The boys had moved 70 of the buffalo to Cody's ranch on the Dismal River. The other 30 grazed in the tall grass just north of the Rodeo Grounds. Cody had hired Monty and two more of Tom's men to ride herd on and bring them into the grounds when he was ready to stage the buffalo hunt.

Today they had nothing to do but enjoy Bill Cody's "Old Glory Blowout." North Platte spilled over into the prairie. People had gathered to see the celebration from as far away as Cheyenne.

Tom deserted Buck and Hawk and fully intended to spend the day with Soft Cloud except, of course, when he was competing. At sunrise they strolled through the Rodeo Grounds. The Pawnee village sat on the north edge of the grounds very close to the buffalo.

Red Cloud's lodge commanded a small rise just east of the Pawnee village, a very good location for him and Still Water and Iron Shell to watch the day's events. Tom picketed Thunder, Storm, and Cloudburst at Red Cloud's lodge. Red Cloud had told Tom he would be honored for the responsibility of keeping an eye on Tom's horses.

They walked by Buck and the men hitching the team to a stagecoach. The first event of the day would be a stagecoach holdup. Buck had volunteered to drive the coach that would be immediately overrun by a band of desperate outlaws. "I plan on givin' those boys a glorious, wild chase around the grounds."

"Don't let them kill you on the first go-round, Buck. Make 'em earn it!" Tom yelled.

At the ground's far end, Tom watched the men set up shooting targets. One young fella had a dickens of a time trying to keep the empty meat cans from falling from the top rail. Finally the boy managed to balance the four cans on the rail.

When the boy turned to walk away, Tom couldn't resist. He yanked his Colt, dropped to one knee, and fired five rounds, sending the four cans flipping through the air and the young boy diving for cover.

"Tom Named by Horse! ... That was a cruel thing to do!" Soft Cloud shouted. "Now you march down there, apologize to that young man, and set his cans back up!"

A crowd had gathered, including Cody but nevertheless Tom tipped his hat to Soft Cloud and hustled to the boy and helped him to his feet.

"I never seen shootin' like that, Mister. You like to scared me to bits! ... You made me piss my pants."

"Got myself in a speck of trouble too."

"I've got to keep workin'. Mr. Cody is payin' me ten cents to keep these targets up all day."

"And a mighty fine job you're doing. I'll be back when the real contest starts." As he walked away, Tom turned to the boy and whispered, "You bet that ten cents on me." He tossed him a wink.

Bill Cody came from behind a wagon. "You do possess many of the same talents as my dear departed friend Bill Hickok. Not only matchless skills with firearms, but also his irresistible urge, that he was never able to suppress, for pulling pranks. You nearly frightened that poor boy to an early grave."

Making no attempt to apologize, or hide the cheek-cracking grin he wore, Tom replied, "I believe the boy will make out all right."

****

Monty and his boys drove the buffalo to the center of the Rodeo Grounds as soon as Buck was finished being shot to death and his stagecoach robbed.

The buffalo were only somewhat cooperative. The crowd completely encircled the grounds as Monty and his boys did their best to contain the now agitated buffalo.

High atop his platform, Dave Perry, who served as the announcer for the day, yelled "If you folks would look to the south you'll see the famous Buffalo Bill Cody entering the Rodeo Grounds on his trusted horse, Buckskin Joe. Buffalo Bill will put on a rousing demonstration of a real buffalo hunt. He will ride Buckskin Joe into the dangerous herd of wild buffalo and kill two before your very eyes."

Cody stormed in and galloped a lap around the restless buffalo. The crowd cheered wildly for their hero. Succumbing to their fervor, Cody galloped a second lap. Then he reined up Buckskin Joe and turned into the herd. With his famous buffalo rifle Lucretia

Borgia, he killed a fine bull with one shot. The crowd cheered even louder. As was his custom, Buckskin Joe maneuvered next to another big bull. Cody fired a single shot. The second massive bull fell to his death instantly. Cody pulled from the herd and raced around it holding Lucretia Borgia high above his head standing in the stirrups enticing the crowd into almost riotous cheers.

"The contestants will hold their horses behind the starting rope," Dave Perry shouted from his platform. "When I fire, the starting rope will drop. The contestants may then mount their horses. They will follow the course marked by our flags across the prairie, circle the wagon where our judges will acknowledge the contestants' numbers, then race back to the finish line. It is a five-mile race, more or less. Raise the starting rope!"

Thirty-two horses pranced nervously behind the rope, held by their riders. Tom stood by Storm, one of the few horses not prancing and pawing.

Buck stood alongside his horse, just as eager. Diablo had been retired a year earlier. He, like Thunder, had sired numerous fine horses and Buck was about to race one of them. This son of Diablo was five years old. Like his father, he was a tall, long-legged black-and-white spotted bundle of fire. Buck had named him Devil. "Faster than Diablo!" Buck bragged often.

Next to Tom, Hawk held the single rope attached to the bosilla of the spotted mare who a few weeks earlier had taken him helter-skelter across the prairie at home. He would ride bareback, as a Sioux. Hawk felt confident she would not be beaten. His grandfather had helped him paint his mare. On her black spots she wore lightning bolts of white clay. On her white spots, painted circles of buffalo blood red. And so that she might see the trail clearly, both eyes were circled with the blood of the two slain buffalo bulls. She also had been sired by Diablo. In honor of his own ancestor, Hawk had named her Crazy Horse.

Dave Perry's pistol sounded. Most of the riders were on their horses by the time the report of the pistol shot had faded. A few struggled with their dancing horses. One man fell from his horse before they crossed the starting rope but his horse ran with the others.

The horses collapsed into a tight bunch, bumping and rubbing each other. Some kicked. Others lashed with their teeth.

Several more riders were unseated.

As Tom expected, Storm jumped to an early lead. But only a narrow lead. A fellow to his right rode a tall Thoroughbred. Good-looking horse, Tom thought, not enough there though to make five miles at top speed. He looked for Buck who was only one horse away and not even 50 feet behind. He found Hawk who was tangled in the crowd. Tom knew that mare. They won't be crowding her long.

Tom was going to enjoy this. He turned Storm loose. He figured other riders would be holding their horses for a little while, saving them for a strong finish. Tom knew Storm had more than five miles of hard running in him. He was content to keep the lead and set the pace. He reasoned if he pushed Storm the pace would be so quick those fellows holding their horses back would release them too soon, and they would fade before the finish. He had taken a few minutes that morning to examine his competition. And he had found nothing in the other 31 that concerned him. Except for one.

Tom and Storm reached the wagon holding the judges in the lead. Two and a half miles to go and the horses were strung out for a half mile. The Thoroughbred held even with Storm. Buck and Devil hung on too. As he made the turn around the wagon and headed straight back for the Rodeo Grounds, he saw a gap widening behind Buck and the other horses.

****

Hawk and Crazy Horse fought their way from the pile of horses. He urged her to push on more than once as they fought to clear space. The mare threatened both horses on either side and soon Hawk had room to ask for speed.

They shot from the bunch like an arrow flies from a bow. In ten strides, Crazy Horse was completely clear of the tangled field, but they were still far behind the leader. Perhaps a half mile behind his father and he would have to guide Crazy Horse through eight or ten more horses between them.

Hawk laid low on his mare's withers and neck. He touched his heels to her ribs. She responded with an explosion of speed. He felt her powerful hooves pound the prairie grass. Hawk guided her between two horses directly in front of them. She pinned ears and bared her shining white teeth. Both horses moved to the side and slowed, allowing her to surge between them.

With each stride she seemed to pass another horse. She intimidated every horse they passed with flattened ears and gnashing teeth. Soon nothing but open space separated Hawk from Buck. But there was a *lot* of open space.

Hawk looked to his left and saw his father round the wagon going in the opposite direction, heading to the finish. Their eyes met and Tom boldly waved goodbye to his son. Hawk watched long enough to see Storm dig in with more speed and pull away from the big Thoroughbred pounding along at his side. Hawk was proud to see his father out in front. But he was just as determined to overtake him.

Crazy Horse stretched her neck and ran faster than the wind. Around the wagon they flew, each stride narrowing the open space between them and Buck. Hawk knew when he came near enough to Devil, he could count on Crazy Horse to take some of the fight out of him. But still he would need to catch the Thoroughbred and Storm.

With less than two miles to overtake his father, Hawk knew now was the time. His heels tickled her ribs a little less gently now. She found the speed he asked for and in a few strides moved alongside Buck and Devil. Buck looked at Hawk and knew he was defeated. As Hawk had hoped, his mare flashed Devil her mean face. He let her pass. Hawk reached and touched Devil's withers, "You are my first coup, Mr. Buck!" He let loose with a victorious war whoop.

He saw his father look back under his arm. He smiled when Tom urged Storm. He noticed too, the black stallion had only a little more speed to give … Storm had begun to tire.

The tall Thoroughbred also had faded. Crazy Horse did not even bother to threaten him as they galloped by. Hawk looked at the rider and frowned in disgust at the little man who mercilessly whipped the tired horse.

With only a few hundred yards remaining before they galloped into the circled crowd at the Rodeo Grounds, Hawk knew if he were to overtake his father he needed another burst from his young mare. Shouting war whoops, he nudged her with several quick, not too gentle kicks. Crazy Horse found a little more to give and gave it. Her nose drew even with Storm's flank. His own piercing blue eyes met his father's. Hawk waved hello.

Crazy Horse flattened her ears, gnashed her teeth—and Storm noticed. In one tremendous leap she pulled equal. The next thundering stride she pulled ahead. Hawk looked back and waved goodbye. In just a few more strides she was more than two lengths ahead of Storm.

Just before she crossed the finish line, Hawk jumped up and stood straight and tall on Crazy Horse's back. He held the rope in his teeth, and waved both arms victoriously in the air.

In that manner he circled the Rodeo Grounds. The crowd cheered wildly. It took Dave Perry five full minutes to gain control. Scarcely any one noticed second across the finish line was Tom on Storm, followed not too closely by Buck and Devil.

Buffalo Bill Cody stood in the center of the Rodeo Grounds.

Still standing upright on his beautiful mare, Hawk turned toward him. Suddenly the crowd began a thunderous roar! Into the center of the grounds rode Red Cloud on Thunder, wearing his magnificent war bonnet with a feathered tail so long it dragged on the ground.

He intercepted Hawk before he reached Cody. Side-by-side in the most majestic manner, they rode to Cody for Hawk to receive his first-place trophy. The crowd cheered so loudly that none of Buffalo Bill's words of praise were heard by Hawk or Red Cloud.

Each from their own vantage point, Soft Cloud, Tom and Buck watched the ceremony through stinging wet eyes.

The End

ABOUT THE AUTHOR

Dutch Henry is a horse advocate, freelance writer and novelist who lives in central Virginia with Robbie, his wife of 40 years, along with one horse and a number of dogs, cats and chickens. He writes about "People and Horses Helping Horses and People" and has columns in Natural Horse and trailblazer magazines. His stories tell of the people and horses who give so much to help others He has also has articles featured in numerous other equine magazine. He is active on Facebook and his Coffee Clutch blog where he writes about horses, birds and nature, the art of writing and, of course , his Coffee Clutch where he begins each day having coffee with his mare Kessy and critters gathered 'round. He enjoys spending time with his wife along with trail riding, bird watching, nature walking and interviewing the wonderful people about whom he writes. He also does "Therapy for Therapy Horses" clinics at equine assisted therapy centers and equine recuses.